THE
HURTING

Lucy van Smit

A MESSAGE FROM CHICKEN HOUSE

The Hurting is a story about the power of attraction – and the consequences of falling for the wrong boy. As Nell's suffocating family drive her to a set of decisions that grow increasingly dangerous, she soon faces a terrifying situation alone. Wolves, kidnap and passion – this book really scared me and is totally unique. Prepare yourself for a heady mixture from brand-new talent Lucy van Smit, an impressive force in frighteningly real fiction!

BARRY CUNNINGHAM
Publisher
Chicken House

THE
HURTING

Lucy van Smit

2 Palmer Street, Frome, Somerset BA11 1DS
chickenhousebooks.com

Text © Lucy van Smit 2018

First published in Great Britain in 2018
Chicken House
2 Palmer Street
Frome, Somerset BA11 1DS
United Kingdom
www.chickenhousebooks.com

Cover and interior design by Helen Crawford-White
Typeset by Dorchester Typesetting Group Ltd
Printed and bound in Great Britain by CPI Group (UK) Ltd, Croydon CR0 4YY

The paper used in this Chicken House book is made from
wood grown in sustainable forests.

1 3 5 7 9 10 8 6 4 2

British Library Cataloguing in Publication data available.

PB ISBN 978-1-911077-86-2
eISBN 978-1-911490-63-0

For all my boys;
Nick, Archie, and our beloved Luke.

To sacrifice what you are,

and live without belief.

That is a fate more terrible than dying.

JOAN OF ARC

PART 1

Love

I

I stole a baby.

The words peck away at me as I climb high above the fjord and stand on Preken Rock. The white night is full with pine gum and birdsong, but I'm gasping and only getting snippets of air. It's the cold mountain wind that makes my eyes water up. Not the hundred metres of nothingness to the sea. Not the sound of his crying.

I stole a baby.

Does that make me a bad person?

Yeah. It does.

I drag his baby carrier off my back, jam it upright between my knees and flip out the metal stand. His dirty nappy makes my stomach heave, but I get the carrier on a flat rock and straighten his fur headdress.

One blue baby shoe falls off like always, I struggle to get it back on, and grab the camera.

'I'll put this right,' I promise him.

He's beyond hearing me. His muffled cries build to a crescendo, and my legs shake like they're possessed, tiny stones twisting into the rock under my boots. I have to crawl to the overhang and make myself look down. No one is there.

Everything spins.

Lights strobe behind my eyes. The purple clouds, the edgeless sky, the fjords and the forest all swirl together and blur past me like I'm on a runaway train. I want it to stop. I've been running for so long, I want it all to stop.

The world just keeps on spinning. And the camera flies out of my fingers. It spins in an arc over the fjord, and snaps back and forth on the strap, snagged on my quartz bracelet. Holy crap. I lose this Leica, and it's game over.

I wriggle back, check the camera still works, scanning the horizon. Norway stuns me, always.

Green mountains drop into the sea like emerald icebergs. And the fjord is so clear, I can see all the way to the bottom. The crystal sea has burnt the grass off the mountains and the bare rock looks like ribs of underwater cathedrals. I used to love all that. But now I know what's down there.

The wind throws tantrums at the wickedness of it all; howling, and hurling matted red hair across my mouth. And I know it's shallow, but I don't want to die like this. I want one more day.

One more day.

It's not so much to ask. Is it? To walk through my life again and appreciate the ordinary stuff. Toothpaste. Hot water. Catching a bus. My family? I never even said goodbye. Never said I loved them. I binned my life like toilet paper, and never noticed.

Skylarks swoop through the Nordic night, singing. Song-flight gobbles up their energy; the skylarks still sing as the sun casts silvery shrouds over the fjord. The Midnight Sun. They call it Black Sun here.

The Black Son? That's him all right. Can I really stop him? Yeah. Maybe. If I keep my head.

The wind drops. I film my last words. 'I'm Nell Lamb,' I say on camera. 'If you're watching this, I'm dead already. Don't freak out on me. It's way worse for me. And I need you to listen. I die, and this baby gets to live, but only if you listen.'

No. No. No. It sounds horribly wrong, a stupid, indulgent snuff-selfie. Who will believe me? What if I bottle it again? What if this doesn't work? What if they find him?

Pray louder than your thoughts, Nell.

My sister's voice is so clear in my head I half turn to hug her. But it's a cruel trick of the wind. I'm alone on Preken Rock. No one will save me. No one will listen.

I tilt my head to eavesdrop on the world around me. Purple shadows lengthen and sneak up the trail, over moss-covered rocks and arrow-straight birch trees. The skylarks stop singing. Hairs on the back of my neck tingle. Then a rush of power surges through the air, over the land, through the forests, and into the rock.

Its pulse terrifies me. *Rage. Rage. Longing.* And all I can hear is the thrashing and pounding inside my own head.

He's here.

2

Three Months Earlier

My British passport has thirty-two stiff pages and each one tells a lie. I scowl at my old passport photo. That ten-year-old tomboy could get me out of this mess, but I'm a hologram of my former self. With that sorry thought, I hammer out the love song on my keyboard. The middle C sticks. I vamp it again. Louder. Dad yells at me to knock it off. So I do. And scribble lyrics in the condensation on the window instead, pretending to be a tough girl who'd scare me witless, if we ever met up for real.

I won't believe in true love.
That's celebrity hype and lies.
This girl's got her eyes wide open.
I'll sing my own lies to the sky.

The song drips down the cold glass and disappears like the rest of my life.

Outside our cottage the views of Preken Rock are gobsmacking. But who can write love songs about fjords? And it doesn't help that the Norwegian mountains look so manicured, so frozen in time, like their beauty got Botoxed. Colour takes on a whole new meaning here. Sounds stupid, but the grass is too green. Its brightness hurts my eyes.

Eleven days of staring at it already feels like a lifetime. Give it time, Dad says. But I don't need a sports lesson in Norway to learn I'm not the outdoors hiking-for-fun kind of girl. I miss Manchester and our dirty red streets. I miss faces. The chat.

I unwrap a Starburst, flick the strawberry wrapper out of the window at Preken Rock. Yep, it's all too splendid here. Too perfect. It makes the muddle of me stand out.

Pulling out my journal, I rework the song. I hum the vocal hook under my breath. It's still crap.

Who am I kidding? I don't do love songs. Never did. Everybody knows love sucks. The only time I got close to a good love song was after a bad dose of Insta-love with Ted at church camp, and my sister Harper put a stop to that. She threatened to tell Dad.

My phone pings.

I glance down at it: *Nell, don't let Harper trump you with her sick card. Get on that flight tonight.*

My best friend Dom is psychic when it comes to keeping up the pressure. Get on that flight tonight? He makes it sound so easy.

But whenever I think of flying back home for the

audition my head just roars: No. No. No. No!

On the flight over, our plane tried to vomit me out of the sky, and the night turned fluorescent green. I nightmare about those jolts and flashes now.

My sister says I scream in my sleep; Harper has to slap me awake and I flap at her in the dark, still falling. I know. I know. Everyone said it was just the Northern Lights. But what if they're wrong? What if there is something up there?

I delete Dom's phone message, and panic about what to do. Fly? And probably die of anxiety. Or stay put?

At least I can't fall out of bed here. My 'bedroom' is a wooden cave. The mattress fits snug against all four walls and I can touch the sloping pine ceiling when lying down.

Great. There's a red spider nesting right above my head. I sit up fast. 'Dad!' I shout. 'Are spiders poisonous here?'

My dad doesn't answer. Of course not. He's with Harper.

I take a deep breath, hook the web on my pencil and catapult the spider out the window. I feel bad about destroying his home, but it's not like I got to keep mine. Even if it was only a grotty terrace house in an uncool part of Greater Manchester.

Ping. Another message from Dom. *You did tell your dad?*

No. Clearly, I haven't got round to telling my dad.

Nor have I told my best friend that his remix of our audition piece is crap. I listen to it again. Yep. Dom's added a climb before the chorus. It's too obvious. Too pop. I wanted a ballad; plaintive, haunting notes, fading to silence. Usually, Dom's genius at remixes and knows what I want before I do, but it doesn't work when we're apart.

'Nell! Turn that racket off,' Dad calls. 'Come help.'

I never get a minute to myself. 'In a sec.'

'Now means now.' My dad goes from zero to sixty faster than anyone on *Top Gear*. I don't think he's any happier about living in Norway than I am, but we all have to make sacrifices for Harper's recovery. But it all happened so fast – our old doctor said Norway had the best treatment for her, so Dad pulled me out of school and the next minute we're living here.

'OK, OK,' I say to him, and crawl through my hatch into the main bedroom next door.

Harper's got that, of course, which I so don't mind. Dad's hung forty close-ups of Jesus's face on the walls, the murky-brown one from the Turin Shroud. And it's bad enough living here without Jesus moving in too. But Dad's not taking any chances until Harper gets cured. He's surrounded her bedstead with miraculous medals and statues of guardian angels, the ones with neon-red lights for their sacred hearts. The total effect is sinister kitsch, like a police incident room got muddled up with an episode of *Father Ted*.

My family is mad for all this stuff, miracles and saints and angels. They believe God can save my sister.

One hundred per cent.

Personally, I think God's too busy causing havoc in other countries to care about the Lamb family. It's not like He even speaks to me.

Anyway, in the centre of it all, on a double bed, lies my older sister with her blue headscarf. At eighteen, Harper has a pale delicate beauty that whacks you in the stomach and makes you want to do anything for her. Until she opens her mouth.

I pull on my black beanie and give her a goofy smile. 'I dealt with the monster spider myself. I'm OK, in case you're wondering.'

'I'm not.' My sister snaps open *Hair* mag. 'Nobody listens to a word you say.'

Harper never lets me forget I'm the ugly kid sister. I smooth my short vintage dress over the thick stripy tights I always wear to cover up my legs. My sister tells any lads interested in me that I've got proper hairy knees. And I'm so rubbish with a razor, she tells Dad I've been self-harming when I attempt to shave them. So I'm sticking with the stripy tights for now.

My dad hangs another picture of Jesus above the door. He works on oil rigs, but fancies himself as a healer, and the more Dad drinks the more he dresses like a religious trainspotter. Today it's a chrome crucifix and his blue fleece, which bulks up his already massive chest and arms. That's not a good look.

'Er . . . Dad?' I take a deep breath. 'Can I talk to you?'

'Not now,' he says. 'Pass me the drawing pins.'

I hand him the pins and try again. 'It's urgent.

About my . . .'

Before I can spit it out, Harper drops me right in it. 'Dad?' she goes. 'Nell says the Turin Shroud's a complete fake. Been carbon-dated and everything. That's not true, is it, Dad? That *is* Jesus's real face?'

'Pray for faith, girls,' Dad commands, dodging the question. 'You need His protection.'

I count under my breath to calm down.

Ping. *You did tell your dad?*

I blurt it out. 'Dad! I need to go back home. Tonight. For an audition tomorrow.'

My dad freezes on the ladder. I stare at his Jesus print wobbling in mid-air. 'Look,' I say. 'It's only for two days.'

'It's Ash Wednesday.' My dad says it like the first day of Lent knocks spots off Christmas.

But in our house it means forty days of no fun. Last year, my dad cut the plug off our telly when he caught me watching Netflix.

'We're going to Mass this morning and that's final,' he says. 'Your sister needs you.'

'OK. After Mass,' I wheedle. 'Harper says she can manage without me.'

At that precise moment, my big sister knocks into the bedside table and her army of medicine bottles crashes to the floor.

Harper always gets poorly when I want something. Then she doubles up, coughing, and I'm by her side in a heartbeat.

'You'll be OK.' I check her chart, draw off a syringe

and inject meds into her PICC line, a catheter that's permanently in the vein above her elbow. I rub her hand until the spasm passes.

Harper's post-chemo now, in recovery after her last treatment cycle, but my sister's hair hasn't grown back and she still gets this bone-deep pain from her weird form of leukaemia.

The doctors say it will pass but she's on loads of meds. We get an automated reminder from the hospital, on a special pager, telling me which one to give her. Me. Not Dad.

I have to coax Harper to take every single one.

She hates the taste of temazepam, and nurses. And Dad hates the smell of hospitals. Between the pair of them, I'm prisoner and jailer in our new home.

'You all right, love?' Dad asks her, keeping his distance.

'Water,' Harper says in a baby voice that makes me want to scream.

Dad grabs her glass. His hands shake, and he spills water over her old Barbie duvet. I groan inside. He's hit the bottle already, and Dad only got back from the rig last night.

'I'll get a towel,' he says, and vanishes into the bathroom.

'He's giving up the booze for Lent,' I whisper to Harper. 'You'll be fine for a few days.'

'You're only saying that to make yourself feel better.'

'Hey. That's not fair,' I say.

'Welcome to my life,' she snaps.

Dad yells from the bathroom. 'Girls! It looks like

someone got murdered in here.'

Crap. Forgot about that.

'It's only hair dye,' I mutter.

'Sorry about Nell's mess,' smirks Harper.

'Mess? It's a bloodbath. That colour never washes out.' Dad carries out the pile of stained white towels like it's a small dead body. 'You're the absolute end. Show me.'

He nags at me till I pull off my black beanie. There's a long, suffocating silence. It's like my dad's never seen a redhead before. The tic in his eyebrow dances. This isn't going to work. I glance at my sister.

'Our Nell wanted to be a pop star.' Harper yawns.

'Songwriter,' I sigh.

'Will you quit peckin' me?' She rolls her eyes at Dad. 'Nell's only gone and got herself an audition at that fancy music school. Dom organized a flight and everything. Well stupid. She'll never get into the BRIT School with her moany old songs.'

I feel the ground disappearing under me, same as always.

'Songwriting?' Dad snorts. 'Who do you think you are, the new Amy Winehouse?'

That's exactly who I want to be.

My phone flashes. Dom again. *Why don't you just tell him?*

I message back. *I did. He won't listen.*

'Give me that infernal phone,' Dad shouts. 'Will you ever learn? You're staying put. That's just the way it is. You can do without this nonsense during Lent. Think of others for a change.'

He seizes my phone before I can duck out of reach.

'No. Please. Not that.' I hate myself for begging, but I won't get it back for weeks. 'It's not fair. You can't make me a martyr. We need a real nurse in. I can't do this.'

'You're just like your mother! Obsessed. Selfish.' Dad clamps his lips together.

I knew he wouldn't let me go without a fight, but I'm caught off guard by how much this hurts.

Dad never talks about *her*.

No one does.

Self-sacrifice wasn't in Mum's bags when she left home.

And nor was I.

'Harper?' I flick my new dyed-red haircut at my sister. 'Come on. You promised.'

Our deal was that Harper gets to do whatever she likes with my hair and I get to go back home for the audition.

My sister rarely keeps her word. I never learn. This time she pulls off her blue scarf. And she scratches her bald head. It gets her most things with Dad.

And it makes me look a total bitch to want more out of life. I stare at her poor white scalp and her beautiful heart-shaped face. My big sister smiles, but her eyes, dark with worry, beg me to stay. This horrible feeling smothers my entire body, like a giant squid. Oh, Harper, what about me? I want to say. My dreams? But I know the answer. There is no *me* in my family.

It's *we*.

Me and Harper.
Don't let Harper trump you with her sick card.
But it isn't a sick card. It's cancer.
And it trumps everything.

3

Norwegian skies are freak shows, full of strange lights and weird sounds. The fjord mirrors everything. The clouds. The red-painted houses. And Preken Rock. The broken old mountain guards the entrance to our fishing village. Harper and me stomp to Mass not speaking. I'm fuming about her breaking her word, but Dad sprints down the narrow fjord road as if church was the best finishing line ever.

The dark wooden church squats on a rock, mad and naked, like Van Gogh built it in a fit of scribbles. The roof and steeple twist in torment, but the graveyard is totally Norwegian, and neat white gravestones bite through the grass slope to Nøyfjord.

'I know it's the only Catholic church for miles around, but I couldn't bear to be buried down there,' says my sister. 'I'd end up as fish food.'

I pull her arm through mine. 'Not if I have anything to do with it,' I say.

We walk on. My anxiety swallows me up whole. What if her latest treatment hasn't worked? What if she never gets better? I can't even go there, and I lock it up in the *room* in my head.

Dad can't resist a sermon about Preken Rock, how the ice shattered the mountain in half and left a sheer, impenetrable rock face protecting the village.

'Protection?' Harper scoffs. 'No one even locks doors in Nøy. Can you imagine that back home?'

'That's why they all have big dogs here. Right, Dad?' I say.

Bang on cue, the priest's brutal husky leaps up against the church fence, barking and jumping up at us like he's on speed.

I freeze. I don't do dogs. I got badly bitten as a kid.

'Breathe louder than your thoughts,' Harper chants. 'Even killer huskies can't get out of that gate.'

'I know that. But my body's got a mind of its own and is scared shitless.'

'Pray for courage,' my sister laughs.

'Yeah, like that will help,' I mutter.

Dad stops to lecture me on my lack of faith. Nag. Nag. Nag. But Harper drags me past the kennel. I look at her in surprise; she loves dogs, Harper does, but letting them out to scare me is more her style ever since I got bitten.

She tries to be a good person, but has to work proper hard at it. Kindness just doesn't come easy to my sister. And she's meaner without hair. Our life's not some fairy tale, where cancer makes anyone in my family a better person. Harper wants to be a hairdresser and it sucks she's got no hair. I let her shave mine off one time, when she first lost hers. For a sweet, painful time, we looked the same. A pair of bowling ball aliens. But then my hair grew back and I don't think my sister has ever forgiven me.

The church is cold. Its paintwork has faded to a soft white inside; and all the pews and walls are decorated in Rosemåling, Norwegian folk art roses. It's quite the prettiest church I've ever seen, more a tall Wendy house really, with a balcony running around the walls.

Everyone toadies up to my dad and whispers in his ear. He's got his frayed blue prayer book out, and pencils in their request. I sigh. My dad is a lay-healer; he's not a priest, or anything. He works on an oil rig, for Chrissakes. But his healing prayers seemed to work on everybody back home, and our parish priest called Nøy's priest, and now everyone thinks Dad is a saint. And he just plays along. Frankly I'm amazed the shame doesn't finish him off. Can't they smell the booze on him? I think it's killing Dad that his prayers can't heal Harper. I take my crucifix off; I'm not going to believe in any God who won't save my sister.

I'm expected to play happy-clappy music during the hymns. I drift off as usual.

If you don't trust me
What do you see?
Not me. Not me. Not me . . .

I think I'm humming the vocals in my head. But Harper taps me on the shoulder. 'You don't get to sing your own songs,' she whispers. 'Not any more.' Then she pats my head as if to say: never mind, at least you've got hair.

My fingers close round the passport in my pocket and I forget the words to the Lord's Prayer, which we only say like a thousand times a day.

Dad troops us up to the altar to get our ashes. Father José glances at my sister's bald head and my dyed-red hair. I swear he calls me a godless sinner under his breath. Sin? I only wish I had the guts to be world-class at that.

Father José is not from around here either. Norway has to import priests; Norway has more billionaires than Catholics. And most of us are foreigners. He marks out the sign of the cross on my forehead – I hate the rasp of his dry thumb on my skin – then he glides back with the communion chalice and places a round white wafer on my tongue. 'Body of Christ,' he says, so disapprovingly I swear he can hear my wicked thoughts.

'Amen,' I say sweetly, to annoy him.

The wafer melts into the roof of my mouth. I say a quick prayer for Harper and ask Jesus to give me the courage to get on that flight tonight.

Sunlight bursts through the stained-glass window. It brings the Archangel to life. His huge wings inflate in the golden bright, and his long sword flashes as he battles Lucifer to save humanity. Dad's face lights up. I feel like crying. He's a total sucker for miracles.

But Harper slips her hand in mine, and I squeeze it tight.

'It's a sign,' my sister whispers. 'Go. I'll be fine.'

'Promise?' I hold my breath, because this really is a miracle.

She keeps me waiting for ages and then she smiles.

My sister looks radiant when she smiles. She's going to dine out on this good deed for months, but it's one of those rare times when she comes through for me that I get a glimpse of how our life could be so different.

We leave Mass. I hike my Dora the Explorer bag over one shoulder and pick up my keyboard. The hairs on the back of my neck prickle, as if someone is watching me. I get that feeling a lot since we moved here – Harper says it puts me right up there with the crazies. I glance around, feeling stupid, rubbing the ashes off my forehead.

'Nell. Leave them,' Dad orders. 'Repentant sinners wear the mark with pride.'

'Dad! That cow Gudrun and my new classmates will take the p . . . No one goes to church in Norway. It's a fact.'

I've only had a week at Vord Skole, but that's long enough to see how the land lies, and Gudrun makes my life hell.

'Don't start, Nell,' Dad says. 'Sinners need protection. Evil walks the Earth.'

'There's no such thing as evil,' I say, unable to zip it. 'Back home our psychology teacher said bad people like psychopaths aren't evil. They just lack empathy. They don't feel emotion or guilt. Not like we do for messing up people's lives.'

I'm not sure my teacher got this bit right. Dad and

Harper never feel any guilt for wrecking my life either, and they're not psychopaths. At least, not certified ones.

'Don't preach your New Age psychology at me,' Dad rabbits on. 'Of course evil exists. Why, the Devil's in all of us, waiting for his chance to pull us down.'

And that's my dad all over. He prays to God, but his money's on the Devil.

Three cars on the narrow fjord road stop for Dad ranting in the middle of the street. Rabbit rabbit. Harper and me stare at Preken Rock and pretend we're not related to him.

'Got it?' Dad says at last. 'You can't just wish evil away because you don't like the sound of it. Now promise you won't rub off your ashes on the way to school.'

'Promise,' I say.

And I skive off to Bergen International Airport instead.

4

The bus hurtles through endless white tunnels, bumping on and off car ferries to cross the fjords. I sit at the back, staring at the bright green mountains, messing up song after song on my keyboard. Running away felt daring at first, but the mood wears off pretty fast without Dom on the end of a phone. Harper promised not to tell Dad until after school, but I keep looking over my shoulder, expecting him to overtake the bus and haul me off.

Hours later the bus pulls into Bergen. Surrounded by mountains, it's the rainiest city in Europe. The harbour is lined with these cute red and yellow wooden houses. I check the airport timetable by the fish market. I've got hours and hours before my flight.

My feet sneak over to Svad's. It's everywhere in Norway: Svad Oil, Svad Mining, Svad Stores – the reclusive oil tycoon Harry Svad owns the lot. Or did when he was alive. Svad's helicopter is missing. Everyone at school thinks he's dead. They're a bunch of ghouls. He's a recluse, right? I bet he's just done a runner like me.

Anyway, this Svad Store is the length of Torgallmenningen and has a honeycomb of golden escalators zigzagging between the boutiques. I think of our cramped dark cottage and slip inside. I want to know what rich feels like. And Dad will never know.

Svad is one of my dad's many blind spots. We're not even allowed to mention it at home. I still don't get why Dad quit, and took a job that pays half as much.

On automatic pilot I find myself in the Food Hall, getting Harper a treat for supper. She's off her food with the cancer, and smoked salmon is all she fancies. But the price is a rip-off and it's stupid anyway; I won't see Harper for days. That thought makes me queasy. My sister hates Dad doing her meds.

Concentrate on the audition.

I try. But my fingers feel lost without a phone and tap the beat on the packet of smoked salmon. *I don't believe in true love.* The lyrics spin around in my head. *That's celebrity hype and lies.* Are they good enough for the audition? I can't tell. Dom usually whips my songs away, before I overwork them.

I wander round in circles, and end up in Shoes, drooling over a pair of tan laced boots, when this security woman in a bulging black uniform appears out of the Food Hall.

'*Stopp!*' she shouts.

I turn to see who she's shouting at, and my keyboard catches her on the leg. 'You under arrest,' she barks at me in English.

Somehow Norwegians never mistake me for one of them.

'Sorry?' I say.

'You are thief.' She grabs my arm. 'I saw you steal fish.'

'What? No way.'

'*Jo!*' the guard insists and opens the pocket on my frayed keyboard case.

'Hey! Careful. That's my stuff.'

'*Nei.* It belong to Svad.' And she pulls out the package of smoked salmon, stuck between the crumpled pages of my music. I've no idea how it got in there.

'Look, I'm sorry, I didn't do it on purpose.'

'She is thief. I saw her steal it,' the guard tells the crowd of shoppers that have gathered around us.

'Hey, that's bang out of order,' I say. 'I'm not even out of the store.'

'This is Svad,' she states. 'We have our own rules.'

That figures. If you're rich you can do what you like. 'Look,' I plead. 'I've got a plane to catch.' I clutch my keyboard. 'I wasn't shoplifting. Please. It's a mistake.'

'*Nei.* Give me your name! Show me passport. You are underage. I call parents.'

'You can't. I don't have parents. Just my dad. And he confiscated my phone, and I don't have our new number on me.'

'He has written his number in the back.' She jabs a finger at my passport. 'You are liar. And thief.' She's got her hand of doom on my shoulder. I panic. Everyone is looking. Shaking their heads. I duck my head. Dad will

25

go mental if I give Catholics a bad rep. But the guard's proper strong, and I don't know what to do.

There's a boy leaning over the shoe counter taking photos of me, like that's all I need, my arrest for shoplifting on social media. The shopgirl's wrapping up a pair of baby boots for him. I know zip about babies, but he's is the last person you'd expect to be buying designer baby shoes. Intense. Dark. Untamed. Like he's just stepped out of the wilderness, and wound up in a shoe boutique by mistake in his huge blue-grey fur coat. I glance around for a TV crew or a film director. He's got to be an actor, or a model or something, but he's on his own, and boys like him never are.

I give him the finger. He puts the camera down. And he stares at me. Green eyes. Sea and broken glass. I try to pull my eyes away, but the more I struggle, the more I'm drawn into him.

Everything else fades away. Just him and me clamped together like two sides of an airlock. Holy crap.

'Miss Eleanor Mary Lamb!' the guard says, loud enough for the moon to hear. 'I am arresting you for stealing Svad property.'

'You can't,' I wheeze. 'It's a mistake.'

The boy, the staring faces, the brightness of shop lights, the noise and the guard's body odour press in on me and I'm seriously struggling to breathe here.

He doesn't take his eyes off me and taps a metal cigarette lighter on the baby shoebox. I recognize the Morse code. SOS. Harper and me used to knock it on the wall between our neighbours whenever we needed rescuing from our messed-up family. It means Save Our Souls – not Save Our Skins, like I used to think.

The boy gives me a wicked grin. He stretches over the checkout and punches the fire alarm. '*BRANN!*' he calls in a deep voice. '*Alle ut! Brann!*' His voice reverberates through the store and crashes down on me. The hairs on the back of my neck lift.

Everything kicks off.

A fire siren rips through the store. The guard spins me around. I want to clap my hands over my ears, but she grips my arms. I look back. The boy has vanished. My heart wilts. The siren is drilling into my brain. Shoppers move purposely to the stairs. Calmly. Like they'd got all day. They put their shopping baskets down. If this were Manchester, they'd leg it. But this is Norway, and everyone's on their best behaviour. Always.

'Move,' says the guard. 'Take stairs.'

The boy stops us in the aisle, arms outstretched, the oversized blue-grey fur coat falling in folds down his body. The baby shoebox in one hand. My eyes blur. The lights brighten. His dark hair ignites into a shining helmet. Blood roars in my ears. He *is* my guardian angel.

The idea is so preposterous it makes me laugh, then my vision vanishes, and there's just this boy standing there in a fur coat that looks way too big for him.

He is so composed, so self-possessed, he quiets everything around him. The guard stops dead and stares, and she was busy shoving me towards the fire escape a minute ago. He dances around us, lifts her arm off my shoulders and plants a kiss on her cheek. The bossy cow actually blushes, and she's old enough to be pulling a pension.

'You're wonderful,' he murmurs to her. 'Escorting absent-minded customers out of the Svad Store when it might be on fire? But it's OK, she is with me. A visitor with foreign ways. I will deal with her, go look after the others.'

The cheek of him. He lies better than Harper. I can't place his accent: definitely not Norwegian – they speak with a staccato hurdy-gurdy rhythm, and this boy has a deep gentle voice. He looks Spanish or Russian, but somehow he's none of those things.

'She is with you?' the guard says, incredulous that this extraordinary boy knows someone like me. She leaves, huffing about rude foreigners.

Our shop floor is empty now, and the alarm stops.

The boy holds out his hand to me. I stare at it. The back of his hand is weathered with long white scars in the tanned skin, but his nails are manicured and spotlessly clean, like he has two personalities in the one hand: one wild, the other civilized; I wonder which side wins that war?

'Come with me,' he says.

He sounds old and young and somehow totally in control.

I don't believe in Insta-love. I don't. It's a sodding myth. But straight up, as I touch his outstretched hand with my sparkly-green bitten fingernails, it's like I've

28

been shot. In that moment, the old me dies, and this other Nell steps out of my body.

I can't move.

'How rude of me,' he says. 'Me Lukas.' He thumps a fist on his chest.

I find my voice. 'You speak English like a Brit.'

'So do you, for a Northerner.'

'Meow,' I say. 'How'd you learn it?'

'I was sent away to an International School,' he says. 'But I grew up on Ulv Fjell. That's Norwegian for Wolf Mountain.' Lukas tucks his chin in the fur coat as if winter came back, and his face is so sad it's unbearable.

'I'm Nell,' I blurt, desperate for him to laugh again.

'Nell?' he says. 'As in Eleanor?'

'Yeah, my gran's name.'

He studies my face. 'Eleanor was the Queen of Aquitaine,' he says. 'She was formidable. Her name means burning bright.'

'So does Lucifer,' I say. 'I'm just Nell.'

He smiles. 'Not to me.'

5

We get stuck in the revolving brass door, staring at each other, trapped between the plate glass. Then we get a fit of giggles as firefighters push past to check the store. The ornate building is dusted with snow outside. Customers crowd around us on the pavement in brightly coloured puffa jackets and bobble hats, so I can't move away from him even if I wanted to. The air between us fizzles. Lukas breathes me in. I do the same.

His black hair smells of bonfires and the outdoors and expensive soap. His face is on fire with laughter one second, but the next his eyes go dark, like a cloud passing over a sun. Then the cloud vanishes and Lukas emerges, dazzling again.

And somehow he looks rich, and yet like he hasn't eaten in weeks; tanned skin stretched taut over his cheekbones, fine wrinkles outlining the sea-glass eyes, like he squints at the sun, or at something far away in the long grass.

'Who leaves town with no coat, a keyboard and a pink

Dora the Explorer school bag?' he says at last. 'Is that the latest fashion in the UK?'

I stand there shivering like an idiot. 'You should try it. Wolf coats and brooding Heathcliff lads are so last millennium.'

'Heathcliff?' He laughs and laughs. Lukas has infectious chortling laughter, it's impossible not to join in. 'That makes you Cathy!' he says. 'Anyway, you must love fish to thieve it.' And he shoves the dripping packet of smoked salmon into my keyboard case.

'Wait up! I didn't nick it.' I hand it back. 'I want nothing that belongs to Svad.'

Lukas stares at me. 'Nothing from Svad? Not many can say that.' Then he rips open the smoked salmon and lobs it over my head into Torgallmenningen Square. Every gesture he makes is graceful and precise, like he's attuned to the environment around him, but so at home in his own skin. He seems to move through the world exactly as he wants.

'I'm sorry to sound ungrateful,' I say. 'But that's a waste of perfectly good fish.'

Lukas smiles. 'Watch.'

A Dobermann is racing across the icy cobbles of Torgallmenningen to get it, dragging a young girl in a hijab by its leash. She's powerless to stop the brute gulping down 200 kroner of fish in one go.

I laugh, or try to. 'Dogs like that scare me to death.'

'Never let them know that,' Lukas says quietly, and he lets out a piercing whistle.

The Dobermann stops instantly, rolls on its back, watching him. Its breath is steaming up in the cold evening air. The girl gawps at Lukas as we walk towards her, and adjusts her hijab. She looks gutted when Lukas conjures up a camera from his coat pocket only to snap away at her dog. She takes in the baby shoebox under his arm and glances at my stomach. I'm wearing a thick Nordic sweater over my dress, no way can she think I'm pregnant. But I suck my belly in anyway and feel my face go red. I focus on the henna-painted designs on her hands.

'So delicate,' I say, like I'm a frigging expert. 'How do you get it so perfect? You stencil it?'

'*Nei*. Freehand.' She's delighted at my interest. 'We paint the pattern in a brown paste and we leave it to dry overnight.'

She pulls out a small pot of henna paste with a tiny paintbrush, and pushes them into my hands. 'Svad had a special offer on,' she says. 'I don't need two. Keep.' She stares at my stomach. 'For baby.'

I want the ground to swallow me up. 'Shh. There's no baby.' I hope Lukas didn't hear, but even with his back to us I swear he's laughing. He busies himself scratching her dog's underbelly.

'I see one in your future,' the girl insists.

'Thanks, Mystic Meg, but I'm never having babies,' I say. 'They ruin everything.'

The Dobermann gives me this vicious look as the girl leaves, and I trip over myself to get out of its way. 'I should go too,' I say to Lukas. 'My flight leaves later tonight.'

But I don't move.

'How come you don't like dogs?' Lukas asks. He's checking his shots, adjusting the contrast, so the Dobermann's yellow teeth jump out against its cavernous mouth.

I shudder. 'An Alsatian ripped my arm open when I was ten.'

'A wolf can do that, if you get careless,' he says, like it's no big deal. 'In our pack, there's always one who's a handful.'

'*Your* pack? You raise *wolves*?'

'Wolves raised me,' he laughs.

'What?' I am amazed. 'And they didn't they eat you? Aren't wolves savage killers?'

'That's a myth.' Lukas tucks the baby shoebox under his arm, and once again this sadness flashes over his face so fast I nearly miss it. 'Most theories on wolf behaviour are based on discredited research from studying wolves in a zoo in Switzerland,' he says. 'Experts, ignorant about how a wolf pack really works, put random wolves together. Strangers. Competitors. Too many alphas. Of course they fought. Captivity breeds aggression. Wolves in the wild rule by respect, not violence.'

'But what about you?' I say. 'You didn't grow up in a zoo, right?'

'No.' Lukas smiles. 'A miner and his wife found me living with wolves when I was a child – I was small enough not to be a threat to the alpha wolf. Alpha is the name given to the father of the pack. Wolves love their young, and when the she-wolf adopted me the whole pack on Ulv Fjell accepted me as one of their own.'

'Oh,' I say, lost for words. Is he having me on? 'That sounds proper . . . erm . . . fairy tale.'

'Yes,' he says, slowly. 'I guess it is.'

I get the feeling he's told this story a thousand times. I steal a look at his fur-lined greatcoat. I never wear fur myself, but the collar and cuffs look quite luxurious, with a ruff of blue-black fur blending into shorter, softer fur inside the coat, and a beautiful dark-grey suede on the outside.

'Is that . . . real wolf fur?' I'm uncomfortable asking. Surely no one who loves animals wears furs?

I don't know how to describe the change in his sea-glass eyes, like a sudden nightfall, sucking up all the beauty and colour. His whole body shakes. Involuntary. Like he's throwing off a curse, and his eyes spit out loss and rage and hopelessness.

'It's a wolf coat,' Lukas says, dead quiet. 'One of a kind. This was made from the pelts of my wolf pups. The miner slaughtered our pack, and had it made for himself. As a trophy. He gave it to me when my little brother was born. A gift. I wear these pelts to honour the fallen. You Catholics would call it a hair shirt, worn as a penance, suffered in silence, never forgotten.'

'How do you know I'm Catholic?' I say, aghast at his story.

Lukas nods at my forehead. 'You have a monstrous black smudge on your face.'

'Ashes?' I squirm. 'I promised my dad not to wipe them off. I sort of owe him today.'

'Then let me.' Lukas presses his thumb gently to my forehead.

My whole world shrinks to that one spot. My skin is memorizing his thumbprint. Every whorl and groove. Shit. I'm in trouble here. This is how girls end up at their boyfriend's football matches, or pretending they love Formula One more than Netflix.

I don't have time for this. I don't. I don't. I don't. I pull my keyboard to my heart and try to remember how much the audition means to me. 'I should catch the next airport bus,' I say. 'Don't I have to be there like ages before my flight?'

His hand drops from my face. 'When is it?'

My skin feels bereft without his touch. 'Later tonight,' I stammer. 'Not too sure.' I daren't look at my plane ticket; part of me half hopes to miss the stupid flight.

'Ah.' He swirls on his toes. 'Come on. I know a shortcut.'

Lukas shoulders my pink rucksack and strides away from the harbour. I fall in by his side, almost jogging to keep up. Shoppers stare at him, and step out of his way like he's a celebrity. Then his wolf coat swings against me, and my knee buckles with happiness. I can't believe how much I want to touch him. I clench my hand and my nails cut into my palm, but it doesn't work. Nothing does.

It's torture not to look. Not to touch.

'So you're a musician,' he calls over his shoulder.

'Songwriter.'

'Any good?'

'I'm off to find out. I'm auditioning for the BRIT School.'

He turns back. 'What?'

'The BRIT School? It's like the best music school for singer-songwriters. Adele? Katie Melua? Amy Winehouse . . . you must have heard of her?' I sigh. 'No? Well, I need to make this flight tonight. It's big. My dad disapproves, but if I get a place, I get funding and my dad can't stop me. Music, here I come.'

'So that's your North Star?' He sounds disappointed. 'Fame?'

And somehow it feels important to make this rich boy understand. 'No. I don't give a toss about fame. Or money. But my writing makes me feel alive. If I don't do it, then I stop being me. I sort of disappear, inside.'

Shut up, Nell. You sound so pretentious.

Lukas just nods. 'I get it. You're an artist. You explore the world inside. You'd write even if your songs never got performed?'

Before I can speak, he turns left and cuts through a park with the biggest municipal lake ever. It's got some Norwegian name that's impossible to pronounce.

'How about you?' I ask shyly, after a long silence. 'What do you want to do?'

'Me?' he says thoughtfully. 'I want to find my missing

she-wolf, Asena, and be the famous wolf whisperer who protected wolves in Norway and stops oil-mining companies exploiting Ulv Fjell.'

'Like Svad?'

'Yes – or the Pied Piper!' He laughs.

I giggle, glad this boy's no fan of Svad, and somehow I believe he can do it. He's just a boy in a wolf coat standing in the middle of a deserted city park with a girl, but Lukas is so centred, so certain inside, his stillness makes anything seems possible.

We run along a wall by the lake, and stop to admire the lone waterfall in the middle. We talk and talk, about nonsense really, but all the while I feel this thing between us humming and knitting the two of us together with iridescent threads, so strong they pull at me until it's like a physical vibration.

It's crazy; I didn't choose this, but meeting him seems inevitable. He's what Harper calls an Old Soul, and it's like Lukas and me have met before. Many times. And it's never enough.

After a while, he turns to me. 'Do you believe in *coup de foudre*?' he asks.

'Sorry?' But I know what he's about to say.

'You know – the French phrase for being struck by lightning. Love at first sight?' Lukas says, like he doesn't know boys never admit this stuff to girls they've just met.

'*Coup de foudre?*' I try to laugh it off. 'Nah. Insta-love is right up there with the tooth fairy and leprechauns, as far as I'm concerned. A cosmic joke.'

Lukas just stares at me. 'Wow. And I thought *I* was crazy. Love is a cosmic joke?'

I squirm. 'Yep. Always the wrong bloke. My best friend falls in love about once a month. It always ends up shite. Every time.'

'And this?' Lukas touches my hand.

My body hyper-jumps and a choked, puzzled look passes over his face, like he doesn't need this either.

'So what's this thing between us?' he asks.

I pause, lost for words. 'Well. Chemistry, I guess.'

Yeah. All sparkle, and no substance. This is my on-going argument with Harper. Love sucks. So how come I feel as bewildered as Lukas looks?

'Next you'll say you don't believe in trolls and fairies,' he says lightly.

God, he's fun. Fit. Unpredictable. 'Some of my best friends are fairies,' I say, trying to keep a straight face.

He laughs and turns away, and the intensity between us lifts. I can't stop smiling and hum *coup de foudre* under my breath. We stroll out of the park and into the noise of Strømgaten. 'Look, it's snowing!' I wave at tiny hard snow crystals, billowing and pirouetting in the street lights.

'It's Norway,' Lukas states.

My cheeks heat up. 'No way. Too old for snow? And exactly how old are you?'

'Seventeen, maybe.' He shrugs. 'The miner and his wife didn't know my age when they took me in. They were rich. One more mouth didn't matter to them.'

'Rich couple adopt lost kid? Sweet.' I laugh.

Lukas goes white. 'They're dead,' he says.

Holy crap.

He strides away down Strømgaten. I chase after him, apologizing, asking him what happened, but the traffic drowns me out. I kick myself for being so tactless and vow to put this right. But there's no time. As we sprint towards the bus station, the blue and white Flybussen pulls out the far end.

'I missed it?' I can't believe I've missed the bus, after everything.

'Hurry,' Lukas calls. 'They wait up at the next stop for hotel guests.'

We race through the station, jumping suitcases and slipping through the tourists. As snow comes down in flurries, Lukas cuts through the Grand Terminus Hotel and we exit out the back. I see the airport bus again, but we're on the wrong side of the road and it's snowing harder now. 'Please forgive me,' I say. 'I didn't know your parents were dead.'

He gives me this intense look. 'Apology accepted,' he says. 'Come with me. I promised I'd put you on that Flybussen.'

He darts into the traffic. There's a screech of brakes, snow sprays up into the air. I blink snowflakes, and when I can see again, Lukas is standing in the bus lane in his wolf coat. A beautiful winter scarecrow, arms outstretched in front of the bus and the tourists on board cheering as if he's just stopped a tank in Tiananmen Square.

I splosh across the road to him. Before I know what's happening, Lukas is pushing me on the bus. I feel him slip a piece of paper into my hands, but the driver is glaring at me and I can't find my ticket and there's no time for goodbyes.

The doors close with a swish. Somehow, my pink Dora the Explorer bag makes it through and crashes at my feet. Lukas turns and disappears in the dark, the wolf coat swirling around his legs, and the loss of him hits me like a blow.

I open his note; it's a torn piece of thick creamy white paper with a rapid pen sketch of a wolf howling.

I can't stop smiling.

The Flybussen lurches into rush-hour traffic.

'*Billett?*' the driver snaps.

But I'm so happy I could kiss him. 'I've got my ticket right here.'

I pop my keyboard between my knees and check my pockets for my purse, then I rummage in my bag. I panic and tip my stuff out on the floor of the bus. Everything gets soaked in melt snow.

'*Billett?*' the driver says, in a voice that's a lot less friendly.

'OK, OK.' I search my stuff again with panicky hands.

But my purse, with my passport and plane ticket, is gone.

6

The crowds thin out in Torgallmenningen Square as the light leaves the sky. He burns her British passport, page by page, firing the brass lighter until the hologram on her photo melts into molten ash. He doesn't give her missed flight a second thought.

Two hours later, he leans against his Ducati motorbike and photographs her banging on the Svad Store's windows, but the nightwatchman won't open up for anyone after hours without money, and he's made sure she has none. Snow pummels her keyboard case. He notes she's desperate to keep it dry. She's not dressed for Norwegian weather. Rain one day. Snow the next. And a heatwave coming. She will find that out for herself, says a cold voice in his head. He nods. But he can't take his eyes off her face.

It's not beautiful, but strong emotions play across it. Doubt. Anger. Loss. He knows them well. She gives up on the watchman and rests her forehead against the plate-glass window. He studies the reflection of her red hair, the fear on her English city face.

This is his pack's favourite bit, watching how prey reacts under pressure. Does she surrender so easily?

She looks around and stares in his direction; a cat that knows it's being watched. But she can't see him in the shadows.

She pulls her keyboard out. He smiles.

She empties a tin pencil case, puts it on the steps and picks out a ballad, head down, like she's playing for herself in her bedroom. He taps the brass lighter on the motorbike. The heartless night walks on past. No one cares about a lost singer. Norway turns a blind eye to foreigners. No one will save her.

Suddenly it's as if she heard him; she stands straighter, shaking the snow off her rat's tails. She lifts her chin and sings like she means it. '*I don't believe in true love. That's celebrity hype and lies.*'

Her raspy voice has something raw and true. He's fascinated by it. She's a different girl now. A survivor. The song feasts on the night, a true wolf's howl.

'*I won't believe in love.*'

Three local junkies creep up the steps. The skinny one in a tartan jacket grabs her arm and, startled, she bellows in his face, 'Don't mess with me, I've had a really, really bad day!'

He laughs at her temper, flips the brass lighter and studies how it lands. Heads, I save her – tails, I don't. She gets the side with the wolf scratch. *Tails.*

The junkies circle her, three giggling stoned Arctic foxes, sizing her up. He sees the moment she realizes the danger and steps out, wielding her keyboard. She'd rather destroy it than let them take it.

He flips the lighter a few times until he gets the side engraved with Svad's name.

Heads.

He guns his Ducati over Torgallmenningen, ignoring the pedestrian only signs. The junkies run for cover into the fish market.

'Need a ride home?' he asks her.

He holds out his hand: gentle, kind, patient – the way he calms a motherless pup. The girl stops with her keyboard in mid-air, and the smile she gives him knocks him sideways. No one ever grins at him like that any more.

'They said Norway is the safest country in the world,' she says.

Not for him. He senses she will be the death of him.

7

His motorbike roars into white tunnels and we take hairpin bends at full speed. Dark mountains flash past. My eyes half close in terror, I lick the falling snow off my face and listen to the wheels sing on the wet road. Flattened against Lukas's warm back, my numb arms clinging to his waist, the danger and the speed and the thrill of him collide. Lukas seems as much a part of me as breath.

Only the force of the slipstream, tugging and tugging on the knackered keyboard strapped to my back, reminds me of what I've lost. My passport. A flight home. The audition of a lifetime.

By the time we get to Nøy, the swirling snow vanishes and our yellow cottage, overgrown with loganberry bushes, appears at the end of the village like magic.

I ask Lukas to kill the engine at the church. Dad mustn't know I was on a motorbike with a boy. I climb off the Ducati, clumsy with cold, but everything in my body vibrating. Lukas walks me to the top of our drive. I didn't want him to see how we live now, renting a run-down cabin in the middle of nowhere, but he insists on walking me to the door.

'You can't live caged up in there.' He touches my cold hands. 'Let's keep on going. Come with me to Ulv Fjell. It's where they found me living wild with wolves. You'll love all the open space. There's no place like it.'

'Me hang out with wolves?' I grin.

Lukas pulls up the collar on his wolf coat. 'I never take anyone there,' he says. 'Don't you want to see where I grew up? Before the humans stole me?'

He holds out his hand to me. My fingers itch to take it and go away with him, then I remember what I am. 'I can't,' I mutter. 'My sister needs me to do her meds. I'm her main carer.'

'But they think you're in Manchester. You'll be back before they know it.'

'How did you . . . ?' I start to say, but the light fades from his sea-glass eyes, and I have to stop myself promising him the world to bring it back. 'I can't. I'm sorry. My family have eyes in the back of their heads. They'd never let me go away with a total stranger. And they're probably right.'

He looks so sad, I almost laugh.

'OK,' he says. 'Let's get acquainted. Meet me at the bottom of Preken Rock tomorrow morning? We can hike to the top in no time. I will show you my Norway, Nell Lamb.'

'You're on.' I curtsy in my sodden dress. 'I'll bring a picnic, it'd be rude not to thank you proper.'

He lets out a yelp and leaps in the air. 'It's a date. Dawn. Preken Rock.'

'Shush,' I whisper, looking over my shoulder.

And with a smile, Lukas steps away.

The cottage creaks as I slip in the back door. I want my bed before Dad's lectures start up in the morning. But he's sitting at the kitchen table, in the dark, with his head on his arms and a plastic rosary tangled in his fingers. His jerky snores sound like he's crying in his sleep. Our mum's name was Rosary. I sigh, and hide the rosary so Harper doesn't spot it later. I tiptoe around Dad, slip-sliding up the stairs in wet socks, and hop down the three steps to Harper's room and the hatch to my bed.

It's too quiet.

I flick on the light. The room closes in on me. Forty pairs of Jesus's brown eyes stare back from the Turin Shrouds. But Harper's bed is empty. I slump against the door.

She begged me not to go.

I shake my dad awake, still in my cold wet clothes. 'Where is she?'

Dad looks so upset that I hug him, and feel his heart thrash inside his barrel chest. I hadn't noticed I'd got taller than him. He hugs me back, only for a moment, but it's lovely, even if he smells of booze. We never do stuff like this. Harper gets all the hugs round here.

'She's in Voss Hospital,' Dad says. 'Something happened with her meds – I don't know . . . she's out

46

of danger now.'

'But she hasn't had an emergency in so long. Sorry. Sorry. I'm so sorry.' I'm gabbling, but no matter how often Harper has hospital scares, each one is an ordeal. We never know when her number is up. This visit. Or the next. Or the next.

It wears me down and I go quiet. But Dad, he likes to go nuts. Tonight he bangs on about my selfishness in general. It takes a while for the penny to drop.

He doesn't know about me running away.

Harper must be bad, if she didn't tell him, and I feel so shit I sway on my feet.

'I should be at the hospital,' Dad says.

Yeah. You should.

But we both know he can't stand them, and used me as the excuse to leave. Then he drank to forget.

'Where the hell have you been?' he says. 'Are you on something? You look too . . . too *happy*.'

Dad spits the word out like it's a disgrace.

Happy?

Yeah, I was. Until I got home.

'And you said you'd knock off the booze,' I mutter. 'Not drink and drive.'

'I didn't.' Dad looks indignant. 'The rig chopper followed the ambulance.'

The crews use them like taxis to hop on and off the rigs in all weathers.

I sigh. 'We need help. You hate hospitals. I'm no Florence Nightingale. Harper needs a nurse. You're

47

making her dependent on me. I can't always be here.'

'Not now, Nell.' Dad clamps his lips.

'What about me? When do I get a life?'

But it's pointless. My life is so unimportant compared to Harper's. I feel bad for even minding; the next few days will be hell, waiting to for the hospital to stabilize her meds, before we can even start any new treatment. Dad must never find out about me seeing a boy. There's an unspoken rule in our house. No lads until Harper gets better. Then Lukas is in my head, laughing, telling me he's too fast to get caught by anyone.

I smile.

'You're so like your mother!' Dad snaps. 'Selfish. Ugly!'

The clout on my ear takes me by surprise. I fly across the kitchen; my side smashes into the sink. I grip on to the taps, and while I wait for my world to stop spinning I spit bright blood into the dirty dishes. I stare at it feeling sick, thinking; it'll be me who clears this mess up.

'See what you made me do?' Dad shouts.

The ringing in my ears gets louder and louder and I zone out, until I'm a speck of dirt, burrowing into the greasy ceiling and this feels like it's happening to someone else.

This is my fault. I'm selfish. My fault. I'm trouble. Trouble. Trouble. Then it comes to me clear as anything. *This is why my mum left.* She couldn't bear to have me around. I'm ugly. It makes perfect sense now. Harper always says I don't listen, I never hear the music behind people's words.

When the boom-box rush in my ears dies down, I wipe my mouth and look at my father for an apology. Dad's lips are moving. I know he's praying for forgiveness. But not from me. From Jesus.

I want to roar and smash dishes. My dad never hits me when Harper is around. He never hits Harper. But would he? If I weren't here? Would he take his frustration out on her instead? I couldn't bear that. Harper needs us.

And I run the tape in my head; Dad never meant to hit me, this only started when Harper got sick. It's the worry and the booze talking. He doesn't know his own strength.

Tomorrow, my dad won't remember what happened.

Tomorrow, he'll be the saintly healer again.

Tomorrow, I'll wish I got blackouts and could forget too.

8

He spends the night on Preken Rock, waiting for dawn and for her. If he lies spreadeagled on the cliff edge and strains his neck he can look down on the little yellow cottage, lost in the shadows outside her fishing village. The Nøyfjord is narrow here, but he can trace the long, dark ribbon of seawater all the way to the majestic Sognefjord. Two hundred metres deep. And beyond that he can see lights on the jagged coastline, a sea-soup of grey seal, bitten rock and barren islands.

He doesn't look down at the shallow waters below the sheer rockface. The dizzying, lethal drop to the fjord doesn't trouble him. It's what hides below the surface that haunts him. And he crawls away, groaning, and lights another cigarette, rolling Svad's brass lighter between his knuckles.

But he can't stop the flashbacks.

The sounds are the worst. The muffled *thwup*, *thwup*, *thwup* of the helicopter blades stabbing betrayal into his heart.

Hate. Hate. Hate. Love. Hate. Hate. Hate. Love.

The helicopter drifting down between the vertical green cliffs. Metal meeting water. No cabins. No boats. No witnesses. Only the purple clouds and the gulls.

For a breath, for a lifetime, the steel skids skimmed along the fjord, balancing on the surface of the water. A mechanical dragonfly. Before cartwheeling into the depths.

Silence.

Then comes the cry again. The unutterable terror as ice water surges into the cockpit to embrace them.

9

Two days in a Norwegian hospital. I sleep on the floor by Harper's bed, doodling wolves in my journal, waiting for her test results. My head and my heart are in turmoil, pulling me in different directions. I never showed up at Preken Rock. Lukas will think I don't care. And I didn't show up at the airport to meet Dom either. Dad confiscated my phone, so I can't even let my best friend know what's happened. I scribble a song in my journal:

It's sunny.
I'm grounded.
Story of my life.

I want to bawl, but I have to stay strong for Harper. Dad's drinking again. Why is he so much worse now we're in Norway?

When Harper wakes, she's so happy to see me, my stomach lurches. I sit on her bed, listening to the hiss of the machines and pumps, afraid to look my sister in the eye.

Her face is chalk-white and blue veins pulsate on her bare scalp. She squeezes my hand. 'Take me home, Nels,' she whispers.

'Of course I will. Soon as.'

'I didn't need to tell Dad,' she yawns. 'I knew you'd never leave me.'

I hide behind my fake red hair and tuck her up. Feeling guilty doesn't come close to how shit I feel. 'I won't leave again,' I say. 'Promise. Please get well.'

I watch the doctors huddle in a group out in the corridor. My stomach tightens with anxiety. We're in the world centre for epigenetics. The study of genes. How they switch on and off. Nothing is fixed in our bodies. I have the same cancer gene as Harper, but mine is not switched on.

Norwegian specialists want to get my genes to do the same for my sister. Imagine. If they can switch her cancer gene off, my sister might be cured for ever.

We need that kind of miracle. Dad and me don't really get how epigenetics works, but the experts say it's their best shot for Harper's atypical leukaemia.

Then they come in and ask me endless questions; like it's my fault Harper reacted poorly to her meds. The cancer nurse makes me go through the new drug protocol, and the doctors give me this look like they can't believe I'm capable of following the hospital pager instructions, let alone doing my sister's injections.

I can't believe that I've been doing it for years either.

'We want to organize a home nurse.' The consultant

stares at me hard and I know I've been silent too long. 'A nurse can look after your sister better. More reliable. Someone with cancer nursing experience.'

Harper plucks at the tape on her IV line. I can feel her brain whirl. She'd never relax with a stranger in the house.

'No,' I say. 'I've got it. Whatever it takes.'

'That is not possible.' He looks so stern. 'A child like you cannot do her sister's medication. We get a nurse in, or your father must do it.'

'OK,' I fib. 'My father will do them, right, Dad?'

My dad looks at me in panic. His hands are shaking. *Did he give her the wrong dosage last night?*

Our doctor looks doubtful, and he confers with the geneticist in Norwegian.

I hold my breath. This is the biggie. Why we came to Norway. Epigenetics. 'I'm sorry, Eleanor,' the geneticist states. 'It didn't work this time.'

There's no small talk. No bedside manner. Just a matter-of-fact statement. I failed.

I look at Harper and I'm screaming inside. She's my sister. My sister. I'm all she's got.

Dad buries his head in his hands.

Harper struggles to sit up in bed. 'What's going on?'

Dad can't speak. *He'll never forgive me for failing her.*

'They're saying,' I rasp, 'they're saying I can't help you any more.'

She's all huge, scared eyes, begging me to deny it and make this OK for her. 'Of course you can,' she whispers.

'No. And they want you to have a nurse in.'

My sister is achingly pretty, with birdlike bones and bow-shaped lips like Dad's. I'm tall and clumsy and musical. I take after my mum. Probably.

Harper holds her breath. And then she is screaming at me. 'I hate you, Nell Lamb. I hate you. Get out. Get out of here. Why do you always ruin everything?'

I turn and run, past the cancer wards, down long pristine green corridors and crash into the day-care room overlooking the pine forest. Dozy patients watch me, unconcerned. They're used to families getting hysterical here.

I hear voices behind me and open a large cupboard and squeeze myself in. I sit next to a defibrillator. No chance it can shock my heart back to life.

I listen to my music and pretend none of this is happening to me. I lock all the mess-up questions in the small *room* in my head. And I throw away the key.

Harper's bay is dark when I go back. She's sleeping. The medics have gone. I take her hand and study my sister's fingers. They're slender and delicate and half the size of mine.

And I do what I always do when she is poorly; I sacrifice something to keep her here, on Planet Earth, with me. I can't lose her. The sacrifice has to be something big. It has to be the thing I hold most dear, or God won't listen. He's greedy like that.

I open my Dora the Explorer bag and find the application form to the BRIT School.

What was I thinking? Me? Going to a place like that? I can't move to London. I tear the application form into tiny pieces, scatter them in a circle around me, then kick them under her bed.

Dad's hung a picture of Jesus from the Turin Shroud over it to protect my sister.

'Satisfied now?' I ask Jesus. 'Give her back!'

He doesn't let me off that lightly.

Lukas.

His voice booms in my head.

I pull out the crumpled wolf sketch, study it, smoothing it out. I was right. Love is a cosmic joke. I look at Harper's poor naked head, its bowling-ball smoothness under the bright hospital lights. My feet drag across the shiny green floor. I put my foot on the Hazardous Waste pedal. The bin opens, slowly. I imagine all the discarded needles, syringes and surgical wipes inside, and I try to throw his wolf note away. But my hand won't let go.

10

The red spider came back. It's making a new cobweb over my mattress like I never left. Nothing else is the same about my life. Dad won't look at me when the nurse calls in, and Harper bullies me at every opportunity in between. We've been home two weeks before she catches me in the bath, 'self-harming' with Dad's razor. My knees are a bleeding stubbly mess. How can we invent the internet and multi-flavoured Starbursts, but not discover a way to remove leg hair without torture?

My sister throws her *Hair* mag at me. 'Dad!' she shouts, jumping to conclusions. 'Nell met a boy while I was in hospital.'

'Bad luck. Dad's in the garden,' I snap, wrapping a towel round me and walking to our room.

'Bitch!' she hisses.

I kick myself for not locking the door. But my sister would have worked it out, sooner or later, from my crop of shaving nicks. She's no good at maths, Harper, but anything to with boys and she outsmarts Einstein.

She does this equation in her head: Nell has Dad's razor + she's shaving her legs = Nell's shagging a lad. 'Remember your promise,' she hisses. 'No falling in love before me.'

I sigh. 'I made that promise when you'd had your first round of chemo. I was out of my mind with panic. Shagging a lad was the last thing on my mind.'

'A promise is a promise,' she snaps. 'Why should *you* have a life, when I *don't*?'

I change the subject fast. 'What do you remember about Mum before you got sick?'

'What do you need to know, Baby?' my sister says. 'How you ruined everything with your non-stop crying? Get over yourself. That's what babies do. They ruin romance; love flies out the window. Our mum was a slutty cow who cheated on our dad. Or she swapped us for an upgrade. Either way, she left. So she's not shaping up for mum-of-the year, is she? Our mum's gone. You still can't say boo to a pigeon and I'm still going to die early. Bald.'

My sister leaves me reeling. But Harper? She switches mood like a TV remote.

'Nell,' she says after a minute. 'Do I need a wig? They say bald is the new ugly.'

'No. I've got a better idea.' I open my bag and pull out the pot of henna paste. 'Want a hand-painted headdress?' I say.

Harper sniffs. 'Oh, go on then. You can't make me look any worse than I do.'

I dip the brush in the pot and I bury the day I met Lukas in the *room* in my head. It's not his fault, but everything has turned to shite since.

'I can paint you a cap in the Norwegian folk style,' I tell Harper. 'You know that decorative paintwork in the church? They call it Rosemåling.'

'Rosemåling?' she says, wistful. 'I like the sound of that.'

So I sketch an Archangel's helmet over Harper's bald head, and I feather the design over her forehead, her head, and around her ears. I use bold, stylized lines. Flowers. Oak leaves. Peacock feathers. Somehow, every line turns into a pair of sea-glass eyes.

'It tickles,' Harper complains. 'But you're not bad at this. Forget singing, become a tattoo artist at my future salon. Paint nails. Who needs the BRIT School? You can sing to my customers and with the hairdryers on, no one will mind your throat-slitting songs.'

'Sure. Why not?' I shrug.

But my heart slides down, like some essential part of me is melting away. The cramped bedroom and the murky brown Turin Shrouds press in on me. Then Lukas's face appears in the prints instead of Jesus. Long, long, broken nose. Full lips. I know every mark and blemish. I met him once, for a couple of hours, and I know his face better than my own. I smile back.

Harper elbows me. 'Focus.'

'Sorry.' I take a deep breath.

Lukas's face vanishes. I thicken the henna into a paste

and go over the helmet drawing again. I want it perfect, and I concentrate like I'm illuminating the most precious manuscript ever.

My sister's skin.

Harper holds a mirror up as I add dots of henna to where her eyebrows once were, and her painted scalp is transformed into something more stunning than hair.

'I look like a flower fairy,' she giggles. It's so lovely to hear her laugh. 'Thanks, Nels,' she says.

Harper never thanks me.

My eyes well up. 'You need . . . to let the henna dry for a few hours,' I stammer.

'Dad once told me that Mum's favourite movie was *Thelma and Louise*,' my sister says, so quietly I almost mishear her. 'Want to watch it after Lent? If Dad ever lets us watch screens again. He thinks Thelma gave Mum the idea of running away.'

'Really?' I act dead cool. I know better than to push Harper for more details.

'Keep my head off the pillow,' she yawns. 'I don't want the design messed up.'

'Yes, ma'am,' I say, chuffed the headdress makes Harper feel better. I hold her upright for hours while she sleeps, and think about Dad. And Mum.

It's dark when I crawl through the hatch to my mattress and pull the duvet over my head.

Why doesn't he come back?

A boy has woken up my heart, and now everything

hurts inside. I sneak my phone upstairs and message Dom: *In love. Going mad. What do I do?*

Dom fires back from the studio. I almost laugh, he's so predictable. The only thing my best friend loves more than musicals and air crash investigations is an unrequited love story. *O.M.G. Put him in a song.*

Then Dom calls me. 'I got the BRIT School to give you an extension. Time to find your passport, or get a new one.'

'A second chance?' My heart soars like a firefly, only to die in the same instant. I listen to my sister's snoring. The best sound ever. What am I thinking of? I can't leave. I unwrap a strawberry Starburst and stuff it in my mouth. You can't even buy them here. 'I don't know who I am any more,' I moan.

Dom sighs in my earpiece. 'Nell, it's not like you had a handle on that before.'

The weeks pass. Harper regains her strength. The last of the snow melts on the peaks. The nurse comes and goes. And Lukas stays away. The new grass is an eye-aching green. And Lukas stays away. Norway nosedives into a heatwave. And Lukas stays away. Everything dries out. It's all the locals talk about. The ozone. The unseasonal sun.

And Lukas stays away.

I can't even google him. As usual Dad's banned screens for Lent, but this year he made me promise on Harper's life that I won't cheat and use them. Now it feels like if anything happens to her, it will be my fault, and I daren't risk using my phone again.

Time always takes on a new dimension when Dad bans screens. But this year I'm falling down the rabbit hole in slow motion; time is hollow, frozen and eternal.

I'm mind-blowingly unhappy and happy in the same moment. I think of Lukas every second. Every minute. Every hour. All day. And night. Every night.

I wish I were exaggerating.

Is this love?

Something more pain than pleasure? Music flies off my keyboard, trying to make sense of the mess inside me. It's hard to keep up and I write song after song after song in my journal, finding a place inside me that I've never explored.

At school I search every face. Looking for Lukas. I know. I know. Of course he won't be there. I horrify myself. I live in a daze. I can't sleep. I don't talk. I won't eat.

'I'm the one supposed to be on the cancer diet,' Harper bitches. 'Don't pine for Dom and that stupid audition.'

'I'm not,' I sigh, lost in my dream world.

'No,' she says, with a sly smile. 'You never shaved your legs for Dom, did you?'

I stare at her.

'Want me to redo your roots?' my sister asks, all innocent.

I hesitate, because if I agree, she'll know she's on to something. And she already snoops through my stuff. I have to hide my journal under the bed, behind the dead red spider, and blow fluff around its curled-up body so it looks undisturbed. Harper mustn't find out about Lukas. She'd ruin everything and tell Dad. He'll go mental I've broken his unspoken rule: the one where I get to sacrifice my happiness to keep my sister safe.

Moonlight picks out Jesus's face on her walls. Forty pairs of brown eyes reproach me for wanting a boy so much during Lent.

'Oh, don't look at me like that,' I cry. 'What is the sodding point of you, when you don't answer my prayers? We don't all have eternity to muck about.'

Ping. Something hits my window. There is again. Stones? Pinging on the glass?

I crawl over my mattress and open the window. Cold night air seeps in and smells faintly of fresh fish. I can't see anyone, but perched on my yellow windowsill is a toy wolf carved out of some kind of quartz, with dark threads running through it.

Did he risk his neck to climb up here for this? There's no note. But I don't need one to get his message. He's coming back. Soon. The stone wolf sits in my hand, I study every marking on its head, and slowly its beauty undoes me.

II

V ord Skole is Nordic cool. The long, mirrored building juts over the fjord, reflecting the ice water and bright-green shoots on the birch trees surrounding the school. We finish before lunch on Wednesdays and students tumble out of classrooms, nattering in Norwegian. The hurdy-gurdy rhythm does my head in, and usually everyone wants to practise their English on me. Not today. I'm halfway down the stairs when I hear his name. Girls from my class crowd around the windows, giggling.

A boy lopes through the birches along the fjord, in a long dark wolf coat.

My heart rate goes stratospheric, then my knees shake, overcome by the shock of seeing him. I want to cry and laugh at the same time. How did he know which school to go to? Or that I finish early on Wednesdays? Can I pull off any level of cool? It's a while before the noise in my head shuts up enough for me to move on down the stairs.

Lukas leans against a birch trunk, smoking. That's brave. Smoking and alcohol are more of a no-no in

Norway than drugs. I slip past athletic blonds in sailing jackets and float over the grass to him, barefoot and carrying my trainers. Of course, I step on a twig and hop to him like an idiot. But Lukas gazes at me as if he can't believe I'm here. He takes my trainers from me, hunkers down and slips them on my feet. He ties the laces up tight and doesn't seem to notice everyone is looking at him, at us.

'I waited for you on Preken Rock,' he says at last, standing up. His eyes fix on mine again, this time accusingly. 'You never came.'

'Harper was sick,' I say, shocked by how resentful I feel towards her right now.

'So we're Romeo and Juliet?' Lukas says grandly. 'Torn apart by family?'

I grin. 'Hope not. They met on the Sunday and were dead by Thursday. We met once, weeks ago, and we're still alive last time I looked.'

His face twists. 'I promised myself I'd stay away from you.'

'Why?' I say, wounded to the core.

'Hello, Lukas, come sailing with us?' Gudrun calls.

Spring is a big deal after the long winter. The alpha bitch in Vord Skole pulls on her outside shoes, blinks blue eyeshadow at Lukas, elbowing her giggling friends to shut up.

I catch the word *trøbbel*. My heart drops. Of course. Lukas knows these girls. Gudrun's exactly the kind to make sure she knows all about him and his business.

'They're sailing to Sognefjord,' I mutter. It's the last thing I want to do.

Lukas shudders. I put my hand out to steady him. His sea-glass eyes lock on mine and the light in them recharges as if he's consuming everything about me. I feel the connection weave between us as strong as before. He gives a tiny shake of his head.

Not here. Not in front of everyone.

He gestures at the birch wood, and I stumble after him into the silvery trees.

Norwegian woods feel older than our ones back home. Bright-green moss covers everything; it grows over rocks, boulders, up the side of trees and shrouds the branches, so the woods feel as if they've been sleeping, undisturbed, for hundreds of years.

Lukas stops in a clearing; the birch trees filter the sunlight a greenish glow. His face merges into the leaves and becomes part of the forest. 'This is all wrong!' he exclaims, touching the young leaves. 'It's too early for spring.'

Global warming, I could say. But I don't. It'd kill the moment and I just want to look at him. He smiles at me. And in that moment I can't remember ever being so happy.

'We got you something,' he says. 'For missing your audition.'

'*We?*' I'm winded by a jealous pang.

'Ulv Pup.' He grins. 'I told my baby brother all about you.'

'Oh,' I say, touched. 'Ulv Pup? What kind of name is that?'

'It's Norwegian for Wolf Pup.'

'What's his real name?'

'Hagen.'

'And *that* means?'

Lukas shrugs. 'Highest Son. But I don't use it. Ulv Pup suits him better.'

'Oh,' I say, and feel sort of sad; my family never used my real name either. Dad and Harper called me *The Baby* until I was twelve. Then I insisted they called me Nell. They were shocked, had never noticed I'd grown up. They rarely noticed me full stop.

'Nell?' Lukas says, and he presses a paper musical box into my hand. It's hand-painted with blue wolves and decorative plumes of smoke. 'That's wolf smoke,' he explains. 'Ancient Chinese armies burnt dried wolf dung in their war beacons. They believed it was too strong to disperse in the air, and could be seen for miles.'

He smiles at my delight, and turns the miniature handle. The musical box plays the tune to 'Yesterday' by The Beatles. Then Lukas slows the tune down and the notes are birdsong sweet. He stops, and I cradle the paper musical box in both hands, like I'm holding a fledgling that might fly away. I can't speak. No one is interested in music at home.

'Someone gave that to me, when I was a child.' He stops himself, knuckling a birch trunk. 'They call these the Watchful Trees.'

'Hmm?' I say, still mesmerized by the musical box.

'All trees have eyes. But especially birches,' Lukas says. 'Trees watch us.'

'Really?' I study the birches. They just look like trees to me. I try harder. In the silver trunks, there are dark round marks that do look a bit like eyes. I shiver. 'But it's just where twigs have fallen off, right?'

Lukas laughs and laughs. I can't believe how happy I feel. How does a feeling this big fit inside one body? He stubs his cigarette out and puts the butt in an empty matchbox. His hands are criss-crossed with white scars.

'Did your pet she-wolf do that?' I ask.

'A wolf is more of a teacher, they don't make good pets.' Lukas looks away. His profile is achingly beautiful. 'The Barnevernet,' he says, 'the Norwegian Social Services, are threatening to take my little brother into care now.'

'What? I'm so sorry. Can't you raise him?'

'One day I will,' Lukas says.

I almost say it's not so easy looking after a sibling, but I don't. I want to ask more, but I don't. Lukas doesn't say anything else about his family. And I don't want to talk about mine. So we chat about music and how I feel about moving to Norway. We talk and talk and talk. Lukas rests against a birch trunk, lighting cigarettes with a brass lighter, and each time he saves the butt in the empty matchbox.

'You shouldn't smoke,' I blurt. 'It can kill you.'

'We have to die of something, might as well be this.' Then he smiles at me. 'Sweet Nell, don't worry. I just like to light up. I don't inhale.'

'Oh,' I say, relieved.

'I'll stop . . . if you sing to me,' he says. 'I want to know why music's so important to you.'

'Here? In the woods?'

'Absolutely. Sing a song just for me, one of yours.'

'You'll laugh at me.'

'It beats laughing at myself.' Lukas taps the paper musical box. 'Come on. We have music.' And he tickles my neck with a birch leaf until I agree to sing the last song I wrote.

Lukas is silent for so long when I finish *Red Spider in My Hair* that I think he must really hate my singing, and doesn't know how to tell me. Then he claps so ferociously I think he's taking the piss. 'You are a songbird,' he says. 'It would be a crime if you never performed. Will your father ever change his mind about the BRIT School?'

'Musical talent doesn't cut it in my family.' I fiddle with the musical box, absurdly chuffed Lukas likes my singing. 'And I can't exactly travel without my passport.'

He flips his brass lighter like he's considering my problem. 'You will need your birth certificate,' he says knowledgeably.

'My dad's lost it . . .'

'Eleanor Mary Lamb!'

I groan. Harper might be sick, but she never loses her piercing voice and it carries clear over the trees.

'That's my sister outside the school. I need to get her home. It's her first day back at Vord Skole. Even a few hours exhausts her. And Harper mustn't see us together. She's blind as a kitten without her glasses, but I swear my sister can see like Catwoman when she wants to snoop on my life. She'd tell Dad I'm seeing a boy in Lent. And I'm already grounded.'

'Want the Norwegian to tell her to fuck off?' Lukas asks, like he can read my mind.

'I wish.'

'*Drit og dra.*'

I laugh. 'Harper would so bust me for swearing. Tell me again how you pronounce it. *Drit og dra?*'

The school bell rings out.

Four times. The chimes linger over the woods.

I sense Lukas is gone, even before I turn around. Will I see him again? How will his baby brother cope in care? I hum along with his musical box, dead slow, until my racing heart chills.

When I look up, the lanky kid from psych class is standing over me. Sven's nice enough; compared to Lukas, he looks so ordinary. And I wish he'd go away.

'It's not safe in the woods, especially with Lukas,' Sven says. 'They say he can call wolves to his aid. And now we have a bad wolf problem. Last week a wolf killed a goat right under a farmer's nose. That's not normal behaviour for a wolf. No one is allowed in the school woods on their own.'

'Oh,' I say, on my feet in a flash.

'Didn't you hear the news?' Sven says. 'They've found Svad's helicopter.'

I almost say good riddance, but it seems a bit mean. The oil tycoon has been missing, presumed drowned for weeks. It's all they talk about ever since we got here.

Of course, Gudrun and her gang find me in the clearing and push Sven aside. They stare at me quite rudely for Norwegians. 'How does a foreigner like you know Lukas Svad? He hasn't been seen in public for months. Ever since his family died.' Gudrun shakes me by the arm. 'Well?'

'Svad?' I say. 'Lukas's family are the ones who died in the helicopter crash?'

'Where have you been? Under a rock?' Gudrun's soft fingers pinch into me.

I smile to wind her up in front of her friends, and think of Lukas's strong lean fingers touching me instead.

'He's heir to Svad Oil.' Berta swings her blonde mane. 'He hunts with wolves.'

'He can hunt me down any time,' sniggers Tove, hugging her pink sailing jacket.

Berta pouts. 'They say he lives on a secret mountain. Ulv Fjell. It's so remote no one can get to it. Can you introduce me?'

'To Lukas? You sure he's a Svad?' I say.

'Yes, Lukas Svad,' says Gudrun. 'Don't you know anything?'

No. Clearly not. Why didn't he tell me?

And then I realize he did. Sort of. He said his parents were dead and were rich miners. Svad Oil owns mines. And this lot are talking about Lukas as if he was some mysterious Gatsby. Maybe he didn't want more of that from me?

'How do you know him?' Gudrun shoves my school bag and I almost drop the musical box.

'Lukas Svad?' I say, loving how his new name fizzes on my tongue.

'Did he say what happened?' Gudrun says. 'Svad's body was found, but his wife is still missing. Was it an accident? Murder? Suicide? What did he say?'

'Probably pilot error,' says Sven.

When I pretend not to understand their fascination with the elusive, grieving heir to an oil and mining fortune, students thin out, disappointed I won't give them any insider dirt.

'Be careful.' Sven looks at me, concerned. 'Lukas prefers his wolves to humans.'

'I probably won't see him again.' I smile at Sven, adding as I remember, 'Anyway, my dad's not exactly a fan of Svad Oil.'

Then we hear it.

A wolf howl.

The sound vibrates though my bones and up into the fjord.

Lukas?

Every creature stops to listen.

The Vord students pull me with them, running out of

the woods, shrieking, laughing, looking back over their shoulders. Thrilled to be scared; thrilled to be alive.

But Harper sits, slumped, alone on a bench outside Vord Skole. Her tired eyes say it all. *You forgot about me.*

12

The dark loves him. It breathes over his shoulder as he runs the Nøyfjord towards Nøy village, feet flying over wet rock and grass, faster, faster, searching the black ribbon of seawater for signs of her. She'll come back, he tells himself. She always does. But her silence haunts him, and the scars on his arm flare up and burn him afresh.

Reluctant. He opens the folder on his phone – *Sleeping Beauty*, he's named it – and watches the film of her red hair floating in the sea.

He knows he should be dead too.

Only, the narrow fjord was strangely warm after the mild winter. Freak weather had saved him from dying of the cold. And Svad's clever piloting saved them from the crash itself. Svad had hydroplaned the chopper over the surface of the fjord. They almost made it to the other side before it sank. Svad saved him; but the tycoon got trapped inside the chopper.

He throws his head back and howls; the grief rips out of him and reverberates off the mountains.

There's no reply. No loving howls of reassurance.

His loneliness fells him. He drops to the rocks, punches out fifty press-ups, the cold gnawing into his hands. He flips on his back and counts fifty crunches, jackknifing his body with a twist, until he collapses on the smooth granite, exhausted.

At the church, a husky races through the gravestones, eager to bully intruders. He grabs its muzzle and slams it in the dirt. The dog yelps and wiggles on its belly, tail down. Game over.

He lies on a grave, marked by a statue of a weeping angel, and listens to the night. The husky curls up on him, its warm body a comfort, and a cruel reminder that his own pack brothers are dead. He knows what he must do. But he finds he dreads the moment when the girl discovers she's been betrayed as much as him.

He saved Ulv Fjell. That's what he did. That's why he did it.

He bivouacs alone that night on Preken Rock and wills himself asleep to dream of running with his wolves on the mountain.

But he wakes in the dark to find he's weeping again, and lights a cigarette; hating how it tastes, but needing the smoke to blot out the smell of blood.

13

Blue skies. Day after day. I have never felt so happy. And I cut school to be with Lukas Svad. Dad will kill me when he finds out.

But who can say no to a boy who's lost his entire family – for a second time?

Lukas doesn't want to dwell on it. He says being with me helps him forget why he can't go ahead with their joint funeral.

Svad's widow is still missing.

So Lukas shows me his Norway. A wilderness of mountains and fjords and savage waterfalls that drum down, so violent, the rocks vibrate under our feet and we stand and roar into the cold spray. Far below us, Japanese tourists wave from the ferries. We give them the finger. They still wave back. Lukas and me laugh so much, I'm up for anything.

He tells me about his wolves and Arctic foxes and their prey. Elk. Moose. Deer. His world is so bewitching and carefree, so unlike mine. Yet Lukas grills me for stories of growing up in a city like he thinks that's even more awesome. 'So what scared you as a child?' he asks, after one of his more outrageous tales of fighting off two wolf pups to save his lunch.

'Everything,' I laugh. 'I was scared of things disappearing. Maybe that's to do with my mum leaving – I don't know. I was too little to know any different, but I hated letting Dad out of my sight back then. We had this one nanny, who would wave him off on his work trips with a smile, but then whisper to us that he was never coming back. Harper still hates nannies. She'd take it out on me and vandalize my dolls, gouging their eyes out. I had to turn them to face the wall at night in case they turned into zombies, and she'd sneak in and turn them back again.'

Lukas whistles softly. 'Is that why your sister hates you?'

'She doesn't,' I say, miserable. 'Harper loves me. It's complicated. She just resents needing me so much.'

'Oh,' he says. 'What about your mother?'

I pause. 'According to Harper, our mum climbed out the window one night and ran away, because I wouldn't stop crying. She never came back. Never wrote. Once or twice a week, I'd wish Mum had left her forwarding address, or sent us postcards or a Christmas card, or anything really, so I could go and live with her instead. She's got to be loads nicer than Dad. He won't even allow a photo of Mum in the house. It's not up for discussion. I panic sometimes, because nowadays I can't even remember her face. Harper just shouts it's my fault Mum left. So

I don't ask any more. As my sister was only little at the time, I bet she doesn't know that much anyway. For years Mum's face was imprinted on my mind and I could fall asleep seeing her smiling eyes. But I can't even remember what colour they were now.'

The way Lukas Svad stops and listens, dead still and focused, always makes me say more than I mean to. He rolls his brass lighter over his fingers. 'Your sister sounds quite a storyteller. Let me tell you why I'll never leave you.'

He walks dead slow in a circle around me, and he never takes his eyes off my face. 'I love your eyes,' he says. 'I love your red hair. I love your throat. I love your long fingers. I love your defiance. I love your kindness. I love your smile.'

I can't see him when Lukas walks behind me, but his spellbinding voice goes on and on. 'I love your shoulders. I love your music. I love your elbows. I love your spirit.'

He stands before me now and smiles.

I thought friends exaggerated about being in love.

They've not even come close.

The next morning, we skirt around the forest above Nøyfjord, and stop on top of a steep meadow. Bergarter Felt. In the pop-up sea of purple-blue-yellow flowers, we spot a roe deer. It's a young buck, with a glistening fox-red hide and small velvety horns, minding its own business, munching lunch. I didn't see Lukas move, but he has his rifle out and his body strums with concentration.

I've never seen a gun before.

'Come look,' he insists, and hands the rifle to me.

It's longer than my arm and smells sharp; gun oil on warm metal. I pull the heavy butt into my shoulder, and Lukas shows me how to line up the sights.

He's so close to me that I breathe him in, and forget what I'm doing.

Then I'm staring down the sights into the roe's gentle brown eyes and this beautiful creature is watching me, trusting me and not running away.

My body shakes. 'Please don't kill it, Lukas.'

He lowers the gun. 'That young thing will grow up and destroy the valleys,' he says, dead stern. 'Deer gorge and trample everything in their path. Only wolves keep them in order. Wolves scare deer away from the open pasture, and the land has time to grow back, riverbanks stop eroding. They get more mice and birds, and small mammals attract kestrel and buzzards, so we have more wildlife. The whole ecosystem thrives thanks to the wolf. But just remember, your Bambi is the real threat to our environment.'

'Wow,' I say. 'How do you know all this stuff?'

'I watch prey,' Lukas says simply. He salutes the ring of green mountains above us. 'It's called a Trophic Cascade in ecology. The addition or removal of a predator. The wolf is the top of the food chain and creates life all the way to the bottom. By killing a few, the wolf saves its world. Yellowstone National Park restored wolves twenty years ago, and they regenerated the land. That's what I'm going to do on Ulv Fjell.'

'Awesome,' I say. 'And there's me who just wants to nail a good song.'

He wolf-whistles at the fawn. The animal freezes; kicks up its heels and is gone.

'You know why we hunters have to cull deer?' Lukas asks me.

I shake my head.

'Because Norwegians shoot all the wolves. This past winter the government shot forty-two of them. Including two entire packs. One time, we had only fourteen wolves left in the whole of Norway. Now they have a Wolf Zone. Not that it stops anyone.'

'So there's fat chance of me meeting a wolf?' That's a big load off my mind.

'Not here.' Lukas's face falls. He locks his rifle on to the Ducati and stares at me. 'Nell, how will you survive the future, if you don't know how to kill to eat?'

'No offence, but in Manchester we have something called shopping,' I say. 'Don't you have dial-a-pizza here?'

Lukas picks a pink alpine flower and pops it in my mouth. His touch on my lips sends a jolt through me. 'Eat. It's purple mountain saxifrage. A Norwegian delicacy.'

I screw my face up at the bitter taste.

He laughs. 'It's sweet if you chew. It's full of vitamins. You need to know what's safe to eat in the wild.'

I feel his warm breath on my face.

He's going to kiss me.

But Lukas takes a deep breath in, and simply asks what music I love best. Lukas goes in for movie soundtracks; he likes big emotional orchestral swells, with as few words as possible. He's proper romantic in an old-fashioned kind of way.

'I like Norwegian pop music at the moment. It's got a cool vibe. They sing in this otherworldly English. Strange, like aliens seeing us for the first time and singing about it to us.'

Lukas swipes over his phone till he finds the song I want.

We share his headphones and sway together in the meadow listening to the last Sigrid hit. We drift into that place where nothing and no one comes close. Only me and him live there. Then Lukas hooks my arm with his and we dance.

We spin and spin and spin, stomping on wild flowers, until we're doubled up from laughing. I flop down, dizzy with head rush and green mountains are spinning around me.

'Ever seen *The Sound of Music*?' I say. 'I played Maria at school. Love that film.'

'I cheered for the Nazis,' Lukas says, deadpan.

'No way.' I sit up aghast. 'Why?'

Lukas has the wickedest look on his face. 'It wound Svad up. Norway was under Nazi occupation in the war. Anything to beat playing happy families.'

I laugh. And lie back, making snow angels in the alpine flowers with my arms, hoping I look cute enough for him to jump me. Part of me is glad when he doesn't.

The way Lukas Svad looks at me is better than sex.

He holds out his hand. 'Nell, don't lie in the long grass. The ticks carry diseases.'

'Eew. What do they look like?'

'A small red spider. You can get Lyme disease from them.'

A small red spider? So much for romance. I'm out of the alpines in a flash, furiously brushing down my legs and dress.

'I didn't see anything about ticks in the guidebooks,' I say.

'There's a lot of things about Norway not in the guide-books.' Lukas moves nearer and I hold my breath again, but he just checks my hair over, looking for ticks like I'm his favourite dog. I sigh.

'Can you wolf howl?'

'Of course.'

'Was that you howling outside Vord Skole? When you came to find me?'

He smiles.

'Can you teach me?'

Lukas tosses his brass lighter and checks how it lands. 'Heads. OK.'

We stand on moss-covered rocks overlooking the fjord, and Lukas throws back his head and wolf howls down to the sea. Then the mountains echo the howl back to us. He does it again and again. My skin shivers.

'I get it,' I say slowly. 'You're modulating the howl over an octave?'

Lukas tilts his head and smiles at me. 'Use your body,

Nell. Not your head. Like this.' He stands behind me, puts one hand on my chest and one on my belly and shows me how to do it. Suddenly music is the last thing on my mind, and my world focuses in on his hands and what they will do next. I can feel him waiting too. His breath on my hair.

And then Lukas sighs, and teaches me there are three key sounds to a wolf howl: a 'woo' an 'oo' and a 'roo'. I am a singer and if there is one thing I can crack, it's singing.

'Arrh oou woooo oooh rooo,' I let rip.

And I swear, far away in the mountains, we hear a wolf sing back to us.

But Lukas just laughs and laughs at my efforts.

'How far away is Ulv Fjell?' I ask.

'It's remote. We keep its location a secret. It's not difficult. Lots of Norwegian mountain ranges have no names. Svad was a private man. Almost a recluse for a tycoon.'

'What was it like up there?' I ask. 'I can't imagine growing up in the wild.'

Lukas is worse than Dad for going deaf, whenever I ask about his family. His sea-glass eyes blank out, like he's somewhere else completely. I touch the white scars on his hand; his skin feels so taut. I could touch him for ever. Lukas kisses my fingers absent-mindedly. I think he's worrying about his little brother.

'I was six when Svad found me, and Asena was just a pup. I held her in my arms so the hunters couldn't shoot her.'

'Asena?' I say, trying to get my head around how he

could hold a wolf and protect it. 'That's a pretty name for a wolf.'

He nods. 'It's perfect for her. Asena's named after a Turko-Mongolian legend when one baby boy survived a massacre by Chinese soldiers and was nursed by a she-wolf.'

'Oh, like Romulus and Remus,' I say airily, like my general knowledge didn't all come from *The Simpsons* and is wafer-thin.

But Lukas just nods and wraps himself in his wolf coat. 'Yes. After that Svad's wife was the closest thing I had to a mother. When I woke up, caked in my wolves' blood, we watched Svad set light to our den so that Asena and I could never return home. His wife kept me and Asena in cages at night for years.'

'*Cages?* She kept you in cages? That's so cruel.'

'No – it was our den, small and safe. She insisted on raising me. Svad's wife brought me back to life, forced me to live when all I wanted was death. Bathed me, dug out my ticks, comforted my grief. She taught me to be human, while Asena grew into a beautiful she-wolf. That was hard for Svad to forgive . . .' Lukas smiles at me. 'It was the only time she stood up to him, and he hated me for that.'

'Why did he burn the den?' I ask.

Lukas shrugs. 'Svad Oil wanted to make Ulv Fjell safe for their miners. They found the biggest deposit in the world of rutile up there. Titanium dioxide. It makes things white. Paper. Plastic. Paint. It's very valuable because it's so cheap to mine in open pits. Even cheaper if you have no problem getting rid of the mining waste – and Svad Oil planned to dump all the toxic waste in Sognefjord. It's so deep they figured it wouldn't hurt our ecosystem.'

'What? No way. Norway wouldn't let them?'

'No. They didn't get a mining licence back then. So Svad slaughtered my wolves for nothing.'

He pulls up the blue-black fur collar of his wolf coat so it frames his long face. When Lukas knows he has my full attention, he pulls up his sleeve and shows me a constellation of fingerprint-sized scars on his forearm. Small marks are burnt into his arm: red and blue; and older, shiny white ones. All brutally etched in his skin.

'What are they?' I gasp.

'Cigarette burns. Svad said I had bad blood.'

'Bloody hell.' I trace my fingers over the puckered skin. 'I'm not going to risk having kids with *anyone*. Too many parents mess up their children!'

Lukas nods. 'True. A wolf pup never comes good after its mother's rejection.'

I blink my eyes rapidly.

'Nell – you OK?'

My stomach twists. I shrug. 'I spent my childhood waiting for my mum to come back to me. I'd sit on our doorstep after rows with Dad, convinced Mum would come get me to live with her. But she never came. I'd fall asleep outside in the dark, clutching my suitcase. Still hoping. Still waiting for her.'

Lukas frowns. 'Did your father move on?'

'He's like me. Can't let go. The longing for someone gets worse as the years pass. What you build up on the outside – confidence, success, friendships, school – it all feels like it's built on thin ice.' Determined not to look a total loser, I pull thistle burrs out of my skirt and grin at him. 'I'm so over it now.'

Lukas is watching my face and I know he sees right through me. 'You're a true artist. You write songs, so you don't lose yourself in the abyss.' He ducks his head, deep in thought, his dark hair falling over his eyes.

Later he wheels his Ducati up the path, kicking wild alpines out of his way. I love how he moves. So, so sure of himself. I want to hear more about his childhood on Ulv Fjell, but Lukas opens the throttle on his Ducati and I think the conversation is over. Then he turns and smiles.

'I have to rescue Ulv Pup from the Barnevernet. He's lost his mother. He needs a real family.'

'Of course,' I say. 'He's your brother – he needs you.'

14

It's been a strange winter with no bite. The year the sea didn't freeze. Svad's funeral sails out of the city and heads to the coast and the burial site.

He stands guard over the tycoon's coffin on the top deck. A Svad Oil fleet shadows the funeral down the fjord. He narrows his eyes, cursing the sleek dark hulls as they smack into the churned-up wake; a seething white, like an open pit, he thinks. *A rutile mine.* Svad's final act of destruction.

They pass silent docks. Wiping the salt spray out of his eyes, he shrinks deeper into Svad's wolf coat when the dockworkers lower their huge cranes in respect.

Should he salute them back? The howl builds inside him. And he's back in the loop of disbelief that this is happening. *How can Rosa be dead and the divers find Svad's body but not hers?*

They sail out to a flat grey sea. The nanny brings him Svad's son. The infant chortles in his arms at the family of humpbacks blowing alongside the tanker. He pinches the baby's leg. Learn respect, he hisses. Your mother is dead.

The baby yelps, but wriggles in his arms, unconcerned.

Anyone can see Svad's offspring is a born alpha. Confident. Inquisitive. Fearless. Svad loved rubbing his nose in that.

Blood will out, Dogboy. This one's bred in the bone. Maybe I've no need of you now?

Rosa kept him, anyway.

He gouges his thumbnail into Svad's coffin so he doesn't cry.

All he wanted was a life that began and ended with his wolves. There wasn't a time before them. His last happy childhood memory was of the pack and him huddled together under the snow.

He closes his eyes. And he's back there. On Ulv Fjell. Skiing with Asena and her pack. His skis clatter over ice moguls, whooshing through the powder, carving straight down the fall line. The wolves loping alongside, effortless grace, raw speed, grinning ear to ear as he tucks into a schuss, skis parallel, a high-speed run downhill to keep up. The arctic wind singing in his face: its never-ending song of freedom. *Schuss. Slalom. Hunt.*

He digs his thumbnail harder into the tycoon's ornate coffin. Everything Rosa built up in him, Svad twisted.

Never forget your blood, Dogboy. You're scat from a wolf den. Why didn't they eat you?

He didn't have the answer to that.

Norwegians were fascinated and appalled by his story in equal measure. A human child living with wolves? No. That wasn't right. Wolves are killers, everyone knows that.

So how come he remembers only their playfulness, loyalty, hunting – their kindness?

He scans the silent sky, half expecting meteors to fall, screeching and roaring that he has saved Ulv Fjell from a tyrant.

But only the sun beats down, unseasonably hot, and everyone on deck sweats and waits for the ceremony to begin.

The captain honours Svad's coffin with the national red, white and blue flag. Wind snatches it out to sea, and the gulls drown out the few words spoken by the minister. He smiles. Svad hated religion; he thought he was more god than man.

Boom. Boom. Boom. Explosions rip into the silence. And the sky is ablaze. Like clockwork, cannons fire along the coast to mark Svad's death. He watches the mourners fidget, uncomfortable with this showiness. Norwegians are not ones to flash their money. Or for small talk. This is a show for foreign investors. Anyone who is anybody is on board. Trade ministers. Ambassadors. Chief executives.

Sailors in dark oilskins pull on the lines and hoist Svad's heavy mahogany casket in the air. No one speaks. No one moves. All eyes are fixed on the coffin as it drops. And sinks below the waves. The sea closes over without a ripple.

For Rosa, he thinks, and throws a white rose on the water.

One by one, the oilmen and ambassadors take a rose

and drop it overboard for Svad's missing widow. This is a bad omen, they mutter. He knows they blame him. They've heard the rumours.

No one can prove a thing. Rosa's son grabs at him and gums the fur collar on his father's wolf coat.

He had to do it, he tells the baby. He had no choice.

Svad's lawyers call him below deck to a meeting in the captain's hi-tech cabin. Borg, the Head of Oil Exploration takes Ulv Pup from him, and cuddles Svad's heir like his new favourite pet. The Norwegian lawyers skim over Svad's will. It's no surprise to them that Svad's baby inherits everything.

But they go into great detail about their plans to expand the mining side of Svad Oil, and develop Ulv Fjell.

He can't speak. It's like his wolves became invisible overnight. Svad Oil wants to dig up their mountain? Clear the area of his wolves, slaughter them? Slaughter Asena. After everything he's done, and it isn't enough.

He glares at the baby – who will grow into another Svad and destroy his land for a quick profit. He won't let it happen. His scarred fingers curl round the brass lighter in his pocket, the worn metal burns into his fist. He stole this, Svad's lighter, so he would never forget his duty.

15

Sunday. Lukas doesn't want to talk about the funeral and spends the day trying to show me how to build a camp. He calls it a bivouac, a shelter that keeps you off the ground and keeps the cold and the bugs out. I'm not strong enough to hack branches down, so Lukas shows me how to use his oversized wolf coat as a groundsheet instead.

Then he makes a snare and catches a Norway rat. The rodent struggles to escape its wire noose, but Lukas talks to it with such gentleness that the young rat ends up trusting him, and relaxes into his hand – until Lukas breaks its neck. I feel sick, but Lukas insists on showing me how to skin it for his supper.

And he gets all worried when I can't start a fire from scratch. I laugh, and promise I'll never go camping without him and his brass lighter. Lukas gives me such a hopeless look. I think he's given up now on me ever learning survival lore.

Purple shadows lengthen on the peaks beyond the green mountains. I'll be in for it, when I get home. But sitting next to Lukas's warm body under a willow tree is worth every punishment that my family can dream up. The early leaves cascade around us like a green waterfall. I peer through them to a cloudless pale sky. It stretches on for ever, and that is how I feel about Lukas.

But how do I write a song about him without sounding a total loser? I hum a new vocal hook, and pick out endless new tunes on my keyboard. I've got it. *Wolf Eyes*. I can work with that. Lukas says wolves are dead playful after a successful kill; they chase each other and play tig. Playful and lethal. That's him. He is resting his head on mine now, watching black-throated ducks cruising in circles on a stretch of dark water under the willows.

'Nell,' he says. 'Tell me a secret. Something real.'

I don't believe in love at first sight. But it's happened. How can that be?

'I told you everything. Dad's a born-again Catholic, they're the worst kind. My sister's sick. I was in a band with my friend Dom, but Dad's dragged me to Norway. I'm not allowed to use the internet in Lent, or my phone,' I say. 'Oh, and no boys.'

But I don't tell Lukas about Dad's drinking, or his hatred of Svad, or my fears that he will lose his job on the rigs. Or admit my biggest worry: that Harper won't get better, and if she dies I will never be able to get back up again. And I wonder how many secrets Lukas Svad keeps from me.

'Nell?' he smiles. 'A secret about *you*.'

'OK. Don't laugh. But when I was a kid, I could fly.'

'What? In your dreams?'

Lukas plays a few notes on my keyboard. I love that he asks me to bring it along. He says time stops when I play my songs. So I risk telling him. 'No, I didn't fly in my sleep. Flying was more like an out-of-body experience. At night I'd fly over Mr Young's garden to the moors. I flew faster than the owls, swooping through the night, landing feather-light on apple trees. I spoke fox and badger and understood hedgehog. I remember animals singing to their young, songs about a human child and how they must be kind to me. Flying in the night garden is my most precious childhood memory. The only time I felt safe. Free. Me.'

I wait for Lukas to burst out laughing.

'My total respect,' he says. I can't stop smiling. *He gets me.* He really does. I love how Lukas listens more than he talks. He rubs his chin, deep in thought. 'An out-of-body experience?' he says eventually. 'Doctors call that escapism. A fantastical search for someone only our subconscious remembers. A ghost.'

'Wow,' I say, impressed. 'Exactly how much therapy have you done?'

'Wall-to-wall counselling to stop me killing my family.' Lukas flips up the collar on his wolf coat and smiles at me.

'You're well funny.'

'I laugh at myself all the time.' He drums his finger on my lips. 'When did you stop flying?'

'School. Harper told me not to tell anyone. She said

kids can't fly. Somehow I got scared of airplanes after that. Tragic. I miss night-flying, cloaked in my long hair.'

'You had long red hair?' He gazes at me like I'm something extraordinary. Lukas loves playing with my hair, twisting it over and over his fingers. There's never a right moment to come clean that I'm not a true redhead.

'No,' I admit. 'That's the weird bit. Dad always cut my hair short.' I don't mention that my childhood head was a nit metropolis, or that I was a tomboy. 'What about you?' I ask. 'Tell me your secret.'

'I have a secret plan to rescue my little brother.' Lukas leans over me, and his sea-glass eyes scrutinize my face so hard it hurts, like I'm staring into the sun. 'Yes. You're the One. I can't imagine a day without you,' he says, and kisses me.

No tongues, or wandering hands, but the world stops. And every cell shoots out of my body, spins round the stratosphere, looks down at me and him under the willow tree and races back into my body, because suddenly, being me is the best place in the universe to be.

Monday morning. Dad bangs on the kitchen ceiling with the broom. My whole bedroom shakes. 'Nell! Get back down here now,' he shouts. 'Breakfast! The nurse has gone.'

He's fixing pancakes for Harper. My dad likes to play happy families for her when he's been away on the rig. The crews work two weeks on; one month off. It's heaven without him. I lug Harper's dirty laundry into the kitchen, humming my new lyrics. *He's my first thought, my last thought, my every thought in between.*

'Nell! Stop singing. You're late for grace,' Dad says. 'For what we are about to receive may the Lord make us truly grateful.'

'Amen,' says Harper, and tucks in.

'Amen to that.' I slip into my chair. 'I'm starving.'

Dad slides me a chipped blue plate across the table and turns back to his newspaper.

'Don't eat bacon,' I say. 'I'm a veggie. I don't eat dead animals with my pancakes.'

'Since when?' Dad says, without looking up from the paper.

'Since for ever.'

'Since *Bambi*,' sniggers Harper.

I smile at her serenely and lift the rashers off my pancakes. Dad used up the last of the syrup on my sister's plate, so I stare at my dried-up breakfast and compare it to Harper's stack, flooded with maple syrup. Neither of them notice I've got a raw deal here.

Yep. This is my life, on a plate. Invisible.

My sister studies the shaving nicks on Dad's face. 'What's with the plasters, Daddy?' she asks, all innocent. 'You got a hot date? Or did your razor get blunted?'

I sigh and make a mental note to buy my own razor. These days my head has been too full of Lukas and his worries of how to rescue his baby brother.

Dad's busy scouring his newspaper, tearing pages in his haste to devour the news. It's one of his many double standards; we're not allowed the TV or internet, but he allows himself local newspapers and the radio in Norwegian. He's up all hours listening to it.

'Anything more on Svad's funeral?' Harper asks idly. 'Vord Skole made the pupils line up along the fjord when it went past. Rumours are flying around about that helicopter crash. Was it sabotage or suicide? Nell says psychopaths don't commit suicide. Is that because they know it's a Mortal Sin?' She smirks.

'Psychopaths don't think like that,' I snap. 'And they're not motivated by emotions. The chopper crash will be engine trouble. Or pilot error. Right, Dad?'

My dad still won't discuss anything Svad. If anything, the tycoon's death seems to have upset him. He folds up the paper like he didn't hear us. 'Girls, stay off the internet and stay indoors. Hunters are after a wolf on the rampage. It's attacking dogs in the woods.'

'That's not normal.' I quote Lukas. 'It's because hunters separated the alpha from his pack; they go crazy on their own. Aggressive. Unpredictable.'

'Will you listen to yourself?' Harper says. 'You give up bacon, the next minute you're the wolf whisperer? You? Who can't pet a dog without becoming a gibbering idiot.'

'A wolf is more of a teacher than a pet,' I say, dead solemn.

Harper snorts.

'Girls, pray you don't cross its path,' says Dad, kissing the crucifix around his neck. 'Evil walks the world right now.' His skin reeks of alcohol. My dad's back to wearing his religious trainspotter clothes. Crap. It will be a dog collar next.

I search Dad's office for booze when he goes to Mass. His paperwork is in such a mess, strewn over the floor like we've been burgled. I don't know where to start. Dad usually keeps his stuff together, tidy in folders.

The first empty vodka bottle is hidden behind a photo propped up against the wall. In the photo, I'm singing in a competition at St Paul's Catholic School. I won that competition and all the ones that followed. Homesick for the girl I used to be, I rummage through an old box of games, looking for my singing trophies.

'Hey, Doll.' I pull out my old American Girl, prop her on my knee and rearrange her white smock. 'How come you didn't get binned like the rest of my life?'

Doll wears my first pair of baby shoes. Blue ones. My mother was expecting a boy, but got me instead. I stare into Doll's china eyes. Annoyed that she looks so trusting, I pull out one of her eyelashes, like it's Doll's fault my life got left behind. Doll blinks back at me. *What am I doing?* She's the only doll that survived my childhood with her eyes intact. Harper vandalized all the rest.

I calm down, search the whole office, pouring away any vodka I can find. I take three empty bottles and hide them in my Dora the Explorer bag. I don't dare put them in our recycling bins.

An oil worker with a drink problem?

That's a big deal in Norway. You can't even buy booze

here easily. They don't sell it in supermarkets. Dad has to go to government-run outlet stores. He goes to a different one each time, so they don't ask questions. Alcohol is banned on oil rigs. He'd lose his job if they find out about his drinking. I won't let that happen.

The house phone, buried under papers on the desk, rings.

'Hey, you.'

'Dom!' I shriek.

'Guess what?' he says. 'I got offered a place at the BRIT School. Piece of piss.'

'Epic.' I clench my Dora bag and the vodka bottles clink together. I am sideswiped with envy and listen to him rehearsing on drums.

'They say Morden is teaching next year.' Dom laughs. 'How brilliant is that?'

We talked about going to music school like for ever. Together.

I can't breathe. All the songs we planned to write. I miss my best friend so much. I miss Dom leaning over my shoulder, jabbing his finger at my journal, finding beauty in words I'd forgotten, strumming them on his guitar, laughing at me, finding our way into a new song while the hours would melt away. It won't happen now.

I focus on clearing up the mess on the floor. I find Harper's birth certificate in a box of medical files, but mine is missing. That figures.

'When you come back,' Dom says, all casual, 'Mum says you can move to London with us.'

'Harper too?'

There's a long silence. We both know his mum can barely remember to feed the cat. She'd never manage with my sick needy sister.

'So where are your new songs?' he asks. 'You always churn them out during Lent.'

'Can't write about fjords,' I mumble.

But I have a journal full of songs about Lukas, and I know it'd hurt Dom to read the kind of love songs that he always hoped I'd write about him one day.

I hear Dom riff, 'I Don't Believe in Love'. It's brutal. He sounds so pissed off with me for missing the audition.

'Look. It's OK for you, knucklehead,' I say. 'You don't have a sister who's sick.'

'There're cures for cancer,' he says. 'Harper was doing fine. What's gone wrong?'

'Her drugs keep going out of whack – we're not sure why. You know how it is. The doctors send in a nurse now to keep an eye on her. Harper was fine when she left hospital, but now she's in pain again. Dad's not coping well.'

'He's not the only one.'

I hear the longing in Dom's voice and feel bad. I've not written to my best friend for ages. My old life is like a black hole, collapsing in on itself, slowly disappearing. I don't notice when I'm with Lukas. He's the only thing that keeps me sane.

'Hey, Dom. listen to this.' I turn the handle on the paper musical box. Slow, plaintive notes fill the room, a ghost of the original Beatles song. 'I'd love to walk out on stage with a musical box and have it play the opening hook, and hear the tiny notes fall like leaves on our audience in the dark, and hope they get the same rush from my music as us. What do you think?'

'That's sick.' Dom immediately mashes up the notes on his guitar. 'Where'd you get it? Don't tell me. Lover boy. Nell? How's it going?'

'Lukas means everything to me,' I say, without thinking. 'Essential. Elemental.'

Dom exhales like a punctured balloon.

Crap. Crap. Crap.

Me and Dom have this crazy pact that if we're not married by twenty-five, then we marry each other. We started life together, top and tail, sharing a big pram in his mum's back garden, and we figured we could end our days like that too. Best friends. I can't imagine settling for that now.

'Of course,' I say fast, 'most of the time I'm stuck with Harper, and we can't meet up.' But I stay up all hours, writing songs. Some nights, I don't go to sleep.

And in the morning, I'm too tired to think of anything but him.

'You're a cosmic joke,' Dom says. 'Blowing life for a boy. You cutting school too?'

'Not every day,' I confess. 'Lukas had the funeral this week. He wanted me to go, but Harper had more hospital tests on her meds and we thought it'd raise suspicions if I didn't go with her.'

'Suspicions?' Dom says. 'What is he up to? Your love story is more secretive than the CIA.'

You promised not to say anything about Lukas's plans for his baby brother . . .

'Did you check out that wolf story for me?' I ask, changing the subject. 'My dad's watertight on banning the internet this Lent. He keeps the router with him. He even burns the newspapers. He says it's just schoolwork, or reading the Bible. I only get novels in under his radar because I'm doing English. I can't wait for Easter Sunday.'

'Right,' Dom sighs, like he knows I'm holding out on him. 'I did find something. A small boy was found on a place called Ulv Fjell ten years ago. Svad Oil were mining the area. No one knew his age for sure. Just a lost boy, living in a wolf den on the mountain. Half-dead. Covered in blood from the massacre of his pack, howling, desperate to keep the last pup alive. It's kinda horrible. The doctors said the boy had some Eastern European language, so they guessed his parents had abandoned him on the mountain as a child, not a baby.' Dom wraps it up. 'He was examined by scientists in hospital. Then the trail vanishes. I can't find any dirt on him. No reporter got near the family who took him in.'

'That was Svad,' I say. 'But if he's anything like Dad says, Svad wouldn't care less about a lost child.'

'I guess they killed the wolves to rescue the kid.' Dom reads me another article on the investigation into Svad's death. 'The lawyers delayed his funeral as long as possible to find all the bodies, but they only found Svad's. They think the wife is still in the fjord. The cause of the helicopter crash has been ruled as pilot error – Svad was the pilot, it says.'

'OK.' *Lukas can put his grief behind him.*

'Now the funeral is over, Svad Oil have got the go-ahead to mine for something called rutile,' Dom says. 'Lukas is going to be a very rich boy—'

I interrupt. 'It's not about the money for Lukas.'

'Don't be daft, Nell. It's always about the money.'

'Don't you ruin this for me, Sherlock. I love him.'

'Get real,' Dom snaps. 'What do you actually know about this Romeo of yours?'

16

He sprints down the path to the yellow cottage in the dark. He tries the door handle and raises an eyebrow. Who locks doors in Nøy? He finds the spare key is in a marigold pot and wanders round their home, claustrophobic, but fascinated by the world of girls. He touches hair magazines and nail polishes, shoes displayed on shelves, and novels piled up on the floor. One lies open on the sofa. *Wuthering Heights?*

He reads the words underlined: '*Whatever our souls are made of, his and mine are the same.*'

He uses his hunting knife to cut out the page, folds it into a neat square and slips it into his coat.

Opening the fridge, he pulls the vodka out of his pocket and hides the bottle on the top shelf. He leans against the kitchen door, annoyed by the dynamics of this family. She's a musician, but doesn't have a piano. Just a cheap keyboard.

A new sweater is folded on the table. He sniffs it. Expensive. She hates pink. It must belong to the bitch-sister. He lifts the coffee pot off the wood stove and pours.

Upstairs, he pads through the bitch-sister's bedroom and peers through the hatch no bigger than a wolf den. His nose twitches. How can she sleep dead to the world? No fear of predators. He can't remember a time when he slept without an ear open for danger.

Unscrewing a bottle of medicine by the bed, he dilutes the liquid again. He's lost count of how many times he's done it and he replaces the lid, curling his lip at the sickly smell. The sick girl is skinhead-bald, but painted like an expensive Russian Easter egg with beautiful faded henna decorations. Something like pity stirs in him.

Trample your weakness before it gets any wings, snaps the cold angry voice in his head.

Abruptly the bitch-sister sits up in bed and looks at him. Did he speak it aloud? Her eyes widen, but they're drugged, unfocused. He holds his breath and wills her back asleep. She opens her mouth. His fingers tighten on his knife. The sick girl straightens her God Squad statues on a shelf and slumps back on the pile of pillows. Her eyes close.

A memory, so painful he can't put a name to it, engulfs him. He remembers playing with toy wooden wolves as a child. Rosa kept them on a shelf for him. He closes his eyes, remembering how much she had done for him.

He senses the eyes in the wall watching him. Forty prints of Christ surround him. He takes his knife, about to stab the point into one eye, but it's like there is a force field around them, something that stops his hand in mid-air.

Instead, he turns her statues to face the wall. He dares himself to stroll through the room, stealing trinkets: a pair of hair scissors with a curved handle, a miraculous medal, a packet of sweets, a plectrum.

Moving through the empty silent master bedroom – unconcerned, he knows their father is out drinking – he searches the wardrobe and finds the document he wants stashed away in a fishing bag. He stares at the names on it for a long time before he steals it.

17

The warm night hums through my open window and I hum back the vocal hook to my wolf song. Up the hill, the church husky barks. A motorbike crunches the gravel at the top of our drive and then free-wheels down to the loganberry bushes. I check Harper is still asleep, then crawl over my bed to the window. Lukas appears round the side of our cottage.

'You coming out to play, our Juliet?' he calls.

I laugh. 'You nailed the Yorkshire accent,' I say. 'But you can't be here. My dad's home.'

Lukas sinks his chin deep into the fur collar and smiles at me. 'I checked. Your father is out for the count, on the kitchen floor. I'm quite safe.'

He didn't say my dad's drunk, but my face burns with shame. 'Please don't tell anyone. He never drank before Harper got sick.'

Lukas nods. I don't think he believes me for a minute, but he looks at me with such love I swallow hard. Even when I lie, Lukas thinks I'm being noble.

He stands below my window, his wolf coat falling in

folds around his legs. It's dark, but he's never looked more beautiful to me. Then he puts his hand on his heart. '*Hear my soul speak. The very instant that I saw you did my heart fly to your service.*'

The words from *The Tempest* swoop and dive in the night air. Lukas knows I love Shakespeare. My heart twists with loving him. In the darkness, the bond between us shines with iridescence. This thing called love. I never believed in it, and yet here it is. Stronger than graphene. One thread to bind us for life. I lean over the windowsill. In the distance, Preken Rock presses in on the night. The fjord is black and silent.

'I'm a prisoner.' I sigh. 'Harper locked me in. She thinks I'll run away like Mum.'

'She's psychic.' Lukas airplanes his arms. 'You're flying away to your night garden.'

'What?'

'I've got a ladder to the stars, against your window.'

'A ladder?'

Lukas stands so still. I know he doesn't doubt for a second that I will go with him.

Harper's snoring. Forty pairs of gentle brown eyes remind me that it's still Lent. No phone. No fun. No boys. But I inch one leg over my bedroom windowsill and find the wooden rungs with my toe. I grab the ladder, blushing. I've only got a white nightie on and the smallest knickers ever.

'You can do it,' Lukas calls.

I don't know how I climb down, but then I'm standing

on cool grass in bare feet and he wraps his wolf coat around me. 'Safe now,' he says, his lips tickling my hair. He kisses the small bruises on my bare shoulder. 'How'd you get these?'

I shrug, ashamed of my family. 'Harper pinches me. If I get her jabs wrong.'

'Another monster who hurts children?' Lukas says.

'No. Just a girl who's scared of dying. Scared of never falling in love.'

'Of course,' he says softly. 'Close your eyes.' He leads me by the hand through the loganberry bushes to our back garden. 'Look now,' he whispers.

It's a starless night, the sky heavy with rain that never falls. But behind our cottage, the apple orchard twinkles with hundreds of candles hung from jam jars and tiny torches on key rings and solar fairy lights, strung along the branches.

'You drew the constellations in torchlight?' I look at him in amazement. 'You did this?'

He loves me. He really loves me.

Lukas runs over the grass and nudges all the candle jars so the garden dances in the flickering light. I clasp my hands over my mouth and work hard to keep from blubbing.

'I wanted to make your night garden perfect. Look, that one's Orion.' Lukas points at the outline of a man, suspended from the trees, with three solar lights for his belt. 'One day, I am going to fly away and land on Orion.' Lukas holds out his hand. 'My lady, may I give you a

108

piggyback to the stars?'

Speechless, I climb on to his back. Lukas grips my knees and he runs through the apple trees, tapping the branches to keep all the lights jiggling. I feel feather-light.

And I'm back there.

In Mr Young's garden. I'm a little kid again with my arms outstretched, touching the stars, my hair flowing out behind me, happy and safe. Then we are floating. Lazily. Spiralling gently, round and round the garden in circles.

'Good as your childhood flying in your night garden?' Lukas asks me.

'Smashed it,' I say, as we drift around in another circle. 'So floaty.' It brings back all the memories: flying over the apple trees, swooping through the garden. The night-time kissing my face. 'Lukas Svad, you're a magician.'

He laughs and laughs. I wish I could bottle his laughter. Lukas runs around the garden again, and I stretch out my arms and the leaves brush against my fingertips. The cold night kisses my face and the candles blur into a jagged golden line. The only sounds are his footsteps crunching on birch bark and our breath, misting together. By the water, there's a swing hanging from an old oak, with long ropes. When we're exhausted with running, Lukas stands me on the swing. He pushes off and we swoop through the night together. 'A dream come true?' he asks.

'Proper fairy tale,' I say.

Lukas leans back and his wolf coat twirls over the

109

fjord. And in that moment I wish time would stop for us and it's just him and me for ever.

'Who'd you wish out of your life?' he asks, as if he can read my mind.

'My dad,' I say, whizzy and out of breath.

Then I feel awful; Lukas has just lost his second family. But he nods. 'What about Harper?'

'Yeah. Her too. Sometimes. What about you?'

He looks at me with such love and smiles. 'I want you in my life. You and Ulv Pup.'

I melt completely. 'You any good with babies?' I ask.

'I've raised plenty of pups. They need exercise. Discipline. And affection. In that order. People always give their dogs too much affection, and not enough exercise and discipline. It's why domestic dogs behave so badly.'

I laugh. 'It's not quite the same thing as raising a baby.'

Lukas stops the swing and looks at me. 'I mean it, Nell. I won't let the Barnevernet take Ulv Pup. The Norwegian Social Services are notorious. Children get lost in the system for years and years. I'm eighteen in a few months' time. I will be his legal guardian.'

'You'd give up everything for your baby brother?' I feel in awe of this boy.

Lukas nods. He pulls me into his wolf coat. I drink in the smell of him. Soap and bonfires and clean clothes. My skin never smells so sweet.

'Pup is the last one left,' he says, dead quiet. 'Will you help? Before he's gone too.'

Gone? That's it. Harper would never let me go into care. 'Of course I'll help,' I say.

'Promise?'

'Promise. I'd do anything for you.'

18

Father José blows out the candles and strips the altar to symbolize the Last Supper. Imagine knowing you were going to die, having been betrayed by your best friends, and not run away?

I couldn't do that. At least I made it through the last week of Lent, forty days without getting caught, but keeping Lukas a secret makes me feel unclean.

Lying in our family is such a big deal. Dad says it used to take a priest and a full confession to repair the damage we do to our souls when we lie. It violates our spirit, he says.

So how come it's so hard to tell the truth?

Dad leaves Mass close to tears, thinking about children dying. I had to sing 'Stabat Mater'. It's a lament about Mary, a mother who loses her only son. I did such a good job it made me feel full of sorrows too. But Father José still made me and the choir stay on to practise for the Easter service.

On the way home, I search the sky for the Northern Lights and forget about Father José's crazed husky, until it launches itself at me through the fence. I sprint up the fjord road to avoid it. My heart is still going ape when I slip through our back door.

The atmosphere hits me straight off. Something's up. Harper shrinks into herself on the sofa, I take one look at her scared face and know that Dad's been drinking. Crap. Crap. Crap. I've only been gone a few hours. And I searched the house for booze yesterday. Where does he get it from?

'Go upstairs,' I mouth to my sister.

It's too late. Dad slams the fridge door, muttering, 'He's my first thought. My last thought. My every thought.'

At first I think he's talking to himself, and then I get it. And my heart stops.

He's reading from my journal?

My dad stumbles into the sitting room, still reading aloud. I stare at my journal in his hands, horrified. 'It's private. How could you?'

But Dad grabs my arm and rag-dolls me as he reads on. I feel him inside my head. Soiling my thoughts. Turning what is beautiful inside out. And killing it.

'Nell spends all her time shaving her legs,' says Harper. 'She'll be seeing a lad.' A sly smile crosses my sister's face as she snuggles back into the sofa. 'His name's in there. Lukas something.'

She gave it to him.

'Harper!' What's happening to us? I want to say; we're meant to be in this together. But the truth is, she's been such a total bitch recently that I've been spending less and less time with her. I feel guilty about it, but Lukas thinks she's paranoid. She blames me for stuff I'd never do, like hiding her glasses or ruining a new sweater on purpose. And she denies pinching the last of my Starbursts, but they're all gone and I sure as hell didn't eat them.

Dad lets go of me to thumb through my journal again. I back into the kitchen, legs shaking, waiting for his outburst.

Here it comes.

'Svad?' he bellows. 'Lukas *Svad*?'

His rage fills the room. I run and try to grab my journal. Dad pushes me into the fridge. Hard. He stomps up and down the kitchen, growling at me, marking out his territory so that no lad can come near me.

'What's your problem?' I say, furious. 'He lost his birth family. It's not his fault he's a Svad.'

'You stay away from him. That's final. He's trouble. I don't want that boy anywhere near you,' Dad says. 'You have no idea how evil shows up.'

I zone out. Crossing my arms over my stomach, I concentrate on the blossom in the garden, listening to the dogs in the village. They bark more and more these days.

'You listening to me?' Dad shouts in my face.

'It will be a baby on the way before you know it,' Harper calls from the sofa.

'A baby?' I snap. 'Can't have that, can we, Dad? You might end up with another me.'

Dad swings a baking tray at my head. He misses. I stare at him, horrified. 'What am I doing?' he mutters, and presses his frayed blue prayer book into my hands. It's like his most precious possession, it has all his healing requests in it. None of them about me. And I want to hurl it into the dishes. 'Swear on that, my girl,' he says. 'Swear you will give him up. You stay away from that Svad boy. You don't leave the house except for church and school. You go nowhere for a month. You see no one. You hear me?'

'*Drit og dra!*' I yell the swear words at him. 'I won't renounce Lukas. I *love* him!'

The weight just lifts off my shoulders; I don't have to lie any more.

'You are just like your mother,' Dad whispers. 'Obsessed.'

I shove his blue prayer book back to him over the kitchen table, furious. 'It's never about me, is it, Dad? You don't see me . . . you just see *her*. It's not right. I don't remember Mum – I don't even know what she looks like – but I well see why she ran away from you. What I don't get is . . . why you kept me?'

Bullseye.

My dad looks proper stricken, like he might cry or something. I laugh at him. And he snatches up my journal and lurches across the kitchen to the sink. I think maybe he's going to be sick over the dishes. Another clean-up job for me.

But Dad folds my lovely journal in two, and he rams it

115

down the sink waste-disposal unit, and he hammers my notebook so hard the room shakes. The grinding noise is like hearing my skin being ripped off. I am screaming inside. *That's my music. All my songs. Lukas . . .*

My father holds me off. I can only struggle, and watch my family destroy everything that matters to me. Years of work and dreams and love.

Harper's frightened face peers round the door. She's shaking more than me, but I push her away.

Dad's bloodshot eyes scan the kitchen cabinets, calculating his chances of finding another bottle. Even now, another drink is more important than us.

Dad locked me in our room for lying to him. Harper and me watch him down in the garden, feeding documents and newspapers and what look like old photographs to a bonfire. Sparks fly into the night as he pokes the flames.

I'm too cut up about my journal to care why he's doing this now. Trust Dad-the-hoarder, who can't let stuff go, to bring his personal stuff to Norway only to destroy it.

'What is he burning?' Harper looks dreadful, but I'm in no mood to play nice.

I snap. 'Why did you betray me?'

'You left your journal on your bed for me to find,' she wails.

'Liar. I never leave it out.'

'You did too.'

I don't answer. 'Oh, get over yourself,' she says. 'Who do you think you are? We're not talking about Jo March's masterpiece novel being set on fire here – this isn't *Little Women* – and I didn't pulp your crappy song book. Dad did.'

'You made it happen!' I shout. 'You can't keep your thieving hands off my life.'

'At least you have one! And you promised not to fall in love with a boy before me.'

'I was thirteen!' I howl. 'You had chemo. What was I meant to say?'

'You promised to wait, Nell.'

She's right. I did. Back then I'd have promised my life away to keep her safe.

'Shut up about it.' I double-check the pager instructions from the hospital, telling me which drugs she gets tonight and in which order. They can change daily and the dosage has to be exact. The nurse checks everything. I concentrate on doing today's injection right. 'Hold still,' I say, as I do her jab in the PICC line above her elbow. Then carefully, I pull the syringe back out of her catheter.

'Ow.' She winces.

I sigh. And stick my arm out. I am pretty sure I didn't hurt her. But Harper pinches me and she twists my skin extra hard. Chinese wrist burns. She only does it on her bad days. *Or my happy ones.* I rub my arm and try not to moan. Some days my skin looks like a human Dalmatian. Harper says it helps her deal with her pain. I know a bruise is nothing compared to her bone pain, but I wish she and Dad didn't have this need to hit out when they hurt.

I stroke her cold hand while the meds kick in. They're taking longer than usual. I make a note in her records, worrying that her drugs are getting out of whack and we'll be back in hospital for more tests before we know it. I know they'll blame me again.

'Not that it's any of your business,' I mutter, 'but we haven't done *it* yet.'

'But you look all lit up inside, almost as pretty as me.'

Sister wars. Who's the fairest of us all? I'm so not playing.

'So what's stopping you?' Harper says. 'Oh, hang on. You think he's still grieving for his dead family?' My sister should've been a professional darts player. Her conjectures are always spot on, and lethal. 'What's it like, Nell?' she asks. 'To be so in love that you turn your back on us?'

'I haven't,' I say, shocked.

'Yes. You've been hijacked by love,' she insists. 'Tell me.'

How can I tell her? How can I tell my sick sister it's love that makes a kiss so great – something so immense, so painful that I don't know how to begin to describe it.

'Tell me the truth!' my sister says.

'Oh, think of what delights you,' I say. 'And multiply that by a cosmos or two.'

'You bitch.' Harper whips off her blue scarf, folds her arms and glares at me. The Rosemåling helmet painted on her scalp has faded to a soft hennaed brown. My sister jerks her chin at a blue-and-white painted china statue of Our Lady. 'I'm eighteen, Nell. Eighteen. And I'm bald. I've got better odds of an Immaculate Conception than a boy falling in love with me.'

'Immaculate Conception?' I splutter, but we both crack up. And I forgive my sister for being a snitch. Completely. Her life sucks way more than mine.

We play cards. Harper cheats. I let her win. My sister unties endless paper curlers in my hair, and brushes out my freshly ragged red curls. Harper likes to play hairdresser whenever she's upset. It's her way of saying that she's a tiny bit sorry for me, but really, she has lost something far worse, so I should get over it. She outmanoeuvres me every time.

'Nels? You don't wear your crucifix – don't you believe angels watch over us any more?'

'I don't believe in all that stuff any more.' I nod at her Turin Shrouds. 'Or him. I'm putting my faith in real people.'

'Well, I believe in angels,' my sister says. 'I sense them at night, watching over me. You're a liar. You feel them. You don't scream about falling out of the sky any more.'

She's right. But it's become a habit, keeping secrets from my sister. I've not had a nightmare in weeks, and I do believe in guardian angels. I know I've got one. He's called Lukas.

19

Norway's gone from winter to summer and bypassed spring. I sit by my bedroom window and watch the bright green grass mottle like overripe fruit. I don't see Lukas. For three whole weeks Dad walks me to school and he picks me up. As for weekends, I'm not allowed out of the house. I don't know how to describe the atmosphere at home. We tiptoe around each other. No one dares tell the truth. And Dad stays sober, so I can't sneak my phone back. But just when I think I can't take another moment apart from Lukas, Dad finds two bottles of vodka in his office.

He drinks all day and goes out to buy more booze.

He doesn't come home.

Saturday morning. Harper wakes early, whimpering in pain. I don't know what to do. Nothing works. My sister's pain meds are useless. She was doing so well when she first came back from hospital – what's happened?

Panicking, I run a bath, fill it with bubbles, light candles and rest her poor head on a white towel. Harper floats. Eyes closed. Waiting for the bone-deep pain to wash away. She can't lift her head and her swan neck's more fragile than a snowdrop in winter. I massage her hands and feet, read *Wuthering Heights* to her. I don't know if she hears a word, but I know water soothes my sister. Our childhood was measured out in bath times. For years, we took them together, giggling, fighting. Harper baptized all our toys, and then she drowned them.

To free their souls, she said.

We'd flood the bathroom with monster suds and Dad never minded the mess back then. It makes me sad to think my family have no happy memories of Harper and me in this cottage. And we're running out of time to make them.

I'm on the phone to the doctor when I see two police-women walking down the drive. The plump one is still eating her breakfast from a bag. I hang up the phone as they approach, and the taller stern officer says they took Dad into custody in Voss police station last night. Drunk driving charges. He'd lost his wallet, and they couldn't ID him until this morning.

Before they give me the third degree, Harper's doctor comes. I take him up to our room and he gives her a shot; the pain melts off my sister's face. Mystified, the doctor checks her meds and keeps me out of the bedroom while he speaks to her.

I don't know what she said, but the doctor takes the opened medicine away to be analysed. He calls an ambu-lance. I'm not allowed in and I go nuts, like Dad does when he's scared. 'Let go of me,' I roar, and flail my fists at the paramedic's chest.

The ambulance doors close on Harper's white face and I realize I'm making it worse. I give her a goofy smile, but I've this sudden awful choking fear that it's me she's afraid of. My inexperience. I think about the way the doctors looked at me in hospital.

A nurse can look after your sister better. More reliable. Someone with cancer nursing experience.

The ambulance is out of sight. I run into the back garden, jump on the swing, push myself higher and higher, until my toes touch the sky and my racing heart deafens me.

The policewomen search the cottage. They find the empty vodka bottles in my Dora the Explorer bag. They come out into the garden and show me. How can I say the vodka belongs to Dad? He's in enough trouble already.

They ask me my age.

'Fifteen,' I say.

'You are a juvenile,' the plump policewoman explains, dead kind. 'We must report you to the Barnevernet. Norwegian Child Protection Services.'

They are going to take me away like Pup?

'No way,' I shout. 'Please. I don't need you. I just need my dad back.'

The officer shakes her head. '*Nei*. You drink. He drinks. This is not good.'

They glance around the garden. I turn and see it through their eyes. It looks a total mess. Every blade of grass, the bushes, and spring-green leaves are smeared an ashy black with bits of burnt paper from Dad's bonfire. The ash puddles in the jam jars still strung along the apple trees for my night-garden lights. Dad's bonfire has made everything ugly.

'We have a heatwave in Norway,' the stern officer says. 'Bonfires are not allowed. There is a risk of forest fires. What was so important for your father to break our laws?'

She pokes around in the barbecue, and from underneath the cold bricks she pulls out a charred photo. 'Is this what your father was trying to destroy?'

I shrug, too miserable to look. How could Dad do that to me? She stares at my face oddly, like this is all my fault. 'What is this woman's connection to you?'

I glance at the photo of a young woman holding a struggling, happy baby. *Me.*

'I don't recognize that woman,' I say truthfully.

But I recognize the blue baby boots. Doll wears them now.

My empty childhood without a mum dominoes back on me. At St Paul's Catholic School we had to write our autobiography. We were studying a bunch of American writers called the Lost Generation and our English teacher showed us some of Ernest Hemingway's short stories as examples. Hemingway wrote a famous one in six words.

For sale: baby shoes. Never worn.

I wrote my autobiography in six words too:

Mum wanted. For baby girl. Unloved.

The teacher thought it was brilliant and read it out. The whole class laughed. Dom slipped his hand in mine and squeezed, till my eyes stopped blinking tears. I found out later that Hemingway committed suicide. Harper says all writers are oversensitive.

The kindly plump policewoman is looking at me concerned. 'Well?' she says.

'I think it might be my mother,' I mutter, and turn away like I don't care. I can't bear to rediscover what my mum looks like in front of them. What business is it of theirs who is at the heart of all this mess? Why Dad drinks. Why Harper is sick. Why I can't study songwriting.

They take the photo away.

'It's evidence,' they say.

'Of what?' I ask.

They don't answer.

I snatch the loganberries off bushes, hurl them to the ground and stamp on them until they turn to a gory mess under my feet and in my mind I turn Mum's laughing eyes into a million mushy pieces of hate.

The policewomen ring the Barnevernet. It will take a while, they say. The office is closed on Saturdays. We watch TV, and wait for my emergency caseworker to arrive. I make them tea, apologize for my outburst and thieve the charred photo back from the kitchen table.

I search Dad's office for my phone, and when I can't find it in his usual hiding places, I work out that he must have taken it with him. I curl up in Harper's empty bed and have a nice long bawl. When I feel calmer I open my bedroom window and breathe in the night air. Even inside our cottage, Nøy has this fresh fishy breath.

'Lukas,' I whisper to the night. 'I need you.'

I know he can hear me.

I'm half asleep, playing with his musical box, when I hear the dogs bark on the hill. A paper aeroplane darts through my window and lands on my bed. My heart rate ramps up as I unfold the crisp paper and read his words:

It's time. I won't let the Barnevernet steal you or Ulv Pup.

I take one last look around the bedroom walls plastered with murky brown Turin Shrouds, and all the space cluttered up with Jesus statues. It feels so empty without my sister. But I always knew I was born for something special and this isn't it.

I lower my keyboard out of my window and it lands in the loganberry bushes. Hanging on to the windowsill by my fingertips, I hold my breath and push off.

Then I drop into the darkness – and into Lukas Svad's arms.

PART 2

The Rescue

20

The Oslo Shards soar above our cafe. Sunlight blazes down the centre, and an intense white light floods the shopping plaza; then fast-moving clouds send shadows skittering across the marble floors. The next second it's eye-achingly bright again and everyone is wearing sunglasses. A white-haired guy is playing piano outside the designer shops.

'Wow. It's like I died and went to heaven,' I say.

'Oslo is a playground for architects.' Lukas spins his lighter on our table. 'More money than sense.' He looks haughty in town, every inch a Russian Tsar, with his wolf coat draped over his shoulder and his black hair as groomed as mine.

Lukas organized a surprise makeover for me. It's so unlike him to think about fashion, but he knows I've wanted long hair for ever, and Harper always cuts it off. So he found a hairdresser to match extensions to the colour of my dyed-red hair. I can't believe my hair's down to my waist now and looks so gorgeous.

After that it was a whirlwind shopping spree. I tried

on the white vintage Dior dress he picked out, and Lukas smiled and said I looked perfect.

He treated me to everything. My whole look is so cool. Long white dress. Tan leather jacket. Laced ankle boots. All vintage. Soft, pre-loved.

Lukas is playing with my hair now, wrapping the new long curls around his fingers. Our waitress is mesmerized by him. She's athletic, Norwegian blonde, but Lukas barely notices her, and she dumps my pancakes in front me in a huff.

My dad makes these pancakes at home, but these ones are smothered with loganberries, sour cream and maple syrup. All for me. Suddenly I'm too choked to eat.

My life on a plate. Perfect.

'You get what you wanted this time?' Lukas smiles.

'And then some,' I laugh. But I can't open my Coke with these long nails. French polish acrylics, they're called. My bitten fingernails are a thing of the past. My hands have never looked so beautiful. 'Can you do the honours?'

Lukas pulls off the Coke tab for me, and he slips the tin ring on my finger.

His knees brush mine under the table. My brain moves into my body and I drift into that space where I can't think of anything but him.

We travelled overnight by train on the Flåm Railway, eight hours through the most scenic mountains in the world, eight hours of bliss. I hug myself. Do Lukas's lips throb from hours of kissing like mine do? He keeps touching his mouth and gazing at me. The Flåm train was rammed for the weekend. I'm sort of glad we couldn't get a cabin; Lukas wants our first time to be somewhere special. Ulv Fjell.

'Can I borrow your phone to call Harper in hospital?'

'Today?' Lukas hesitates. Then he passes me his phone. He doesn't take his eyes off me as I punch in my sister's number. She doesn't pick up. Maybe it's just as well.

How can I explain that it's love that makes a kiss so brilliant? The way Lukas looks at me? Nothing tastes as good as that feels.

'Don't let her hijack your freedom,' he says, watching my face.

'I won't.' I laugh. 'I feel like Ariana Grande with this hair.'

'She's nothing to hang on a Christmas tree.' Lukas smiles at my bemusement. 'You're more than a pop star.' He passes his phone back across the table and shows me this Renaissance painting of a girl with long red-gold hair, stepping ashore from a boat-sized seashell. Starkers. Except for a skimpy shawl.

'Botticelli's *Birth of Venus*. The Goddess of Love and Beauty,' Lukas explains.

'Gorgeous,' I say. Except she's so not. Her body is weirdly elongated, with death-white flabby legs. I sigh and push the sour cream off my pancakes. 'Who is she?'

'She is the first female nude painted in the Renaissance. Simonetta Vespucci. The most beautiful girl in art history.'

Lukas says it like there's no debate, and instantly I'm jealous of a girl long dead. 'Botticelli loved her, yet they could never be together, for she was already married. Botticelli painted this picture a decade after Simonetta died tragically young. He never forgot her face. Thirty-five years later on his death bed, he begged to be buried at the foot of Simonetta's grave.'

I can't stop smiling. 'Love lives on, even when the girl dies?'

'Exactly. Together. For ever.'

We gaze at each other. The waitress fusses over him with his coffee pot. Men in the cafe sneak looks at him. I smirk and absent-mindedly scroll down his phone. 'Wow. Your photos are in folders. Oh, *Sleeping Beauty*, is that me?'

'No. Don't open it.' There's something in Lukas's voice that makes me look up.

'No more secrets.' I duck out of reach and open the folder.

'Nell! Give it back.' Lukas lurches over the table.

'Ow. That hurts. You're crushing my hand.'

The waitress smirks. I concentrate on his nails. He got a manicure. Harper says they're strictly for girls, but somehow on Lukas, a manicure looks powerful. Rich. I've never known a boy wash his hands as often as he does.

'Sorry.' Lukas kisses my fingers and takes his phone back just as it rings.

He talks in Norwegian, pushing his dark hair out of his eyes, tapping his brass lighter on the table. He hangs

up. 'Nell, I'm sorry. I know I said we'd have Ulv Fjell to
ourselves, but someone inside the Barnevernet has tipped
me off.'

'What's happened?' I dread his answer. 'Tipped you off
about what?'

Lukas's face is alight. 'The Barnevernet are at our
house to collect my little brother! They don't know Ulv
Pup is here in town with his nanny. We have to act now.
Take him with us to Ulv Fjell.'

'What, today?' My heart plummets.

Lukas is like an extreme roller coaster; every day I feel
a rainbow of emotions – joy, envy, delight, hate, longing.
Right now, delight has been replaced with anxiety and
disappointment. 'We're rescuing him today?'

Lukas nods, calm, focused. 'You see the boy by the
piano player?' he says quietly.

I look around the crowded plaza to the exit. 'That's
him? The kid in green boots?'

'No. That's the nanny's son. Ulv Pup is in the pram.'

'Where's the nanny?' I say. 'She should be with them.'

'I know.' Lukas smiles at me. 'Let's change the plan.
We can't wait till Ulv Pup gets home. We take him from
here. It's risky, though. I need to stay out of sight from the
CCTV as Svads are too memorable. But no one will
recognize you like that.'

As Lukas explains his new plan, my Coke goes flying
over the table. He moves his brass lighter out of the
mess. 'I can't just take Ulv Pup from a shopping centre,' I
splutter.

'You promised you'd help. He's lost his parents. He needs to be with family – me. You'd do anything to save Harper.'

'Of course. Can't you just talk to Svad Oil about your plan to adopt him when you're eighteen? Maybe they can make the Barnevernet wait a bit?'

'They wouldn't listen to me.' Lukas flicks his brass lighter and stares at the flame. 'His last nanny burnt his elbow. And this one? What kind of nanny leaves a child alone in a shopping centre? Trust me. The Barnevernet will take him and have him grow up in care. Would you let that happen to someone you loved?'

'No.' My legs are shaking so bad I can't stand. 'Lukas, please. We do this and it will spoil everything. Ulv Pup's a baby. A person. We can't just shoplift him.'

'Nell? Don't push me under the ice,' he says softly.

'What?'

'I can't go under now.' Lukas pushes his chair back, and with one graceful move he swings his wolf coat over his shoulder and glances at the CCTV camera. He tilted it up to the ceiling when we got here. Lukas does that everywhere we go. He hates being caught on camera unawares; always know the direction of the bullet, he says.

'Where are you going?' I say, senseless with panic.

'I'll do it myself. I should never have got you involved.' Lukas cradles my face like I'm the most precious thing he's ever seen. 'You never had a mother. You don't know what love means. What family really means. I do. I'm leaving now.'

'Leaving?' The room is spinning faster and faster. I focus on the sugar bowl. It's got blue and white stripes and has tiny air bubbles trapped in the glaze.

How do I breathe without him?

'Wait.' I look into sea-glass eyes. 'I'll do it.' I jump up and Lukas catches me as I trip in my new boots. I'm frantic; but his heartbeat is clockwork-slow. This is nothing to him. Nothing. I'm overreacting again. Why am I always so oversensitive? 'Don't go,' I whisper. 'I'll help you. Of course I will rescue him.'

Lukas pulls away. 'No. I can't risk it. You're too gentle – too kind.'

'I can do it.'

He turns to the plaza. Ulv Pup's pram is still being guarded by the small boy.

Lukas tilts his head and studies my face. 'OK. You will never know what this means to me.' He puts dark sunglasses over my eyes. 'No one will see you. People only see money. Glamour. Not the person.'

Every instinct in me is screaming: *Nell, don't do this. Run.*

And I don't listen.

135

21

Each step requires so much effort that I have to concentrate on my balance. I walk across the marble plaza like I'm playing Grandmother's Footsteps. Shoppers and tourists glance at my celebrity hair, my designer sunglasses and soft leather boots. But they don't see *me*.

Lukas was right; glamour *is* the best disguise.

The little boy in green wellies is kicking the pram wheels, bored out of his head. His eyes light up when he spots me. He's about six, with a stuffed toy dog under his arm.

Swallowing hard, I pop a strawberry Starburst in my mouth and focus on the plan. 'Want one?' I offer him the whole packet.

'*Takk.*' He grabs the sweets before I can blink. So much for Stranger Danger.

Focus on the baby.

I peer in the pram. Ulv Pup watches me with button eyes. He's cute for a baby. The works. Red-blond hair, dimples and smells better than fresh bread. Stiff white jacket and stripy blue tights. Brand-new leather shoes. I recognize them. Lukas bought those for Pup. And my doubts melt away. Those blue shoes prove how much Lukas loves his kid brother.

But I don't recognize the girl who is carrying out this rescue. This other strange rebel girl, in unfamiliar expensive clothes, lifts Ulv Pup out of the pram. A baby weighs a ton. Lukas's instructions play in my head.

Take time for the surprise factor.

'Let's play a game of hide-and-seek,' I say to the little boy in green wellies, and borrow his toy dog.

I tuck it under the pram blanket, leaving just the top of its soft furry head on show. It's a perfect colour match for Pup.

Walk away. Don't run.

Everyone else carries on like normal. The piano player sings on with his eyes closed, shoppers hurry past, and the little boy's going for a world record for sweets-scoffing. My sunglasses slip down and I catch his eye by mistake.

'Are you his new mama?' he says, in a piping voice that carries through the plaza.

I point to Ulv Pup's nappy. 'No . . . but baby needs the toilet.'

The boy clutches his willy, hopping from one foot to the other. 'Me too!'

'What?' I say, aghast. No way. I point at the toy dog in the pram. 'Can you look after him?'

'Like this?' He cradles his arms, cuddling a pretend baby. He's so much better at this than me.

'Perfect,' I say. 'Clever boy.'

And I walk away.

Ulv Pup snuggles into me, like he totally trusts me. I feel so shit; I can't remember his real name. I wrap my arms around his cannonball little body and start praying. *Sweet Jesus, get me out of here.* I feel something pulling and pulling at me, begging me to take him back. But my bond with Lukas is stronger, and I keep on walking.

I make for the car-park stairs as planned, but a lift door opens, and I take that down instead. The crowd noise vanishes. I look at my watch. *Only three minutes?* I pace up and down. The doors open and I lurch out, hyperventilating.

The underground car-park lighting is crap by Norwegian standards. I peer into the gloom, searching for Lukas. The darkness feels like it's stalking me, prowling over the empty cars. I step back into the light, panting.

The lift smells surgically clean, and of course it reminds me of Harper and the ambulance.

Concentrate on Ulv Pup. What did Lukas say to do next?

I remove the sunglasses and Pup whips his head off my chest. He glares at me like he's only just realized I'm not his mum. His cries echo off the underground walls. Then he arches up over my shoulder, struggling, making this horrible screeching noise. It does my head in and I've already got the worst headache ever. I sing softly to him, but the baby roars back in my face and pushes me away like he hates me.

And he's dribbling this horrible goo through my white dress. I stare at the stain, blinking away tears to see two blurry figures walking towards me. My heart stops. They're in dark uniforms, striding through the car park. *Politimenn.*

They have guns strapped to their belts. *Holy crap.* They've come to arrest me.

'*God ettermiddag,*' one officer says, peering at the baby.

'Good afternoon,' I stammer.

Ulv Pup's acting like I tasered him, jerking and fitting in my arms. He's so ungrateful about being rescued. I lose it then and push the screaming baby at them.

'I don't want him. Take him back.'

I hold my breath; dizzy, relieved it's all over. But the policemen look at one another and laugh at me. They are still laughing when they take the staircase to the plaza. Ulv Pup stares at them too, hiccupping in misery. I don't know what to do. I cuddle his plump foot.

Shit. I've lost one of his new boots.

I turn and see it lying inside the lift. The doors close.

The blue baby boot disappears.

Somehow, losing something precious that Lukas bought him seems the end of the world. It's only been six minutes. I can't do this. I can't save a baby. Not even for Lukas. I can barely look after myself.

As I press the button to call the lift back, a jeep screeches through the underground car park, Lukas driving with one arm dangling out the window, looking totally chilled.

I stagger towards it, cuddling Ulv Pup. Lukas's eyes lock on mine, but if anything the jeep picks up speed. The noise of the engine merges with Ulv Pup's crying. I can't move. A parking ticket is flapping back and forth on the windscreen. I can see the dust on the wipers and the broken bumper.

'Lukas!' I scream.

There's a squeal of brakes. Everything is flashing and spinning, and the jeep skids to a stop. I keel forward, put one hand on the bonnet, yelp and whip it away, leaving a sweaty handprint in the hot grime. He had the engine running all this time?

'Are you trying to kill us?' I gasp. 'I'm going nuts here. Where've you been?'

Lukas simply vaults over the jeep door and kisses me. 'You did it!' He glances at the lift. 'In the jeep. Someone's coming. That will be the Barnevernet.'

'Please. Take Ulv Pup.'

But it's too late. The lift doors open. Six hefty lads tumble out; they're drunk, kicking Ulv Pup's blue boot like it's the Premiership. It flies across the car park and they dive after it, rolling by the jeep, arms and legs flying. One lad makes the connection between the screaming baby and his baby shoe. He picks it up by a filthy lace and drops it into my hand. '*Beklager,*' he mumbles. *Sorry.* Then he runs to their car, shouting at the others.

Lukas steps out of the gloom once they've gone. I try and put Ulv Pup in his arms, but the baby keeps shrieking at me and I drop his shoe again, and it rolls under the jeep

140

and I'm scared witless of this kid. But Lukas? He places one hand on the baby's head like he's the frigging Pope and whispers, 'There are no cows on the ice, Ulv Pup, calm down.'

And the baby gulps, and shuts up. His whole body relaxes under Lukas's hand like he just got the best head massage ever. 'How did you do that? You take him. He hates me.'

'Settle him in the boot. I brought the dog basket.'

'What?' I gasp. 'I'm not putting him in *that*.'

Lukas shrugs. 'I slept in one.'

I feel sick. 'It's not right. He's not a dog.'

'You're always so kind,' he says. 'OK. Have it your own way.'

He helps me up into the jeep, but the seat belt won't fit round me and Pup.

'Shouldn't he have one of those baby-seat-thingies?' I ask.

Lukas sighs. 'Ulv Pup has a perfectly safe dog basket in the boot.'

I try to breathe louder than my panic.

We speed out the exit. The Shards reflect the sun and seagulls in the mirrored windows. The light hurts it's so bright. We drive by the plaza cafe. The same waitress is busy chatting up the same customers. The same little boy in green boots is pushing the same pram, puffed up with excitement. The nanny comes out of the shop, still on the phone. Still laughing. Not a care in the world. How can

141

she not know Ulv Pup is missing?

'My plan worked.' Lukas whoops softly. 'Thank you, Nell.'

No one ever thanks me at home.

And my heart is so pumped it's like there's too much of me to fit in my body.

'You were right. No one seems to care about Pup. They haven't even noticed.'

Lukas nods. 'People are only half alive compared to wolves.'

We drive alongside the nanny's little boy. I protect Pup's peach-soft head and duck down off the seat. I'm squished on the floor. Pup's eyes scrunch up tight like he wants none of this either. 'What next?' I whisper.

'We have to get out of here first.' Lukas brakes hard. He can't pull out on to the main road. The lights are red and beyond them the traffic is bumper to bumper.

I check the wing mirror again. The boy sneaks another sweet. He nudges his mother to get her attention, but she ignores him.

Impatient, the little boy pulls the cot blanket back with a squeal of laughter. His mother stops. Now she's staring at the pram. Her phone falls in slow motion to the ground. She picks up the toy dog, its feathery copper tail shaking, and for a moment she does nothing. Then she drops the dog in the pram and screams like she's been stabbed:

'Babyen! Babyen! Babyen!'

Sweet sweet Jesus, please, please, change the lights.

The nanny smacks the Starbursts out of her son's hands and shakes him. '*Hvor er han?*' she yells. I'm pretty sure that means: where is he?

The little boy pulls away with his stuffed dog, crying. He sees me. His mouth drops open.

'Lukas, he's seen me.'

'He won't say anything,' he says calmly. 'He's too scared of his mother.'

The boy wraps round the woman's legs, pulling on her dress and turning to look at me, but she drags him back to the plaza. He tugs at her again. She slaps him. Hard. In the face. Three times. Everyone in the cafe is staring at them. *No one hits kids in Norway.* What a bitch. Then the lights go green, we pull into Tollbugata, and the nanny and the little boy disappear out of sight. I wiggle back on the seat, panting, and cuddle Ulv Pup.

Lukas punches the air. 'Mission accomplished!'

'Oh my God. Did you see? We got her little boy in trouble. She's horrible. I get why we have to rescue Ulv Pup from the likes of her.'

'That's parents for you. Always there to knock us down in our hour of need.'

'I wish they didn't use small children as weapons.'

'Children are always used as weapons.' Lukas smiles. 'I'm learning to fight back.'

143

22

Lukas and me sing raucous, awful versions of 'We're on the Road to Nowhere'. We giggle, hysterical, like we robbed a bank and escaped a high-speed car chase. We drive out of the city with the roof down. I wish I had a scarf, as my hair whips my face whenever I turn around, expecting to find the police on our tail.

'Relax.' Lukas smiles at me. 'What can they do? Arrest us for caring?'

We pass the Opera House and the port, and when Lukas takes the E16, I feel dead weird, anxious and pumped. Pup lies on my lap, stiff with disapproval.

'When do we let them know he's safe?'

'Soon.' Lukas scans my face. 'Don't worry.'

'Pup makes minutes seem like hours.'

'Alphas are hard work,' he sympathizes. 'Don't spoil him with too many cuddles. And I have a gift for your bravery.'

'I'm no hero,' I say. 'My head feels like it's going to explode.'

'Courage is exactly that. Feeling the fear, but taking action anyway.'

I steal a look at Lukas to see if he's taking the piss; sometimes he's as bad as Harper for doling out the drivel. Lukas looks his usual assured self, and rummages in the glove compartment. The jeep drifts over the lane and clips the edge of a roundabout. I yelp and grab Pup. He howls. The jeep swerves back on to the road, cutting up two cars. Lukas ignores their shrill horns, still hunting for something in the glove compartment.

'Don't worry, little one.' I tickle Pup's lip. 'Steering's overrated. He's better on motorbikes. But you're safe with Lukas.'

'How dull.' Lukas laughs. 'You sure about that?'

'For the record, you're about as safe as a hand grenade, but I don't want Pup squawking again. I never know what's going to happen next with you.'

'I thought you loved me for my turquoise eyes.'

'Any chance you could keep them on the road?'

'Not with you in the jeep.'

'Cheesy,' I say, but my heart somersaults when Lukas looks at me like that. He tugs a small package out from the glove compartment. A coach horn blares in my ears. Pup roars.

'*Drit og dra!*' Lukas flips the driver, and drops the red box in my hand.

My heart is at cardiac, but I smile back.

The leather box has gold edging. It looks vintage and is the size of a fountain-pen box. I've always wanted to write songs with a proper pen. The box looks so beautiful that I don't want to open it. In case what's inside is not as lovely. That's usually the case at Christmas. I get all excited and then Dad's present turns out to be something totally duff.

'It's not a Steinway, sadly,' Lukas says. 'Couldn't get a grand piano in my jeep.'

I love how he gets me. My fake nails fumble with the scarlet ribbon. I give it a yank and the contents of the box fly out and land against the windscreen, skidding up and down the dashboard. But it's not a pen; it's a strange, fancy quartz bracelet, attached to a gold ring.

Lukas asks politely, 'You prefer a pony?'

I laugh. Our gag line for spoilt rich kids. 'Any chance of a matching tiara?'

'Next time.' Lukas slams his hand over the sliding bracelet and hands it back to me. 'It's a goddess bracelet,' he explains. 'Put the ring on your finger first. Then the quartz stones go over the back of the hand, like a spider's web.'

I can't do it up and hold Pup, so I let it swing loose on my wrist. 'Wow. I'd get mugged for this bling in Manchester.'

'Bling? Those are worth a small fortune.'

Lukas smiles as my jaw drops.

'You're kidding me?'

'Rutilated quartz.' Lukas sounds so disapproving, I want to laugh. 'It's a type of quartz valued for those beautiful needles of rutile inside the gem.'

'Oh,' I say and get goosebumps when I read the inscription inside the box:

For ever together.

Love really is a cosmic joke. It trumps every rational thought. It's more real than other people. Or our families. It's bigger than my dreams. I never thought I'd think like this. Nothing comes close.

Later, I notice my white dress feels damp, and Pup is crying. His face is red, and snot oozes from his nose. He's obviously been crying for ages. Only, I've stopped hearing him.

The road twists down the mountain; I count thirteen hairpin bends in one terrifying drop to the fjord. Pup lies heavy on me, sleeping. I can feel his heartbeat with my fingertips. Nothing scares me as much as he does.

The clock in the jeep says we've had him two hours.

Two hours.

'Lukas? Shouldn't we be telling someone Pup's safe?'

He doesn't answer and taps the steering wheel with his brass lighter. Then he notices me staring and stops, but when I look away, I hear him tapping it again.

I study how the quartz bracelet webs over the back of my hand. *He loves me. I know he does.* And the enormity of him in my life overwhelms me. I'd do anything for him.

An awful smell fills the jeep. Pup's awake. He's gone red in the face and looks impossibly pleased with himself. 'He's nuclear,' I giggle. 'He beats Harper for pongs.'

I peel Pup's gummy fingers off my dress and groan.

He's so red and chubby and wrecks everything he touches. 'Call someone,' I say. 'I've got a bad feeling.'

'OK,' Lukas says. 'We're near the ferry stop. I'll call the nanny and tell them.'

I'm stunned this is so simple. Lukas takes a sharp right. We pull into a hamlet with a white beach and red-painted wooden houses. Perfect. Norway exhausts me.

Lukas hands me a 500-kroner note. 'There's a store next to the jetty. Get Pup nappies. Clean clothes. Leave his posh stuff in the changing room. He won't need it where we are going. Trust me.'

23

He films her in the vintage white Dior dress as she disappears inside the supermarket by the fjord. In the white dress and with long red hair, she looks so like Rosa he feels dizzy with grief. Svad's infant son stares at him over her shoulder. He scowls back. Guilty as charged, Ulv Pup. He flips Svad's brass lighter and checks how it lands.

Heads.

Sullen, hating himself, he sends the film of the girl and baby to the NRK news desk. *Frame her*, the cold voice says. And he moves all the photos of her to his Sleeping Beauty file. Then he breathes in the fresh salt air and closes his eyes.

Instantly, he's back there. On Ulv Fjell, skiing to keep up with Asena and his wolves. The wind singing its never-ending song of freedom. *Schuss.* Slalom. Tuck.

But the bored seagulls call him back to the car park, and he's caged in by neat Nordic shops and yapping tourists. With pent-up energy, he polishes the jeep's paintwork. He's meticulous. And he leaves her handprint on the bonnet.

24

The store smells of pickled fish. Everything is a rip-off price. Dad said Norwegians paid over thirty quid for a pack of butter a couple of years back. Sixth richest country in the world and the idiots ran out of butter at Christmas.

There are like a million different kinds of nappies. I've no idea which ones to buy. They're done by weight. I'd need an engineering degree to work out which one Pup needs. He's small but well hefty. Does he weigh ten kilos? Or twenty? 'Don't you dare leak on me,' I whisper. 'This is a quick in and out job.'

Pup grabs at my quartz bracelet and puts it in his gooey mouth. I pull it off him. Pup screeches. Everyone in the shop turns.

'Hello?' A yummy mummy is speaking to me in Norwegian.

I move away. But she follows me and asks in English if I need help. I nod at the row of nappies. 'I don't know which ones he needs,' I admit.

'Your baby looks about nine or ten months,' she says.

150

'Is he crawling?'

'No,' I say, meaning, I've no bloody idea.

The mother tsks and hands me a packet of nappies the size of a microwave.

'*Takk*,' I say, through gritted teeth.

'*Ikke noe problem.*' She switches back to English when I look even more befuddled. 'There is baby room at the back of shop.'

I shudder. 'No way. I'm not changing him.'

'Your mother has done everything for you?'

As if.

In the changing room, I feel awkward undressing Pup. He's a boy and his bits should be private, right? I get his nappy off and he pees like the second the cold air gets to him. A golden spray arcs over my shoulder. I duck, but then his crap gets all over my hand. I gag. And he's the one who screams? I open the new yellow onesie and remind myself to pay for it later, but Pup turns into Houdini when I try and get all his arms and legs in it. How can it take ages to dress a baby? By the time I'm done we're both sweaty and cross.

'I can't mother you,' I grumble.

Pup gnaws on his fist, looks me in the eye and farts. Brazen, brazen muppet. How can he be so happy when he's not wanted? But I'm on a roll. I pick up baby milk, a bottle and even baby wipes to prove I know what I'm doing.

'You want bag?' the cashier says, busy watching a TV

above her till.

I hand over the 500 kroner. The cashier keeps her eyes on her hospital soap and ignores me while I pack up my shopping. Pup gets in my way again and the bracelet catches on the bag.

The cashier notices the goddess bracelet; suddenly she has time to help me untangle the bag and coo at Pup. She can't take her eyes off me now. I want to laugh. Bling? Is it that simple? Look groomed and powerful and everyone wants to be your new best friend. I could write a song about that. *Faking it. Making it.*

Laughing to myself, I glance up to see my face on the TV screen. I look around for the CCTV camera, and my heart stops. There's no CCTV in this store.

It's a newsflash.

I'm on the sodding NRK news. I watch myself float across the plaza in the white dress and sunglasses and take Ulv Pup from his pram. Me. On my own. No Lukas. If they saw him in his memorable wolf coat, they would know it's all OK. He's family.

'*Savnet barn. Kjenner du denne kvinnen? Ring politiet.*'

The subtitles are repeated in English.

'*Missing baby. Do you know this woman? Call the police.*'

The report ends with a police officer holding out Pup's baby shoe in his hand.

'*A ghost walks away with the Svad baby,*' the subtitles say.

Ghost? Whose ghost? Dazed, I stare at the close-up of Pup's boot. I blink, unable to take it all in. I stare at the policeman on the telly. '*Kidnappet,*' he says.

Kidnapped?

The floor lurches under me.

Ulv Pup's head is banging into my chest and I'm nearly out the glass doors when I hear the cashier yelling at me. I think my heart is going to burst, but I look back. The casher is waving my change. A metre above her head, the TV has footage of me in the underground car park. What if she looks up? No. *She can't. Not if she keeps looking at me.* I force myself to walk back, locking my eyes on hers. Smiling. She smiles back when I tip her. I turn to leave and can feel her eyes drilling into my back.

Outside. I'm gulping air as if I'm drowning. 'Lukas!'

The sunlight crashes into my eyes. I can't see him anywhere.

'Lukas!'

Then his arms wrap round my waist and I lean into the safety of him.

'We have to go back. I'm on the news.'

'Shush. You're safe now.'

'But the police think I kidnapped . . . him!' I am jabbering with terror.

'It's OK,' Lukas says, with such gentleness in his voice that I blink away my tears.

I focus on his eyes. Sea. And broken glass. Until the ground stops spinning. 'But I saw myself on TV. *Me. Nell Lamb,*' I sob. 'Carrying a stolen baby. We have to go back.'

'Nell,' Lukas says softly. 'Calm now. I called the Barnevernet. I fixed it. You were right. We can't look after a baby. Their welfare officer is on her way to collect him. She will be here any minute. It's over. They promised she'd hire a new nanny. Someone kind. And to prioritize my request to adopt Ulv Pup when I turn eighteen.' He frowns. 'Can you believe, Svad Oil never passed on my request to adopt him?'

I shake my head. I'm so relieved this nightmare is over; but I can't hug Lukas and hold on to a wriggly Pup. It's not the baby's fault, but I'm so mad at him for getting me in this mess. What if my family see the news? I start worrying about Harper in hospital and my dad in custody, and how my family will fall apart without me. But Lukas is so calm, so certain. Gradually my heart slows. Everything is going to be fine. It's just me and Lukas now.

And the relief seeps into me like an illicit drug.

25

Lukas and me are little kids again, playing on a beach, chasing waves cold as snow. We need a ferry to cross the fjord. Lukas photographs me stepping ashore from a rowing boat and he calls me his Botticelli Venus. A Goddess in Love? Me? Nell from Manchester?

Then we curl up together on towels, drinking warm vodka from a bottle in a paper bag, making plans, talking nonsense. We giggle and talk about everything. Everything except him.

Ulv Pup.

Every time my mind tries to puzzle out why Lukas changed his mind, I slam the door in my head. I don't want to spoil our first whole day together.

It's OK now. It's over.

Pup's safe. He's with the Barnevernet. I know that. Social Services collected him from the cafe. Lukas told me to keep out of sight, so I didn't get into trouble. I didn't need telling twice. I whipped off the killer boots and disappeared off down the deserted beach with my stuff and the towels. Out of sight of the cafe, I pulled off my leather jacket and kissed the quartz bracelet before zipping it into a side pocket in my Dora the Explorer bag.

Keep it safe in there, Lukas said. Don't lose it.

I sunbathed and went out like a light. He was swigging vodka, and reading a copy of *Vårt Land*, the Norwegian newspaper, when I woke. He folded it away and didn't want to talk about Pup. I think Lukas feels he failed him. And I didn't dare ask what the Barnevernet said about me. I'm just glad it's all over. Someday I'll ask Lukas what it was all about. But not today. And I won't talk about Harper or Dad either.

'Allow me.' Lukas kneels to strap on my vintage boots. He's so chivalrous, not like the boys back home. I look up at another Norwegian painterly sky and drift off into that space where the only thing that matters is being with him.

A ferry glides down the fjord; the passengers wave to us, happy, unhurried.

We drive on and park the jeep on the bottom deck. I'm mainlining aromas from the cafe and wondering how Lukas can go for days without eating when I could scoff my body weight in chips. I ignore my rumbling stomach, and go to put the towels in the jeep.

'Don't touch the boot!' Lukas orders.

'What?'

I let go. The boot catches me in the face. I hop, hold-ing my cheek, trying not to cry. Lukas snatches the

156

towels, throws them in the boot and slams it. Then he is holding my face, covering it with kisses. 'Sorry. Sorry. Sorry. It's got a faulty hinge.'

In the end, I'm laughing so much it stops hurting.

'What was that in the boot?'

'Nothing,' he says, kissing my wet salty hair, my bare wrist. 'Where's your bracelet?' he murmurs.

I jiggle my Dora the Explorer bag. 'In here. Safe.'

'Wear it for me.'

But when I look, the quartz bracelet's not in the zipped pocket. I prop the bag on my knee and check it a second time. 'I know it's in here,' I say, determined not to get upset.

My face burns when Lukas sees my clutter of Starburst wrappers, make-up and half-eaten biscuits. By the time I search every pocket a third and then a fourth time, Lukas is tapping his brass lighter on the jeep.

'My lovely, lovely bracelet. I don't understand. I put in in this pocket here. I know I did,' I say, gutted.

'You sure? You promised not to lose it,' he says. 'It's very special.'

'You have to believe me,' I say, frantic. 'It was here. In here. Someone's stolen it.'

'There was no one on the beach,' Lukas says. The tight look on his face plucks my heart out. I'm choking back the tears now. 'Shush now.' He presses his forehead against mine, but I can't stop shaking.

'Maybe it's in the boot, with the towels?' I sob.

'No. I shook them out,' Lukas says.

157

'Can you forgive me?' I crush acrylic fingernails into my palms.

'Nell,' he holds my face, kissing me over and over, 'no bracelet is worth one of your tears.'

I feel the warmth of his hands and his calmness, his assurance flows into me and my body relaxes against his, trusting, hoping, longing to believe he forgives me.

'I can still give you my surprise,' he murmurs. 'I booked you a flying lesson.'

'What?' He never mentioned *flying*. 'In a plane?' I try to keep it together.

'I booked Svad's Cessna to get us to Ulv Fjell.' Lukas looks so chuffed with himself, as if he's giving me the best treat ever. 'You good?' He kisses my bare wrist again; it feels so naked without his bracelet. 'I thought you'd be more pleased,' he says, pouting.

'Thank you,' I smile, managing – just about – to hold back the tears.

The ferry pulls out to the middle of the fjord, the swell of the sea and my love for this boy surges through me.

Of course I can do this. I can do anything. Be anything. As long as I'm with him.

We drive off the ferry, and an hour later Lukas pulls into a bright private airfield littered with small planes. A cold sweat snails down my back.

'Is this for real?' I gasp. 'I was thinking more Heathrow. A proper airport?'

'This is a Norwegian airfield,' says Lukas calmly.

'What about the pilot instructor?'

'That will be me,' he says.

'Oh my God.'

Lukas laughs and laughs. 'You are quite safe. I have over a hundred flying hours. You collect the paperwork and I'll go get the parachutes.'

Parachutes?

An engineer in orange overalls walks me over to a dark-green Cessna. Single engine?

Holy shit. No second propeller. No back-up?

My head is spinning. The flimsy wings are held on to the fuselage with struts. Rods. Thinner than my own legs. And there are no steps. The engineer puts his foot in the wing strut and climbs in. I copy him and the whole plane shudders when I drag myself up into the cockpit and collapse on to the pilot's seat.

'Everything is in order,' the engineer says. 'You paid in advance. Enjoy your flight.'

'*Takk.*' I keep the surprise out of my voice. How can they ask so few questions? Everyone's so trusting in Norway. This was less hassle than buying nappies. Every inch of the walnut dashboard, the walls and the ceiling, are crammed with instruments, switches and knobs and meters. I grip the Z steering wheel in front of me. It looks straight out of a computer game. Suddenly I can't breathe. My chest tightens. I'm going to be sick, like last time. And we've not even taken off.

The engineer hands me a clipboard. 'You can complete the flight check?'

My hands are sweating as I take it from him. I can't speak. Is he bonkers? I swear he thinks it's me who's piloting this thing. As he jumps down, the engineer gives my thin clothes a stern look. 'You have misread our strange weather. There is a storm coming. Tomorrow. Don't get lost in the mountains in those.'

No kidding.

The boots pinch, so I take them off. And I'm out of that plane faster than a skydiver.

The red windsock snaps back and forth above the hangar. I dash inside and see the jeep parked in the corner. If I find the quartz bracelet, Lukas will be so happy. I can wriggle out of this. I cup my hands against the windscreen. Crap. He's left my keyboard on the back seat. I need that. Then my nose prickles. The jeep reeks of bleach and the sweet wrappers and crumbs inside have been tidied away. In the wild, Lukas always puts his cigarette butts in matchboxes; I think covering his tracks is second nature to him.

He's wiped the jeep clean, but missed my smeary handprint on the bonnet. It spoils the whole effect. I go to wipe it off when I hear a shuffling noise in the boot. My skin goes cold like a ghost walked through me.

After a couple of serious yanks, I get the jeep boot open. My eyes adjust to the dark as I rummage through the damp, sandy towels, telling myself all I will find is the missing quartz bracelet. But my hand touches something else, something cold, something that moves, and is very sticky, something so scary the hairs on my arm spring up like they've been electrocuted. I slam the boot down and back away, retching sour vodka fumes on the hangar floor.

'Lukas?' I holler, desperate for him to make this OK.

I make myself go back. And open the boot.

Ulv Pup is curled up in the dog basket. The wet beach towels cover his eyes and nose, but I can see a plastic dummy is taped to his mouth with bright blue sticky tape.

Dead slow, and whimpering, I lift the towel to see his eyes.

26

Ulv Pup's eyes are closed. Relief washes over me; he's not been harmed, not blinded. Not like I was panicking, imagining the maimed, empty eye sockets of my vandalized dolls. Zombie dolls. His poor eyes are only crusty with sleep and tears. I want to run away and pretend this isn't happening, but he's in my arms before I can think. 'Shush, Pup. It's all right.'

But it's so not. The tape's stuck to his mouth. I tear it and ease the dummy out.

Breathe, Pup. Please. Please. Breathe.

Pup's floppy, but his belly is warm, and that's a good sign, I think.

'Help,' I squeak. 'Help me, somebody. Please.'

Lukas sprints in, silhouetted against blinding sunlight from the hangar doorway. 'I told you to stay away from the boot. It's not safe.' He pulls me away from the jeep and tosses Pup's dummy in the dog basket. 'Give Ulv Pup to me.'

'He's not breathing.' My legs are shaking. 'I can't think – I'm so scared.'

'He's playing possum.' Lukas rips off the remaining sticky tape. The red marks on Pup's face sicken me, but he doesn't cry.

Lukas sniffs Pup's skin. 'He's fine. He's had his medicine. That's all.'

'Medicine? Stop.' I step between Lukas and the boot. 'What did you give him?'

He dives around me. 'The usual. Nell, can you move? Ulv Pup needs his rest.'

'Oh my God. Look at his lips. They're going blue.'

Lukas scowls. 'You're overreacting.'

'No,' I say, bricking it. 'Let me try CPR.'

'What?'

'I did rescue stuff at school. But Pup's smaller than the dummies I practised on.'

Lukas holds the baby in one hand. 'The patient's all yours, Dr Lamb.'

He's so calm I want to hit him.

I put my whole mouth over Pup's and his nose. I breathe into him. *Slow.* Pup smells sour, sickly, but I'm too terrified to feel squeamish. I watch his tiny chest inflate, but when I lift my mouth, my breath sighs out of him.

'He's fine.' Lukas tucks the hair extensions over my ear and whispers, 'Good job.'

'No. He's not breathing on his own.'

I try again. Lukas says something about us being late, but I don't listen.

Pup's so small; he seesaws on my heart. I concentrate

on his chest. I do three more breaths, three tiny compressions, each time counting. *Dear God, I'll be good. Promise. Let Pup live.* Nothing happens. I breathe into his mouth again.

This time a faint rasp comes from Pup's throat and his lips pink up. Relief turns my legs to mush. Pup's eyes blink open. I think he has trouble focusing on me. 'He needs to go to hospital,' I say, bending over him. 'How could you gag him?'

'Gag him?' Lukas raises one black eyebrow as if I'm nuts. 'The dummy falls out of his mouth. His nanny tapes it on so Ulv Pup doesn't lose it. That's all.'

He could have choked to death.

'We're taking him back, right? He needs a hospital.'

A shadow passes over Pup's face; his button eyes widen in surprise. Instinctively, I move to protect him, but forget to duck myself.

'Nell, watch out!'

Something smashes down on the back of my head. There's a moment when the blood goes cold inside my skull, dripping over my brain like a cracked egg. I think I'm OK. Then the pain explodes. And I am drowning in darkness.

Pain sirens through me. It hurts to move, but it hurts more to stay put. My knees are crushing into me; I stretch out. Bare feet touch cold metal. Panicky thoughts stream through me. Why is it so dark? Why can't I tell if my eyes are really open? Is it a terrorist attack? Am I dead?

Where's the light? What's that ringing in my ears?

Stale air presses in on me, thick as a blanket. No. It's not a blanket. It's hair. Me, with long hair? I sit up too fast, and smash into more metal. More pain. I see stars. Hear music. I can't breathe. I touch something round and squishy. I grip on like it's a lifeline. Am I trapped in here? Buried alive?

Focus. Get yourself out of here.

I force my hands to explore, and these strange long fingernails screech across the metal. I bite my nails, don't I? These nails cut into me when I grip on to the squishy object in my fist. I can't play the keyboard with these. I'm a songwriter. A songwriter. Never forget that. I turn my head, waiting for the spinning to ease up. It stinks in here. I sniff. Wet dog? I'm in the dog basket? *Oh my God.* No. No. No. I can't be in the boot of our own car. Suddenly I find I can't breathe, and my world dissolves into black.

When I come to again, I bang feebly on the boot. 'Help!' I croak.

Voices. Elephantine thumping above me.

The boot's shaking up and down, but the door won't open. It goes on for ever.

A voice shouts, 'There's a short cable by the lock. Pull hard.'

Eventually I find it. I pull. There's a blinding light and Lukas, pulling me into him, covering me with kisses. I'm shuddering, and clinging to his shirt like I'll never let go.

'Nell, I've got you. Quick. Move away. They should fix that lock.'

'Wha-ha-ha-happened?' I mumble.

He hugs me. 'Don't you remember? The boot crashed down. Knocked you out.'

'Did. Did. Did someone hit me?'

Lukas looks so shocked I feel bad for asking. 'No . . . the hinge just broke.' He cradles my face with huge hands. 'God, I adore you,' he says, with such love my breathing calms. 'You were out cold. I put you on the dog basket and then the lock jammed.'

I'm looking out at rows of small aircraft. Airport? 'But why . . . are we . . . here?'

He frowns. 'What's the last thing you remember?'

Strange worries play hide-and-seek in my mind, and my brain lurches after them, trying to make sense of random images.

A starfish? Jumping waves, cold as snow? A quartz bracelet?

'Nothing makes any sense. I've got stampeding buffalo trampling on my brain.'

'I can fix that.' His strong fingers massage my head and neck. I think of Harper then, and the pain she gets when her meds won't kick in, and pull myself together. A bump on the head is nothing compared to what she goes through.

Then, over his shoulder, propped against the hangar, I see the baby.

And a blue shoe.

Memories swim to the surface and a tsunami of them crashes over me. Lukas catches me as I buckle. 'Why's he still here?' I sob.

Lukas sighs like he's told me a hundred times. He smooths hair off my forehead. 'You keep forgetting,' he says.

But I remember. Waves. Cold as snow. Drinking vodka. I grope my way to the truth. No. Pup wasn't with us on the beach. I can't keep quiet about that.

'You definitely told me the Barnevernet took him, didn't you?'

Lukas tilts his head and gazes at me. 'He's lost his mother and his father.'

He says nothing else. He is so calm. So certain he's doing the right thing.

I promised to help him. I promised.

27

Fear crawls over my skin like an army of ants. The white silk dress sticks to my back and Pup sticks to my chest. I wait in the cockpit and stare ahead at the sun roasting the airfield. The wind bowls along, snatching up dust and bleached-out newspapers and shoving them in the fence. They hang in mid-air, impaled on the wires. I see Lukas drive the jeep out the hangar. He waves and disappears round the building. He's only been gone a couple of minutes, but whenever he leaves me alone with Ulv Pup, I feel like something awful is going to happen. I finger the lump on my head. Lukas's touch took the headache away, but the extensions don't help; they are pulling on my scalp like a scolding sister.

I keep forgetting why I'm doing this. I wake up over and over again, like from a bad dream, shocked at what I've done, but unable to change it.

That's one thing I wish I could unlearn from today; how cowardice makes me unable to think for myself. Yeah, fear of humiliation, worrying what other people think, obliterates me. It wipes me out. I need to write that down before I forget it again. Writing stuff down always helps me think it out, when I can't hold all the stuff in my head.

I rummage in my bag for my journal, before I remember it's gone for good. I've somehow lost track of myself again.

Lukas looked stunned when I told him Dad destroyed my life's work in the kitchen waste-disposal unit. I thought Lukas was going to cry when I told him I'd lost all my songs and it felt like the best part of me had died.

But safe inside my copy of *Wuthering Heights* is the charred photo. I've not had a chance to talk to Lukas about finding the first-ever photo of me and my mother. I take it out now and look at it.

I seem such a happy chubby baby, chewing on my blue shoe strap. Pup looked just like that this morning. I can't work out my mother's face. I'm surprised to see she looks kind. Harper said I ruined everything with my crying, but Mum is playing with my foot and smiling like she loved being with me. Why did she leave? Did she ever regret it? Was it the worst decision of her life, and somehow Mum couldn't find a way to come back?

Or did she walk away and never look back?

Pup squawks and tries to snatch the photo off me. I glare at him like it's all his fault my mum left me. I hide the photo away again, before he ruins it.

He arches up over my shoulder like a wild thing. I peel him off and sing softly to him. Pup just roars back in my face and pushes me away. He hates me. His damp curls are plastered to his head; the yellow onesie is filthy with engine oil and dirt. It's hard to remember the pristine baby in his pram from this morning. He makes me feel so guilty.

'You hungry?' I sigh. 'I'll find you a bottle, but lighten up, I'm not your mother.'

I know that's mean, but it's not like he can understand me, or anything. He's Norwegian. And Pup doesn't let up. Nothing I do is good enough, or fast enough, for him. There's no space to move in the cockpit. I hook the strap of my Dora bag with my foot and drag it towards me, but the joystick digs into me and pushes me off the co-pilot seat. Pup goes mental, until he sees me pull out a bottle of baby milk.

'Tah-dah, this what you want, my precious?'

The milk feels warm and looks a funny colour, but Pup snatches the bottle out of my hands and shoves it in his mouth. He sucks hard with his eyes closed tight like it's the best drink ever. Its sickly sweetness makes me want to gag. I risk moving him to the cabin chairs behind us. I grab Lukas's wolf coat off one seat and strap Pup in carefully.

'You stinker. I swear your nappy's twice the size it was an hour ago. Behave. No more squawking.'

Pup turns his head and acts like I don't exist.

'You ungrateful little savage,' I say, hurt. I got dissed by a baby? I clear up his mess anyway, and shove it in the nappy bag.

Suddenly I grip my legs so hard the acrylic nails cut

into my knees. I stare at my pampered hands and feel like this is all happening to someone I don't know.

Breathe. Breathe. Don't panic.

Pup gives a piercing wail. He's finished the bottle and can't hold it up to get the dregs. He's as hopeless as Harper. Sweat dribbles down my neck.

My sister never goes to hospital to have tests without me. I need to speak to her.

Fur sticks to my damp fingers as I slip my hand into Lukas's wolf coat pocket. He hates me touching his phone, but I've seen him tap his security code out a thousand times. Can I remember Harper's new number? My mind blanks. That headache again.

I look out at the blue sky and feel the warm wind on my face. This should've been the best weekend of my life. I've never been anywhere. And I'm in a knockout country with a hot boy, and a baby pouring cold water over everything.

As I fiddle with Lukas's phone trying to magic up my sister's number, I scroll down to a folder called *Sleeping Beauty*.

That's one of Lukas's nicknames for me. He says he woke me up with a kiss. I grin. That's so like Lukas to cast himself as Prince Charming. I tell myself everything will be OK; if I can anchor myself in our memories. I often wonder why he's so secretive about his photos.

And I know it's wrong but I open the *Sleeping Beauty* folder.

A gust of wind rattles the Cessna's door and I whip

round, feeling guilty as hell. Dressed in orange overalls, Lukas looks like a mechanic, but he lopes along like he owns the place, strolling down the rows of aircrafts. I almost didn't recognize him with that cap pulled down over his hair, but I'd know my keyboard anywhere. And I think if I could just get my old Lukas back, everything would be all right. He smiles.

Mortified, I put his phone back.

Lukas swings into the Cessna cockpit. I wish I was graceful like him. He pulls off the orange baseball cap, slides his long legs under the pilot seat and snaps on a three-point harness.

The way he smiles at me, I forget Pup. I see only him.

'Nell, look what I found!' I stare at the golden gems sitting in his hand. The goddess bracelet. Lukas slips the ring over my finger, fixes the chains over the back of my hand and clips the bracelet on my wrist. 'Better now,' he says.

'I don't get it.' I touch the quartz stones. 'I lost them, didn't I? On the beach.'

'You've got concussion,' he says gently.

I pretend to admire the goddess bracelet, but really I've forgotten why it's so important.

Lukas kisses my wrist. 'Come on. Time for your lesson. Your fear will vanish when I teach you how to fly.' He dangles the ignition key in front of me. 'See this? The Cessna's tail number is written on the tag. We're A006RB. You use it to identify your aircraft to the flight tower.'

The blood rush is so loud I can hardly hear what he's saying.

Lukas turns on the two-way radio. '*Kontroll, Alfa zulu zulu, seks romeo bravo,*' he says. '*Ber om avgang pa Rullebane Delta.*'

Runway D is empty, but the control tower tells Lukas to stand by. He narrows his eyes. 'They like to throw their weight around up there.' He taps his lighter on the walnut flight deck. 'Watch me. You put the key in the ignition and this red button, to the left of the joystick, is the master switch. Got it?'

I nod, trying not to puke.

'You see the mixture knob?' he says.

'The one that looks like an old lipstick tube?'

'Yes. Push it all the way in, to maximize the fuel in the engine.'

'The switches look so old-fashioned,' I say. 'They're not even digital?'

'It requires more skill.' He smiles. 'This is the throttle. Crack that open a quarter.' He puts his fingers over mine and shows me how to do a quarter turn.

The whole plane rattles like Dad's old washer-drier.

'What's that?' I ask, panicked.

'Just the gyros.'

I look at him blankly. 'Aviation fans,' he says.

'Oh. Right. Aviation fans. That makes complete sense.'

He grins. 'OK, we're good to go. Turn the ignition key to the right, like this.'

The propeller throbs into life. I grip the armrests. In front of me, the co-pilot joystick moves all by itself, like a ghost has hold of the controls.

'Lukas Svad, we're not really taking off in this thing, are we?'

He laughs and laughs. 'We've been talking about this all day.'

'We have?'

'Yes. Show time.'

The Cessna taxis down to the yellow line in the middle of the runway. A voice crackles over the radio: '*Alfa. Zulu. Zulu. Seks. Romeo. Bravo. Returner til basen.*'

'The control tower wants us to go back?' I say, hopeful.

'I never turn back.' Lukas flips the radio off. 'We're good to go.'

The wheels hit every crack in the cement; the impact jolts through my teeth. 'You OK, Ulv Pup?' I say, but the baby's eyes slide off me to stare out the window.

An engineer runs out of the office. He sprints across the airfield to cut us off. And I really, really hope he catches us up.

'We're at seventeen hundred rpm.' Lukas pulls on the joystick. The nose of the Cessna lifts and we clear the perimeter fence. I look down and wish I hadn't.

'Oh my God. Oh my God. Oh my God!'

The airfield is a cot blanket of tiny pale squares and toy-sized houses. Then it disappears out of sight and we fly over the fjord and on out to sea.

We're a gnat flying above the ocean. Then Lukas dips

the wings; the sea and sky become one and the endless blue dwarfs me. I lean into Lukas and I feel his certainty. His skill. He wasn't lying when he said he could fly. He loves being up here. My hands haven't stopped sweating since take-off, but right now, up here, it's so peaceful and he's so magnificent, love feels bigger than fear.

'The stars are out,' he says. 'Your night garden in the sky.' He flips a series of switches and the next thing we're floating, gently spiralling.

One by one, the stars blink in the pale blue, unaware of their cosmic beauty. Lukas looks at me and his smile is bigger than the sky and my whole body hums.

Above us, a plume of rocket vapour seems to split open the sky, the sunlight ignites the white tail and turns it into a golden fluffy line from the sea to high up in the atmosphere. The light is something else. Neon. Blinding. Godlike. 'Wow, look at that,' I say.

'It's a contrail,' Lukas says calmly.

'A what?'

'A condensation trail from aircraft thousands of feet up.'

'It's beautiful,' I say. 'It looks like a crack in the sky. I wish we could slip into another dimension and escape.'

'Crossing a threshold? This calls for raw speed.' Lukas pulls hard on the joystick.

The Cessna shoots up, shaking, rattling to get more altitude, and the velocity presses me into my seat. Then we are on our backs, upside down. I want to scream, but my mouth is rigid with terror. My ears pop. Pup roars.

Lukas whoops. 'Twelve thousand feet. You up for a dive through the clouds?'

'Yeah,' I gasp. 'I'm up for anything.'

He takes his hands off the Z steering wheel mid-air. The Cessna rolls and Lukas acts like it's no big deal. 'Your treat,' he says. 'Push in the co-pilot joystick. All the way.'

'What? I can't fly this.' I panic.

'You can.' As he presses my hands on to the joystick, his skin warms mine and there's no space to tell him how scared I am.

I push. And push. And push. The Cessna stalls. There's this sickening quiet. Even Pup quits crying.

The Cessna is motionless. Abruptly, we nose-dive.

The plane picks up speed and we spin straight down through the cloud. Spinning and spinning. I can't see the sea. We're in a whiteout; flying blind, diving down the centre, every sound muffled, the sky squeezing, suffocating us.

'Where's the sea?' I yell. 'Do I pull up?'

'Wait.' Lukas forces my hands down.

I forget to breathe. It's just us and the dive. Suddenly we spin out into the sunlight and I sigh in relief. But we're still plummeting, falling from the sky. The rush is something else; my body rips apart, trying to be in two places at once, and my stomach gets left in the cloud, way back. All I can see is the sea and sea and more sea. The sparkle on the waves dazzles me, but the sea looks so solid. Deadly.

The shadow of the Cessna darkens the water. Lukas is

still staring at the waves, like he's seen a ghost. Is he thinking of them? The helicopter crash?

'Lukas!' I pull on the joystick, but it won't budge. 'We're going to die.'

'Not today.' He yanks on the joystick; the nose of the Cessna comes up. The engines protest. His arms are shaking with the effort to keep us out of the water. He's left it too late. Sea spray foams over the windscreens, the back of my throat burns. I taste salt on my lips and look over at Pup. He stares back at me solemnly with his chocolate-button eyes. He has no fear. I send a prayer home. *Harper, I'm so sorry.*

Lukas pulls out the throttle, flips a Bakelite switch and the wings level with the horizon.

Oh my God. The adrenalin rush. The relief.

'Light me a cigarette?' Lukas hands me his brass lighter.

My heart is beating so fast I think it's going to burst out of my body, but I feel so alive I'd follow Lukas Svad to hell and back, if he asked.

28

We fly west. Neon clouds race across the pale evening. Lukas pulls me into his shoulder; his knee is pressing against mine and I can't think of anything else. We morph into us. And if I don't look at Pup, I can pretend he's not here, ignore the shame leaking into my bones. An hour later, Lukas pushes me back into my own seat. 'Get ready for the descent.'

'You're joking? The last town was miles away.'

'And you didn't recognize Preken Rock from up here.' He laughs.

'What?'

'Preken Rock?' he says. 'We flew over your home to come here.'

'Oh?' I say. 'So we went all the way to Oslo and back to rescue Pup?'

'Yep,' he says.

I take a deep breath and look down. A narrow fjord is dotted with red-painted homes, small farms and barns. Then comes a beast of a mountain.

As we fly up, time rewinds itself; fat rivers narrow into

fast streams, plunging waterfalls dry to a trickle, the trees thin out and scree slopes become a tide of shadows, swirling around a peak, sunset-pink.

'Ulv Fjell,' Lukas says over the engine whine. 'I know it like the back of my hand.'

I look closer. 'That's a hell of a white crater down there. What an eyesore in the middle of a nature reserve. Is that the open pit? Rutile? It's as ugly as its name.'

Lukas doesn't answer. Crosswinds wallop the Cessna, pushing us sideways. The noise is something else, fists pummelling on the fuselage. 'We'll drop out the sky,' I cry.

'It's only turbulence.' But Lukas is frowning in concentration.

'The airfield warned there's a storm coming,' I remember. 'Forgot to mention it.'

'Good to know,' he laughs. 'It will make the descent interesting.'

The Cessna dips again. I feel sick, but nothing fazes Lukas. I wipe my sweating hands on my dress and turn to check Pup's harness is on tight. The baby gives me a bored look and stares out his window.

'Where's the runway?' I ask.

'There isn't one. We use that firebreak. Got to get this right, or we end up as soup. Relax. I've seen Svad do it loads of times.'

'What?' I pinch his arm. 'You watched? Tell me this isn't your first time.'

Lukas shrugs. 'First time for everything.'

Another crosswind punches the Cessna. 'Oh my God,' I sob. Another jolt. And my heart hammers me, desperate to get out of my body and go somewhere a whole lot safer. But Lukas ignores how we're being buffetted from side to side.

'We approach the airstrip at a right angle,' he says. 'Textbook. Bank to the left and fly parallel to Ulv Fjell.'

I watch darkness creeping over the mountainside. 'Can you see to land?' I fret.

'Not really.' He frowns. 'My family liked to keep the location secret. But there are concealed lights that should turn on once we pass the radio mast.' He rubs his black hair. 'How do you like your touchdown? Hard or soft?'

'In one piece,' I snap, gripping the armrests.

He smiles.

Below us, the airstrip lights up. It looks proper ramshackle; the runway overgrown. You wouldn't find this place from the air, if you didn't know it was here.

We float down. Lukas lands the Cessna as lightly as a moth, then the wheels rattle over the long grass.

'Oh my God,' I say. 'You did it. You're amazing.'

'You're too kind.'

He focuses on holding the Cessna steady. Trees in white blossom flash past. We're in the middle of nowhere and they edge the forest like frothy white lace. Wind snatches the blossom and throws it up into the night. Directly ahead, red arc lights are flashing, warning us to stop. As the Cessna gets closer, the blossom swirls up white, but drifts down stained bright-red.

'Look. The lights,' I murmur. 'It's turning white flowers red.'

Lukas nods. 'Renaissance red roses represent suffering. Svad planted white cherry blossom up here for his wife. White means purity. He liked to think of her like that.'

We're running out of airstrip – the Cessna's heading straight into the ravine barrier.

'Lukas!' I beg. 'Brake. Please.'

'Thought you'd never ask,' he laughs.

When the Cessna stops, my heart is just about climbing back into my body, but Lukas looks as if he'd do it again in a heartbeat. His face is stained crimson by the arc lights.

'You are an absolute devil. You trying to kill us?'

'Death doesn't scare me.' He laughs. 'It's living that's hard.'

'Wow. You give Nietzsche a run for his money.'

'You learnt about Nietzsche in school?' he says, curious.

'Yep. Psych class. My old teacher in Manchester had a thing for psychopaths. I thought they were exaggerating. They'd have a field day analysing you.'

'I hate doctors, especially shrinks.' Lukas pouts. 'When did words fix anything?'

'Well. There's *I love you* and *sorry* for starters – you can go far with those,' I say, expecting an apology for scaring me witless, but Lukas swings out of the Cessna, whistling.

'What are you waiting for?' he says. 'There's no Flybussen up here.'

I laugh and climb down into his arms, shivering in my flimsy white dress. Wind savages the cherry blossom, pulps it into the red arc lights, and then drops it into the ravine like a child bored by a new toy.

'It's snowing petals,' I marvel.

'There won't be any left come morning,' Lukas states.

The arc lights switch off, plunging the mountain into darkness. Lukas draws my arm into the sleeve of his wolf coat and for a moment we have one arm in each sleeve. I could stay like this for ever, listening to his steady heartbeat.

The mountain yawns above us, a black hole in the stars. It smells crisp, even better than fresh flowers. I'm humming that idea into a song when Lukas suddenly says, 'Svad loved astronomy. His wife called me "the hunter in the sky". You see the three stars in a row? That's Orion's Belt – Orion was a great hunter in the old tales. My family told me you can hear the stars talking to each other up here.'

'You miss them a lot?' I think Lukas loved his Svad way more than he realizes.

Lukas ignores my question. 'Can you hear them in the stars?'

We listen together.

'Maybe we can't hear them, but what if they can hear us?' I say.

The night sky is sequined with stars, and they pulsate. *On. Off. On. Off.* Like they're breathing. Like they're genes switching on, switching off. Like we're all connected.

Hard to believe these are the same stars I see back home. Manchester nights are bleached orange by street lights. I catch my breath. 'Oh. Is that a shooting star?'

Lukas nods. 'Technically it's a particle of dust, burning up in the atmosphere.' He slips the rest of his wolf coat over me. It hangs down to my ankles.

'You old romantic,' I say. 'But the bigness of this place, the mountain and the stars, is how I feel about you. There is nothing I couldn't love. Nothing I couldn't forgive.'

'I knew you'd get it.' He tucks my hair inside the wolf coat and gazes at me like he can't get enough of my face. He kisses me then. Crushing my lips, as if we only ever get this one kiss. My heart explodes and I'm everywhere, and right here with him.

From the Cessna, Pup emits a glass-shattering screech.

'Boy, he chooses his moments,' I groan.

Lukas drags Pup out of his seat by the scruff of his neck, and Pup stops crying.

'Hey. Careful,' I say. 'He's not a real wolf pup.'

'He is,' says Lukas, and puts the baby in my arms.

Pup kicks me in the stomach and snatches at the falling petals.

'Whoa. You are one fierce baby.'

Pup smells of piss and sour milk, but I'm so happy I plant a kiss on his plump foot. Of course, he hooks me on the chin with it. I'd almost admire his spirit, if he weren't such a total pain. But Harper's got this so right. Babies nuke romance.

*

Fog covers the mountain airstrip fast, I swaddle Pup in his cot blanket. This mountain is a beast now. It feels alive. Unpredictable. And I'm jumpy as shit. Something shoots out of the bushes, I shriek and hug Pup tighter. A grey shadow darts through the trees. Lukas leaps after it and disappears in the mist.

'Cut through the forest, keep up,' he calls.

'Lukas! Is that a wolf?'

He doesn't stop. Moonlight picks out his tall athletic body, loping through the trees, swirling the ground mist behind him. I stomp on, trying not to hate what he loves. This forest is Lukas's back garden. He doesn't trip over roots, or bang into saplings like me and he never doubts that I'm right behind him. But Pup weighs a ton, and now I've got the keyboard on my back too and I'm no silent stalking cat. The forest floor crunches under my feet like it's made of cornflakes. Trees blot out any starlight; their trunks loom out of the fog like lamp posts, branches whispering: *You don't belong here. You're not one of us.*

An owl hoots. I stumble and the moonlight shines on Pup's filthy face. His eyes are bright, but he's taking in everything.

This morning, his world was his pristine pram. I pull his blanket up tighter.

'I'll make Lukas radio the police. Get you home,' I promise. 'Soon as.'

Pup sighs. I get the distinct feeling I bore him.

Somehow he's in his element out here, but I'm so far out of my depth I don't know how to get back to shore.

We leave the forest and Lukas points at a structure on a sort of huge crane, towering above a compound. It's like a border control, a watchtower, but suspended in mid-air. Black. Dangerous. And exciting. 'Cool,' I say. 'Who lives up there?'

Lukas looks at me like I've forgotten his birthday. 'We do. It's our home.'

29

Lukas unlocks a gate and we slip inside the compound. The smell hits me right off, odour of wet dog and old rain and forest rolled into one. We walk past rows of empty cages; sheds with skis and quad bikes and sledges. Lukas sprints up, taking the metal steps three at a time. Lugging Pup, I huff up after him, my heels catching in the treads. I'm swaying with exhaustion when I get to the top. Lukas shoulders open the door. Inside, a glass cabin floats in mid-sky like we're suspended between the stars.

'Blimey. How does it stay up?' I ask, as my legs turn to mush.

'It's cantilevered; anchored one end.' Lukas flips the light switch. Nothing happens. 'Generator.' He gives me a torch and disappears back down the stairs.

'Hey! Don't leave me, I'm not good with heights or the dark or babies,' I mutter.

But he's gone. Pup grizzles. The torch produces a narrow beam of light and I explore the crushing darkness like a burglar with tunnel vision, tripping over wolfskin rugs and oak tables, battered leather armchairs and a wood stove.

A Steinway grand piano? It looks so out of place. How did they even get it up here? They'd have needed a crane. I sink down on the piano stool and pick out a few notes. It's perfectly in tune. A frigging *Steinway*. Lukas never said anyone in his family was musical.

Pup settles into me and claps his chubby fists as I play 'Don't Believe in Love'. For the first time since we met he stares at me with something like respect.

The kitchen's dead simple, just an oak chopping bench really. No dishwasher or anything modern. Wolf photographs cover one wall. I shine my torch to get a closer look.

'Whoa, Pup. That you? No way.' The photo shows a baby asleep with a wolf, its chubby arms wrapped around the massive ruff of blueish fur. The wolf has its chin on the child's bare back and watches the camera, alert, protective, ice-gold eyes outlined in black lashes. The thought of being that close to a wolf brings me out in hives. Someone must have trusted that wolf. And I don't need to see the baby's face to know it's Pup. But who would risk their child to take that photo? No parent.

Lukas.

It hits me for the first time . . . how he never looks at Pup, never touches his little brother, unless he has to. I wonder if somehow he blames Pup. Because how you touch someone is how you show love, right?

My reflection ghosts up in the window: the big red

hair, the white dress, a baby on my hip. This so isn't me. I can't work out how to feel any more – I thought today would be the happiest day of my life, but I'm jangled by panicky thoughts; about this baby, about Harper, about Dad, about not keeping up with Lukas or understanding why I went along with this. The more I worry, the more the lump on my head throbs.

Pray louder than your thoughts.

Great, Dad. Like that will help.

In the bathroom, Pup and me stumble over a claw-footed bathtub some idiot put in the centre of the floor. I wobble backwards, and knock into an antique gramophone player.

'Ouch,' I groan, rubbing my ankle.

The generator kicks in, the lights snap on and I wince at the brightness. An oil painting dominates the room: a Renaissance naked girl with long red hair, stepping out of a seashell. It's a sodding fake Botticelli. 'Not fair his muse looks so clean when you and me are sticky gum.' I grumble.

Pup yawns in my face. He smells of sick. 'You're proper gross.' I say. He scowls at me and I have to laugh.

Back in the living room Lukas hunkers down in front of the wood stove, scrunching up a *Vårt* newspaper. He flicks his brass lighter and the paper catches first time, the photo of a shrew-faced woman on the front page disappearing.

I catch the headline: *SAVNET. Missing.* 'Who's that?'

I yawn, and dump Pup down on the chair nearest the stove.

'Not Svad's chair. No one else sits in it.' Lukas slams the stove door and flames leap up against the blackened glass.

'Who plays the piano up here?' I ask.

'Pup's mother,' he says. 'She could play anything. One of the best bits of my childhood was listening to her play Chopin. She wrote music when Svad wasn't around.'

'And she raised you and Asena too?' I say. 'I thought you said she was a geologist?'

Lukas doesn't answer.

I sigh, and move Pup to the wolfskin rug. He roars the minute I move away. 'Blimey. You'd think I'd trodden on his hand.' I'm too tired to pick him up, but Lukas's staring into the flames like he's reading a horoscope. I plonk the baby back on my hip, and instantly his cries turn to hiccups. He's worse than my sister for manipulation.

'Can I use your phone?' I ask. 'Harper must be frantic.'

Lukas ignores me.

'Hey. Don't give me that. You promised,' I say. 'I need to know if she's OK.'

'Maybe. Later,' he says. 'You love her? Don't you?' He gazes at me. 'Even when she's a bitch to you?'

'Of course; she's my sister, no matter what. And I won't say anything. About, you know . . . all this.'

Lukas raises one black eyebrow. 'Oh, I know you won't.'

Our eyes meet. I feel his certainty in himself.

'Tell me your plan,' I say. 'I got Pup here. But I can't

stay with him indefinitely.'

'I thought you wanted to escape your family.'

'I do. But I can't abandon them. Imagine how hurt they'd be.'

Lukas shrugs and opens a beer. He takes a long swig and hands it to me. I don't mind. It tastes of him. 'You clean Ulv Pup. I'll cook.'

'I'll cook, Tarzan. You change him. It's your turn. And if you love Pup so much, how come you never cuddle him?' I cross my arms and give him some attitude. God, he's cute. Then a black look crosses Lukas's face and makes me think it's not worth it.

So I bathe Ulv Pup. Well, that's one word for it. But it'd be easier to wash a cat in the kitchen sink. Pup howls and flails and scratches me. I save him from going under the water, twice, but I'm soaking, starving and cross.

The white dress is wrecked and my back's aching by time I get Pup's legs and arms dried and back inside his onesie, then button it up before he wriggles out again. I can't help but kiss his button nose. He beams back at me. And I feel dead chuffed.

Lukas has got a stew going on the wood stove, and it smells incredible. This time I avoid Svad's empty chair and settle Pup down in the rocking chair by the window. 'Sit tight. And I'll go find you a bottle,' I tell him. Then I stare in astonishment as Pup yowls and tries to throw himself off the chair. I pick him up. Pup stops crying.

I take a deep breath. 'Lukas. He needs milk. You got a microwave?'

He laughs. 'No. Use the kettle. I'll go milk the goat.'

I shudder. He's out the cabin before I can protest, and Pup arches his back again like I'm tasering him. I sigh. 'You frigging dictator. You only care about your milk.'

The kettle looks well older than Dad, and when I plug it in, the lights blow. Of course they do. I shriek. Pup hollers. He buries his head in my chest. Darkness menaces me and for a split-second, I wish Harper were here with me on my hot date.

30

He had hoped it would help, coming home, to Ulv Fjell. But nothing silences the guilt yipping and savaging his heart, and in despair he kick-boxes the empty wolf cages. Again and again, his feet slam into the birch poles. He steps back, only to see her smiling, trusting eyes. He dreads seeing the look on her face when she finds out he betrayed her. When she finds out who he is.

The flashbacks come back. The chopper falling. Their screams.

It's not his fault. Not his fault. This problem only happened because his best solution didn't work out, and now it's become a bigger problem, and he never meant to fall in love with her – and now the boy still has to die.

'Don't judge me,' he whispers to her. '*Faen ta deg!*'

He lashes out at the cage door with a wild punch.

The impact judders up his body; a burning pain explodes in his fist. Blood?

No. No. No. Don't look. Don't look. It's too late. He feels it, leaking out of him. Blood. His own blood. His head swims with the rapid drop in his heart rate.

His knees buckle, and he barely feels the cage floor smack his face, or the wolf dung soaking into his hair. He only hears his childhood soundtrack:

Get up, Dogboy. Up. Get up. On your feet. It's only blood. I won't have a blood-phobic weakling in my house.

He tries to stay upright. Tries to please Svad. He tries and he tries. But the sight of his own blood always destroys him. The light twists into a mottled kaleidoscope, and he groans as the dark terrors take him.

31

Our cabin door creaks open. The night air rushes in.

'Lukas?' I say, nervous. Silence. 'Lukas? That you? You've been gone ages.'

I wrap my arms round Pup and back away into the kitchen.

A figure grunts and stacks logs by the wood stove. I shine my torch and sigh in relief. 'Stop playing games, Lukas! I'm too freaked. I can't even sleep in the dark at home.'

He smiles. 'I know. What happened to the lights?'

'The kettle fused the electrics,' I snap. 'Can you fix them?'

'No. I used up the last fuse. Stay put. We've got candles.'

Soon the cabin glows like a solar system. Lukas dances around the kitchen, lighting candles that smell of cinnamon and orange, and placing them along window ledges. His excitement is contagious.

'I've got that fluttery feeling I get at Christmas,' I say.

'Waiting for Santa. You know, when something wonderful is going to happen and the excitement builds and builds, till we get to unwrap our presents.'

Lukas shrugs. 'Christmas was never like that for me. I was lucky if Svad fed me.'

'Oh,' I say, lost for words.

Pup drinks goat milk with no fuss, pumping his legs at the bright flames in the wood stove. We take him upstairs to a bunkroom, on a landing above the kitchen. Lukas wants to put him on the top bunk, but I refuse and pull out a drawer from an antique chest. I pop Pup in that with some towels. I watch him as he falls asleep.

No matter how hard I try to feel chuffed about rescuing him, this panicky feeling gets trapped inside me. What was I thinking of? Rescuing a baby? We don't know how to look after him.

But I have never lived on the edge, never dared defy my dad, never asked what makes me happy. And I can't go back to sleepwalking through my life. Lukas Svad woke me up. I close the bunkroom door behind me and leave the old Nell in the room. I don't want her spoiling everything. Tonight is about Lukas and me. Pup can wait; until tomorrow.

Lukas has thrown warm red blankets and a bunk mattress out on the observation deck.

'Why's that outside? I ask, mystified.

'Special night.' His face looks proper tender. 'Thought you'd like the comfort.'

I blush. 'Hey, we got a toasty fire going on in here. We don't need to bivouac. There are no parents to stop us sleeping in front of the fire.'

His nose twitches. 'Too stuffy. I never sleep up here.'

'You're kidding me? Not even in winter?'

'Svad didn't want me getting soft.'

'Wow. Norwegians are tough. That'd be child abuse in the UK.'

'It's normal where I come from.' He smiles. 'Svad's wife recreated the experience of a wolf den in the cages, after she rescued me from the hunters. Asena and I played down there in the meadow. As we got braver, we roamed the forest, hunted elk, fished, swam in the water-falls, but we always came back to our cages at night. When Asena was four, Svad's wife brought her a mate – a rescue wolf from Scotland. I was ten when Asena had her first pack. Her pups were born in the cages down there. I slept with them all the time, skied with them in winter to keep up as they ran through the snow.'

'Wow,' I say, feeling about one hundred per cent inadequate.

Lukas hugs me tight. 'Nell, imagine a world where it's safer outdoors, and you know exactly where you belong, you trust your senses more than what you read in a book, every hair on your body is alert, your skin is a multisen-sory force field, and every member of your pack trusts you, fights to the death for you. They share and play and love – and you fit right in.'

Something in Lukas's voice changes; it's not deep any

more, it's high and fast like a small child. He towers over me, but somehow he sees his world through the eyes of a six-year-old. Everything is very black and white, no grey areas, and I think he will always have that little boy inside, who believes a wolf den is the best place in the world.

'You know something?' I say. 'You've got me thinking. I've decided, I'm going to track Mum down when I go home.'

He gives me a strange look. 'Parents aren't all they're cracked up to be, you said.'

'I know. But I can't go on hating Mum all my life. I need to forgive her.'

'And I need fresh herbs,' Lukas says. 'Go down to the compound and pick me some rosemary.'

'Rosemary?' I sigh. 'What's for dinner?'

'Local specialty,' Lukas says. 'Elk. We hang the meat out to dry like biltong.'

I pull a face at him. 'Thanks. I'll stick with cheese.'

'Try it first. I'm a master chef,' Lukas says, deadpan, and pours more red wine in my mug. We laugh like it's well funny. I've never seen Lukas cook anything, other than grilling Norway rat over a bonfire. We collapse on the deck outside the cabin, kissing and giggling. I can't remember how much I've had to drink, but soon I badly need a pee.

I hold tight to the tower railings, and edge down the metal steps. I'm good, I tell myself, as long as I don't look down the thirty-metre drop. The wind gives vicious tugs on my hair. I hope the airfield was wrong about that storm; I don't want to be in this groaning tower when it hits.

I find rosemary bushes by the abandoned cages and crush needle-sharp leaves in my hands. The pungent smell reminds me of Harper's favourite shampoo. I snap off another bunch, suddenly furious that my sister never had the chance to experience anything like this.

The wind has chased the clouds away, and the mountain stares down at me, haughty and magnificent, crowned with diamond-bright stars. I sing back as loud as I can:

> *'What do you see?*
> *You don't see me.*
> *Not me. Not me. Not me.'*

Deng-deng-deng. Something hurtles between empty wolf cages, crashing through the dark garden. It attacks me from behind. *Deng-deng-deng.* I shriek, turn to see two evil red eyes. I'm halfway up the stairs before I hear the goat bleating like it's laughing at me.

Lukas is dancing in the bathroom. He's wearing a wolf headdress attached by fur straps that swing against his chest. Spellbound, I watch through the window as he tangos around the bathtub, drumming on a skin drum. It's like he's dancing with wolves that only he can see. He dashes around the tub, graceful one moment, then

198

holding the drum above his head and jumping to one side, chasing something round and round the room, stopping only to throw back his head and wolf howl. Maybe I'm drunk, but the drumbeat and the wild dance feel ancient and magnificent and totally Lukas.

He opens the big bathroom windows with a flourish. Cold mountain air steams up the glass and I breathe him in. I could recognize Lukas Svad blindfolded. Woodsmoke. Expensive soap. Always super clean. He pulls me over to the gramophone player.

'I want you to hear something special,' he says, and hands me a glass of red wine.

I sip it, but the more Dad drinks, the less I do. When Lukas messes with the gramophone, I pour my wine into his glass. He doesn't notice. 'This is a recording of my wolf pack,' he says grandly. 'Wolves hunt at dawn and dusk. In the valleys, local farmers play this recording to stop intruder wolves killing their cattle.'

'Music as a weapon?' I laugh.

'You don't believe me?' Lukas raises an eyebrow at me, indignant. 'I assure you the recording of our pack howling scares off any predators. Even human ones.'

'Love it. Great idea,' I say gamely. He nods, satisfied, and directs the horn trumpet out the window. The vinyl crackles; the hairs on my arm stand up.

'*Arrh oou woooo oooh rooo.*'

The ghostly howling bounces off the bathroom walls, disappears out into the night and echoes off the mountain.

'*Arrh oou woooo oooh rooo.*'

'Wow,' I gasp. 'They're calling each other home, like Cathy lost on the moors and Heathcliff calling, calling. Come home. Come home. Come back to me.'

'Exactly,' says Lukas. 'I am calling the wolves home to me.' And with a wild laugh, he spins me around and we dance and hop around the bathtub, wolf howling and stomping and throwing bubbles at each other. We yip and yap along to the next track. Lukas explains these wolves are teasing each other, playing after a successful hunt. I'm laughing so hard my stomach aches.

'Howling's their jazz, isn't it? Wolves adapt their song, changing notes to fit their mood, each other, like a blues singer.'

'Music – or survival?' Lukas gazes at me. 'How can we see things so differently?'

Then comes a real-life howl off the mountain.

Lukas lights up. But the sound sends a shiver down my spine. Danger. Danger. Danger. Another round of howls; this time in a lower octave and the harmonics modulate up and down, waves stretching on and on to the horizon, never breaking.

'That's a distress howl.' Lukas frowns. 'There are hunters nearby. From the mine. I need to track them tomorrow. Before his death, Svad swore my wolves wouldn't be shot, but with . . . with him and his wife gone, Svad Oil can do what they like. I won't lose another pack to their greed.'

I gaze at his beautiful face. 'You really love wolves,

don't you?'

'They're my life,' he says simply. 'Everything I know, I learnt from them.'

He pulls my arms towards him and we spin round the bathroom again, dancing faster and faster, until we over-balance and fall, tumbling into the bath, fully dressed, laughing as water sloshes over the side, snuffing out the candles on the floor.

'It's a Trophic Cascade,' I laugh.

'And I'm the big bad wolf at the top of the food chain,' Lukas growls.

We snort with giggles as the room darkens to a single candle, flickering under the Botticelli painting. Candle-light sends shadows leaping over the oil painting, making the red-haired Venus look like she's about to step out of her picture and slip into the bathroom with us. I sweep my hair up like hers; this look of wonder crosses Lukas's face. The glass wall that's been between us all day drops away, it's just him and me in this room, and all the ghosts depart.

Lukas is washing my foot with rose-petal water like I'm sacred. It makes me want to giggle, and I think of Jesus washing Mary Magdalene's feet and wonder if the story of her being his wife is true. I believe in every miraculous thing right now.

My hands slide over Lukas's chest. His skin feels so fit through his wet shirt, it's a crime he wears clothes at all. My fingers freeze. There's something ridged and hard below his shoulder blades. 'Show me,' I whisper.

Lukas hesitates. He peels off his wet orange shirt.

His skin is criss-crossed with scars; long curved welts run the length of his back to his waist. I trace my fingers over the white scar on his shoulder. 'Who did this?'

'I got careless. Play-fighting. When I was little.'

'Your wolves?' I say. 'They tore up your back?'

Lukas smiles like it's no big deal to be mauled by a wolf. I can't speak. My fingers read the story written on his skin. It's the story of a childhood I can't begin to understand. But he thinks it's normal.

'You want more wine?' Lukas says. 'Or are you too sleepy?' He's been drinking both our wines and his glass is empty again.

I shake my head. 'Sleep's the last thing on my mind.'

A look of annoyance flashes across his face so fast that I must have imagined it.

'How could Pup's mother let wolves torture you?' I say carelessly.

This time, I don't imagine it. Lukas flips. He pushes my hands off and snarls. 'Money bewitched her like it does everyone.'

'Lukas?' I say, scared.

But the boy I love is gone. The sea-glass eyes rage at me. I shrink back in the tub. Why is Lukas looking at me as if he hates me? Slowly, his eyes ice over. I see only darkness inside him like someone's turned his lights off.

'You OK?'

He won't look at me; he's shaking his head, putting

fingers in his ears, blocking out voices. Then Lukas sinks up to his chin in the bathwater. 'She tricked me,' he mutters.

'Who?' I'm shaken to the core.

He closes his eyes. 'You'll find out.'

Pummelled inside, I mumble something about needing to pee and slip out of the bath. The white dress cling-wraps my body and the sodden extensions pull on my scalp. Distressed, confused, I compare my bedraggled figure to the Botticelli painting. Two tall redheads, long white bodies, long toes and manes of long red hair.

What's the fascination with Botticelli's pin-up girl?'

'She was perfect,' Lukas mutters. 'Untouched. Like you.'

My heart sinks. *Untouched?* Perfect. He's put a spotlight on the liar in me. I've kept my big mouth shut about Ted at church camp until now. It was just a fumble anyway. No biggie. We didn't even get my kit off and I'm not sure that really counts.

But am I a dead ringer for a girl from hundreds of years ago? A fantasy virgin? Botticelli obsessed about his Simonetta. Would Lukas bury himself thirty-five years later in my grave? Or dig me up again, as Heathcliff did with his Cathy? Yeah. Lukas would. He devours me. He wants to know everything about me. But how can he know me, if what he loves is based on a lie?

Don't be stupid. Don't tell.

Of course I don't listen to myself.

'Lukas?' I say self-righteously. 'There's something I have to tell you: I'm not her. Your muse? I should have

203

told you before. I'm . . . not a virgin.'

He doesn't answer. My neck prickles. I turn around, slow.

My Lukas has vanished.

'Lukas?' I say, puzzled. I didn't hear him get out. I walk to the tub and peer in.

The water's stained a dirty cloudy pink. Rose petals lie crushed and wilted on the surface. And below them lies Lukas Svad.

I can't see his face clearly. At first I think he's holding his breath like a deep-sea diver. His dark hair halos around his face and a memory from long ago stirs in me, but it keeps slipping out of my grasp.

I shake his arm. 'Lukas? Stop it, you're scaring me.'

But he doesn't move.

32

Plunging my arms in the bath, I drag Lukas's head out of the water. I can't hold on. His shoulders slide under again. Water surges over the side. I climb in and pull Lukas into my arms. I fight to keep his chin above the water while I scrabble for the plug. But the plug fits flush and I can't fish it out. There are three bath knobs. One of them must work the plug. I press the middle button. The water rises. Shit. Shit. Shit. I press another one. The water stops. I look at the panel again, take a deep breath and press the last button. This time the bath water goes down. Lukas flops back against me. He's breathing. It's OK. It's OK. I stroke his face. And I collapse on his chest, bawling.

He nearly drowned.

It's my fault. Lukas didn't know he was drinking my wine as well as his. As I climb out the bath, soaking, I knock over the wine glass, and it shatters on the floor. The shock kick-starts my heart. But Lukas, amazingly, sleeps through it all. Broken shards scatter across the floor. And in the base of one fragment sits a white chalky residue.

I run my finger over it. Taste it. And spit it out. I recognize it instantly. *Temazepam*. It's a tranquillizer.

Scummy bathwater drains away from his body and conflict builds in me. Did I tell him that doctors give temazepam to Harper? I crush the tablets in water for her so she can swallow them when her mouth is sore. The sedative knocks her out on her bad days – though it's not been so effective recently.

Why has he drugged my drink? My heart hammers in sudden panic. *Why?*

I search the bathroom, and under a towel I find the battered box of temazepam.

My shaking hands drop the box twice before I read the name on the prescription.

Rosa Svad.

Rosa? Oh my God. This is so messed up.

I turn the temazepam box over and over in my fingers. Lukas never said Svad's wife was called Rosa. Had I told him my mum's name was Rosary? That's just a weird coincidence, right? But then I realize how Lukas never calls Pup's mum by her real name.

Not once.

Svad's wife.

The bathroom feels arctic. I go to close the windows and they resist like they've a mind of their own. I give up and stand freezing in the wet white dress. I've never seen a night so black. Wind wails around the dark mountain, snapping at the forest. And the stars wink down at me, like I'm a joke to the whole universe.

Lukas is too floppy-heavy to pull out of the bath. I find blankets and tuck them around him. I lift his wet head and let it sink back on a pillow. Part of me wants to crawl in the bath with him, but I'm too afraid. Afraid of why he wanted to drug to me. Afraid of why he is lying. Scared of hearing the truth when he wakes.

I stroke his hand while he sleeps, like I do with Harper. My fear drains away when I touch the cigarette burns on his arm. How could Svad do this to him?

I peer closer. Some burns look more recent than others. I trace out the constellation of Orion. One burn mark looks brand new; a shiny, angry, weeping red.

Lukas did this to himself? To cope with the pain of being him? Self-harming is commonplace at my old school. I write music to find myself; other kids cope by cutting themselves to forget the pain of who they are. And it gets me wondering: did Lukas do all these burns? Or just continue what Svad started? And go on hating himself?

Then I worry about Pup: what if Lukas hurts him too?

I run up to his bunkroom. Sleeping in the mahogany drawer, Pup looks like a cherub, but he's the scariest thing on the mountain. Pup burgles my head. One thought of him and the *room* inside my head pops wide open and every scary thought flies out.

The fire is dead. I open the glass door to the wood stove, blow on the ashes. They glow red for a second, then fade to black. I grab *Vårt Land*, the Norwegian newspaper Lukas brought, tear out the sports pages and twist them into plaits. I place them over the embers, wait for them to burst into flames and then dump on a birch log. I slam the glass door and sit back, trying to sort out my head. I think back to the TV news report in the minimart. The police described me as a ghost. Panic knots my gut. Who did they think I was? Certainly not Botticelli's Venus. I was just a British schoolgirl with long red hair who walked out of a Norwegian shopping centre with a baby. Do the police know it was me who rescued Pup? I spoke English in the car park to those policemen. It's only a matter of time before they join the dots. A missing redheaded Brit who ran away from the Barnevernet? The girl suspected of messing with her sister's medications? Will they think I'm a dangerous baby abductor?

Then comes the knockout thought. *Did Lukas frame me?*

Those photographs of me in Oslo didn't come from a CCTV camera. That's why he never shows me his photographs. I sit back on my heels, sick to my stomach. Why did he do this? Dom says it's always about the money. No. No. No. I'm being stupid. Pup is family. Family. Lukas will have a perfectly good explanation for this.

I smooth open the scrunched up *Vårt Land* to calm down. The front page has a posh Norwegian young mother holding a newborn. The baby boy is wearing blue shoes identical to ones Lukas bought Pup. I flatten out the newsprint to read the headline.

Rosa Svad. Drept.

Rosa Svad. Murdered?

The newspaper batters itself in my hands like a frantic dying moth and I'm only aware that Rosa Svad is tall, even for a Norwegian. And beautiful. Red hair. High cheekbones. Grey eyes. I tilt my pointed chin and study the way she tilts her head. Then I twiddle with my long hair and study how Rosa's mane of red curls falls over her shoulders. Exactly like mine. A horrendous thought hijacks me, and it's like I'm being strangled, I can't catch my breath. Shut up, shut up. I drag myself across the oak boards and pull out my bag.

The charred photograph of my real mother is inside the leather notebook.

This mum held me up in her arms and smiled for the camera. It seems a lifetime ago when the policewoman found my christening picture in Dad's bonfire.

I crawl back across the floor to the wood stove, whimpering gibberish. I pull the heavy wolf coat around my wet dress and compare the two photographs. In the newspaper one, Rosa Svad's face is thinner, sharper, with fine lines around her grey eyes, but her pointed chin is identical to the mother in my photograph.

I tell myself the women in the photographs could be related. Sisters? Right? Or cousins? Or a coincidence? Yeah. Absolutely. Harper says all gingers look the same.

But I recognize the white Dior sixties dress.

It's the same dress in both photos. And Lukas chose an identical dress for me? *My mother's dress.*

209

I start to laugh. I laugh and laugh. Until the truth deals another knockout punch and I'm rasping and flapping on the floor. What twisted game was Lukas playing at? I pull off the damp dress and hurl it into the wood stove. It snuffs out the flames and smoke billows out into the room. From the newspaper photograph, Rosa Svad watches me and hugs Pup's foot as if she'd never let go, like she once did me. All lies. Harper said Mum took one look at me, climbed out of a window and did a runner. Mum left me. And she never got in touch. Never sent me a card. Never tucked me up in bed. But she posed for my christening photograph, cuddling me in her arms, before I ruined everything and she disappeared.

Absent-mindedly, I gnaw on an acrylic fingernail; it tastes nothing like the real thing. It's totally fake – like the rest of my life. Everything Lukas said to me was a lie.

I bet Rosa is the real reason we came to Norway. Why Dad hates Svad. No wonder Dad started to drink again. And for the first time, I realize how tough it's been for my dad, loving Mum when Svad stole her away. And now I've done the same thing as Mum. No wonder he went mental when he found out about Lukas.

Lukas left his brass lighter on top of the *Vårt Land* newspaper. He would never, ever leave this out by accident. Lukas always covers his tracks, always tidies up after himself. But he knows I never read newspapers, and he couldn't risk me missing this, so he drew my attention to it. More games. Fury jacks up inside me. I grab a grey fur cushion and tear at it until feathers fly. The sense of betrayal overwhelms me. I found my mum, but it's too late. She is dead. And he knew and didn't tell me?

Lukas's quartz bracelet fits over my hand like a web, a priceless trinket. And Rosa Svad is wearing an identical quartz bracelet in Pup's photo. Everything Lukas gave me came from my mother? The clothes. My hair. My nails. Everything? Why? Blood is roaring in my head. I can't hear my thoughts, except the one that's yelling loudest. *He lied to me.* Everything he's said is a lie. My whole life's a lie. Suddenly I want Dad so bad; I need him to put this right. The cabin creaks. The night creaks. Bile rises in my throat. I open the wood stove and spit a mouthful on the smouldering dress. It hisses back in my face and I slam the door. I listen to the wind. I'm alone in this world. There's no one to tell me the truth. No one I can trust. No one.

I ransack the whole cabin, opening every cupboard and drawer. I find no photos of my mother. No letters. No computer. I shake out all the books on wolves, searching for answers, and all I do is twist myself in knots.

Who was she?

Why didn't I ask Dad more questions when I had the chance?

The master bedroom smells of roses. My eyes well up. Walls and mirrors are covered in a distressed gold leaf, so the room gleams, tasteful and subdued. I shine my torch over the double bed and see photographs turned face down. I pick one up after another. Portraits of Pup and Rosa. Rosa and Svad. It's a kicker to see the way she looks at them. Did she ever look at us like that?

My torch picks out Rosa's clothes thrown everywhere – piles of hunting jackets with padded, zipped pockets, warm waistcoats and cashmere shirts and silk dresses lie strewn over the floor. She's a slob. Why else would she live like this?

I pull on a cashmere sweater and soft stretchy leggings. Her clothes fit me perfect. I slip on a pair of gold sandals, take four steps and gaze down at them. Heartbroken. This is the first time I've played dress-up in my mother's clothes. No. Don't cry. Don't think. Don't. Remember something happy. But I can't.

Every happy memory I have is of Lukas. His betrayal eats into me. My mother raised him and Lukas must have known. And I told him how not knowing my mum was like missing the start of a movie. You never catch up; never truly understand the film, or the characters. And I never understood my life, why my dad can't love me but never lets me out of his sight. Why I love singing and he doesn't. Every time I had tea at a friend's house I would watch their mum, watch how they made cakes and smiled and loved them. I never knew what that felt like. And Pup will never know either.

I stagger back up to his bunkroom. Somehow, Pup looks completely different to me now I know he's a half-brother. My brother. And that single wondrous thought makes me happy, in the same way a single candle lights up a huge dark room. Careful not to wake him, I push up his onesie sleeves.

My little brother has chubby smooth soft white arms. Pup has no burns. No bruising. No signs of abuse from a cruel nanny. What have I done? This wasn't a rescue. It's abduction. And for the first time I unlock my biggest fear.

Does Lukas love me?

I can't breathe. Once the tears start, I can't stop. I can't even cry right. Tears don't trickle out my eye. My face contorts. I howl, gulping air and tears, jerking as if my heart is cracking open. Pulling Lukas's wolf coat off its hook, I bury myself in his smell. Sleep sneaks up, and rescues me. But in my dreams I never stop falling.

33

He has the dream again.

Rosa's long red hair floating behind her, as she drowns. She battles the sea, churning the crystal water with her arms and legs. She sinks down. Tiny bubbles trickle up her face, pushing against her skin as if trying to get back inside her. Her white feet beat in time with the current. Petals from her bouquet billow around her dress. The quartz bracelet gleams on her wrist. He dives back down to get it.

Her eyes open.

She can't see him. She can't. She can't. The angry voice bawls at him: 'Let her go. Leave her. She. Betrayed. You . . . You . . . You . . .'

He swims up. Sunlight jackknifes off the rocks and dances through the water.

He wakes at dawn and finds he's in the bathtub, drugged and tangled in wet blankets. Rosa's daughter gave him pillows and blankets?

He loses it then.

And howls.

34

The wolves wake me. I sit up gasping and the shock of last night crashes in on me.

My mother raised Lukas. My mother is dead.

I focus on my baby brother, snoring in the wooden drawer, until enough of me is back in my body to feel human again. I lean over and stroke Pup's sleep-soft face. His skin is butter-smooth perfection and smells so good you want to gobble him up.

I catch sight of my reflection, and recoil. Does anyone like who they see in a mirror? A scared girl stares back at me with wild grey eyes and celebrity-style long red hair.

How could Lukas do this to me? Mum left us because she fell in love with a Svad, and now I've done the same terrible thing to my dad and Harper?

I won't let Lukas turn me into another Rosa.

I run downstairs and rummage in the kitchen drawers. Back upstairs, I twist my tangled red hair extensions into a ponytail, and hack it off with the bread knife. The screech of hair on the blunt blades puts my teeth on edge, but I go at it in a frenzy, and by the time I finish, the extensions are on the bunkroom floor and my real hair is in clumps around my ears. I look about ten years old. A redheaded Dennis the Menace.

Pup opens one eye. I shake my new mop at him. He claps his hands and roars with laughter.

'I know. I know. It's a total cliché, cutting my hair off to reinvent myself,' I say. 'But it creeps me out. He made me the double of the dead mother I never knew.' I squat down to Pup. 'Sorry, sorry, darling. I keep forgetting my mum is your mum too.' I kiss his chubby hand. 'I can't imagine her abandoning someone as cute as you.'

Pup burps in my face, clearly bored to pieces by our family tragedy.

'Hey, stinker.' I peer in his mouth, impressed. 'Your first tooth's come through.'

I stroke his face and Pup beams at me. He is the sweetest thing. I find him another bottle, Pup snatches it off me like I'm running room service, and settles back down for another marathon kip. Thank God he's not one of those babies who never sleeps.

Footsteps dance across the roof. I stumble outside, pulling on my boots and one of Svad's fur overcoats. The fresh air socks me in the face.

It's the first time I've seen Ulv Fjell in daylight. Over the forests, a thin pink line appears and the dark mountain hunkers down over the meadow. It took a battering from the winds, but what's left of the white alpines unfurl and turn to face the dawn. If it weren't so dangerous here, it'd be magical.

I scan the edge of the forest, searching for wolves, when I know a wild one is inside the tower, with me.

The metal walkway sways as I walk. I grip the railing and shuffle along, calling his name. Lukas doesn't answer.

A neat, folded paper aeroplane swoops low over my shoulder, the tail on fire.

My mother's eyes smoulder at me. He stole Mum's photo? Anguished, I snatch at air trying to save the photo, but it nosedives to the meadow, still smoking.

'You coming up?' His cigarette glows as he flicks ash. 'Best view ever.'

'This is high enough for me,' I say, miserable.

'You didn't need to cut your hair off.' His voice sounds so sad. 'It suited you.'

'How could you do this to me? I thought you loved me?'

'Nothing can stop me loving you, Nell. God knows, I tried.'

He leaps off the roof and his body flies. My heart's in my mouth, but Lukas lands safe on the railing and strolls along it, hands in pockets. His showy performance infuriates me. He looks as alert as always, and shows no side effects from the temazepam.

'You'll fall,' I mutter. 'Good riddance.'

The long wolf coat swirls as he spins on the balls of his feet. '*Nei.* I can do this with my eyes shut. Svad beat me if I held on. I learnt fast. He pushed me off once to check my reaction time.'

The ground below swims at the thought of him falling. 'Maybe Svad didn't like liars?' I hurl his brass lighter at him. 'Or betrayal.'

'Temper, temper, my love,' Lukas says, catching the lighter and pocketing it. 'Rosa betrayed me. You wanted to find your mother. I gave you the truth. How do you feel, knowing I had your cruel childhood with Svad, instead of you?'

I'm too stunned to speak at first.

'Cruel childhood? You had my mum. Did it ever occur to you that maybe Svad didn't massacre your pack for profit?' I snap. 'Maybe Svad thought he was saving you from savage wolves?'

Lukas stares. Had that thought really never occurred to him?

'Think about it,' I say. 'How long could you have really lived with wolves? Wouldn't they have turned on you? Eventually? Maybe Svad didn't kill them for greed. He killed for love.'

'Love?' Lukas steps from the railing, so gently he floats down to the deck. 'What would a greedy, ruthless oil tycoon know about that?'

'It's not the people we hate who drive us nuts, is it?' I snap. 'Why did you make me steal Svad's son? The police think I kidnapped Pup.'

'He's your brother. They can't arrest you for that.' But Lukas can't look me in the eye. 'Anyway, it's too late now,' he says. 'Walk the railing with me. It'll take your mind off things.'

'Lukas Svad,' I say, strumming with upset. 'I'm taking my baby brother home.'

'This is your home,' he says, puzzled. And he gazes at me with such love in his face my heart twists.

'Did my mother ever mention me to you?'

'Yes,' he smiles. 'All the time. I carved you toy wooden wolves. Rosa said I'd meet her daughters and we'd live together on the mountain. Svad, and your father, put a stop to that. But when Rosa drowned I fulfilled her wishes – I brought you home.'

He's lying. I don't know which bit, but every instinct is screaming: liar, liar, liar.

Lukas reads my face and clicks his fingers at the mountain. 'This is my world, Nell,' he says softly. 'I swore to save it. One day you will understand.'

'No. I'll never understand your lies. Take us home. I don't belong here. Your Rosa is not my mum. Someone who should have loved me best? Put me first? Don't you get it? What kind of mother abandons her baby?'

'A she-wolf.' He laughs. 'No. Actually, nothing makes a she-wolf abandon her pups.'

'Is my life a joke to you?' I rage at him.

'No.' He looks at me with such longing it takes everything I've got not to bury myself in his arms. And I see the same conflict in him, the turmoil under the surface. He flips his brass lighter. 'Come on. It's time you conquered your fear of heights. Try it up here. When you feel small, do something brave. Fear stops people from living.'

I sniff. 'Stop playing games. Nothing will get me to risk my neck.'

'There are worse things to risk,' Lukas says, thoughtfully. 'The trick is to forget about the height and never look down, keep your eyes focused on the rail a metre or so ahead, keep a slight bend in your knees. Risk makes us feel alive. Each step reminds us not to sleepwalk through life.'

I stamp my foot. 'I don't need to walk the plank to prove I'm alive. I'm hurting too much to be anything but.'

He holds out his hand and smiles. 'You can ask me anything about your mother,' he says. 'One step. One question.'

35

He draws strength from her fear. Heights don't bother him, but Rosa's daughter is terrified. She clambers on the log pile and kneels like she's praying. She grips the railing with both hands. It was a mistake to look down – she's frozen, unable to move an inch. But he's impressed; she'll do anything to find out the truth of who she is. He flips the lighter and stares at the SVAD inscription. Her luck's just run out.

No. He pushes the voice away. 'Nell! Give me your hand. Look at me. Not down.' He weaves his spell over her. 'The railing's wider than my hand. And there's a ledge on the outside with a metal net, to catch snow and stuff falling off the tower. It's not as perilous as it looks, as you'd land on that if you fell, and I won't let you.'

She wobbles up to standing and grips his hand like she'll never let go. 'What was my mother like?' she asks.

'Kind. Rosa loved life. She dazzled everyone. Partied late, but always up early. A lark, longing for the new day. A geologist who loved wolves, her piano, and new experiences.'

'Why didn't she see us?' her daughter says in a small voice.

'Take another step first.'

Her white toes grip the rail, then they slide a fraction and her whole leg judders, as if electrocuted by fear.

'Rosa chose her crown over motherhood,' he says. 'You have to understand something about Svad: he doesn't like to share. He forced Rosa to choose between you and him. She thought he'd relent. Svad never did. He threatened your father. Svad told him he would take his daughters away if your dad ever contacted Rosa. Svad used you as a weapon.'

And it cost Rosa her life.

Now her daughter nips her fingernails into his hand as if she can hear his thoughts. 'Every word you said to me was a lie. All your questions about my mum? You already knew the answers. Were you laughing behind my back? How could you be so cruel? Why? I loved you. I trusted you! You knew I grew up believing my mum didn't want me. Believing I wasn't good enough. Mum left me unworn baby shoes, and a half-life, like a punctured lung. Every breath hurt when I thought of her.'

Her legs shake, but she takes a bigger step. Trusting herself. Trusting him. And somehow that maddens him.

'Next question,' he snaps.

'How exactly did Rosa betray you?'

Loosen your grip.

It happens so fast. One second, her daughter is silhouetted against the pink sky and the next she's falling, arms

222

windmilling, terror pulling her mouth into an ugly rictus.

'Lukas!' she cries.

Sacrifice her.

And he steps away, his heart stretched beyond enduring; memories domino in his mind. His massacred pack. Asena. Rosa. Death. No burial rites. No goodbye.

No goodbye?

He leaps up and seizes Svad's overcoat and drags the girl back over the railings, back into his arms. Not her time, he tells himself, not her time. His heart lifts, ecstatic, happy that she didn't fall. How is it possible to love and hate someone in the same moment? Is he starting to believe his own lies?

'It's over,' he says to her. 'Let's start again. Don't let Svad ruin everything.' He curls up on the deck, kissing her fingers one by one and staring at Rosa's quartz goddess bracelet.

Her daughter buries herself in his chest, breathing him in, but he's the one who feels saved. 'I want to go back,' she begs him. 'Please. Take Pup to the police.'

'Shush,' he whispers. 'Listen. Can't you hear them?'

He leaps across to the railings and stares down at the forest. He gives a soft yip.

A grey wolf steps out of the forest.

'We can't leave now.' He laughs in wild triumphant delight. 'My wolves are home!'

PART 3

The Sacrifice

36

In the cages, Lukas strips and rubs his skin down with the filthy rags he wears when he works with his wolves. He pulls on thick dun-coloured trousers and straps on leather armlets to protect his wrists. He waves, smiling and dancing through the cages.

'Your job,' he calls, 'is to crank the main spring on the gramophone and play my wolf recordings. Change the needle each time or you'll damage the seventy-eights. The track lasts three minutes. Play it every half hour. When the wolves appear you can watch me from the deck. I can't believe this day has finally arrived.'

Nothing fazes him, I realize in amazement. He's obsessed with his wolves. He doesn't get how awful this is for me.

How do I tell Harper that we have a dead mother, and a very much alive baby brother who we didn't even know about? Does my dad know Mum is dead? Is that why he's been drinking so much since we got to Norway?

And if Lukas Svad actually loved the real me, he'd be right here, in front of me, talking, telling me the truth.

Comforting me. Instead he locks the compound gates behind him like Dad, as if I'm stupid enough to run away with my baby brother with wild beasties on the loose, and he strides across the meadow, calling his wolves with a yip-yip-yipping sound.

Nothing happens.

He sits all day on a rock in the meadow. I never saw Lukas Svad keep so still.

Between wolf recordings, I snoop.

Lukas never did say why Rosa betrayed him. I'm guessing it was just the shock of being usurped by Pup in her affections. Parents always have favourites. I should know, I tell Pup, and plonk him firmly on my hip. We've already searched the cabin better than Harper could, and this time I check the generator shed, on the deck below the cabin.

The shed is dark. It has a consumer board full of switches. But Dad taught me how to fix a fuse. He's away a lot, and Harper's sick a lot. So I knew straightaway that Lukas had flipped the mains power switch off. I pull the red switch down. A dim light comes on. I race into the cabin to switch off any lights that would give me away.

Lukas has left his phone behind; he said wolves don't like the smell of technology. In the kitchen drawers, I find a charger that works and plug it in. Please. Please work, I beg it.

There's no signal. I skulk back to the bathroom. The wolf record has stopped, the needle bounces on the surface with a nasty crackling noise. I put Pup down and change the damaged needle again, and wind up the main spring to replay the track.

'*Woo woo oo oo oo ruh.*'

Pup giggles. Even he could sing their wolf song off by heart by now.

When we get tired of watching and waiting, Pup and me hang out at the grand piano. In the music stool, I pull out a bunch of silly baby songs for him, and underneath I find a gold leaf notebook of handwritten music.

The music is elegant, notated in a fast deft hand. My heart races, and I flip through the book checking the pieces of music. Some titles are labelled *January*. The others are *August*. Nothing else. Just alternating months. *January. August.*

Harper's birthday is in January. And mine's August. Are these Rosa's songs? There are fifteen tunes called *August*. My spirit soars. Mum wrote music for me and Harper? Maybe she missed us after all. Maybe she loved us.

The Steinway's voice has a rich honeyed tone, incomparable to my ratty old keyboard. The ivory keys become extensions of my fingers and call the music out of me. The more I play Rosa's tunes, the more her songs take on a life of their own, and I get lost in their stories. Some are childish, happy tunes; others are gut-wrenchingly plaintive.

I feel sorrow and loss pulsating in the rhythm. Did Mum love us? I stop, breathless and giddy. Pup's body relaxes into me. I think he's heard this music a thousand times.

He fiddles with my quartz bracelet. My heart swells with love for him. He's all button-eyed innocence. A brand-new life for the world to mess up. I kiss his cute little nose. 'You don't have parents to mess you up, but I promise to love you.'

His starfish hand shoots out and pulls on my red hair. And he won't let go.

At dusk the wolves come.

Eight wolves appear over the hill; they stand in a semicircle on the crest and stare down at Lukas. Has he seen them? I stand on the top deck, screaming inside: *Run. Run.* Of course, Lukas doesn't as much as twitch. I fret, and pray. Hold Pup. Hope like mad that Lukas knows what he is doing. The sky darkens before the wolves move closer. They sniff the air, skitter away if Lukas stirs at all, but slowly, slowly they approach.

One huge grey wolf sits on the flat rocks opposite him. Still a good fifty metres away. Three younger, playful, males dart nearer, until the grey wolf snaps at them to get back. They grovel an apology and wiggle away on their bellies in the long grass.

In the centre of it all, Lukas sits rock-still, submissive, but radiating calm and certainty. I can feel the joy beaming off him. But I get more and more wound up, and can't bear to watch. Every time a wolf moves closer, I bite down on my knuckles. In the end Pup picks up on it and bellows. The wolves startle. Lukas turns and scowls at us.

I put Pup down for the night. Lukas warned me it's

going to take time before Asena's pack accept him again. I sit at the piano, picking out Rosa's tunes with one hand and scroll down his phone. I open his *Sleeping Beauty* file. And suddenly the cantilevered cabin floor lurches under my feet. I can't believe what I am seeing. It's Preken Rock. Filmed underwater. Ethereal. Sunlight knifing through the sea, bouncing off submerged rocks fused together like an inverted cathedral. But, oh my God. Sinking down, in a white dress, is a woman, her red hair floating behind her. Sunlight flashes over her quartz goddess bracelet. A hand with a white scar moves through the water. He holds her hand and removes the bracelet. No. No. No. She floats down. He swims up.

I drop the phone and bury my head in my hands. The ill-fated goddess bracelet catches in my hair. I pull it free, but I can't get the bracelet off my wrist; the more I yank it, the more the chain cuts into me and the net of quartz sparkles over the back of my hand: a glittering web of betrayal. I am drowning as the panics and the fears and the terrors come after me; wave after wave crashes over me. Don't think. Don't think. I ram and cram and push the thoughts into the *room* in my head and shove the door closed.

My shaking fingers perform chords on the piano; they hammer out the notes, over and over, until all I can hear is C major playing in my head.

Shadows move over the cabin walls, and vanish through the floor-to-ceiling windows. I don't how long I sit before

I notice that the battered radio in the kitchen has both a headset and a handheld microphone. Could it be one of those two-way radios? It looks well used, and it makes sense as phones don't work up here.

I stagger across the darkening cabin and check Lukas is still in the meadow communing with his savage soulmates. The late-night sun is low and casts an eerie red light over the eight wolves. It transforms their grey pelts into mythic creatures. One beast has his huge head on Lukas's shoulder, and even from here I can see the bliss on his face. The other wolves creep closer. Watching. Waiting. I think they trust him now. And that makes me sad, because I so don't. I lock the cabin door and tackle the two-way radio. It's so old; I've never seen anything like it. I put on the headset and say into the microphone: 'Help. My name is Nell Lamb.'

No one answers. I mess with all the prehistoric dials, and eventually tune into a man speaking Norwegian in a staccato hurdy-gurdy rhythm. I beg him to rescue us.

Why doesn't he hear me?

My mind blanks out.

I am ten years old again, tapping Morse code on the bedroom wall with Harper. SOS. Three dots. Three dashes. Three dots. A continuous string of notes without a break. Three dots. Three dashes. Three dots. Three dots. Three dashes. Three dots.

I tap the SOS code on the microphone. I tap it for ages, not knowing what else to do. With liquid hands, I fiddle with every switch and dial, while all the time I'm tapping SOS. Three dots. Three dashes. Three dots. My long acrylic nails tap it out.

My mother's hands. Then I can't stop the flashbacks. I see her long white fingers fluttering in the fjord as she drowns.

I cry into the radio, 'Please. Help me.'

No one responds. I give up, and throw the headphones down.

I find the Leica and film the footage of Rosa drowning from Lukas's phone. It's the one place he won't search. His own camera.

Later I see a switch on the two-way microphone. How could I not have seen it before? I flip it and scream into the mic.

I hear a gruff male voice reply. 'Hello?' he says. 'Please identify yourself.'

I sob. 'My name is Nell Lamb.'

'*The* Nell Lamb?' he says, like I'm famous. 'Stand by.'

The radio crackles; it sounds like he's talking to someone else his end. I hear the word *politiet*. Police? I start to relax. It's going to be OK.

The man comes back on. 'Nell Lamb is a wanted criminal. She kidnapped Hagen Svad.'

I hiccup, miserable. 'That's me. It's a misunderstanding.'

'Where are you?' he demands.

Dread seeps into me. 'Please,' I beg. 'We're trapped. Wolves. They've surrounded our cabin. We can't escape on foot. We're on Ulv Fjell.'

'Ulv Fjell?' he barks. 'We have no Wolf Mountain in Norway.'

'You do!' I wail. 'The location is secret. You can't see it from the air. I'm trapped with my baby brother.'

There's no answer . . . just a weird static crackling sound.

I rack my brains to convince him. 'We are near Svad Oil's open pit mine. The rutile one. Hello? Hello? Can you hear me?'

The radio goes dead.

Shit. Lukas has cut the power. Then the locked cabin door handle rattles, and I almost scream.

37

He's on the cabin roof now.

Pup.

I race to get to my little brother first, but before I can reach the spiral staircase Lukas swings in through the kitchen skylight and lands dead quiet.

'They all came back except Asena. She'll be with her new pups now,' he says, like I give a shit about his wolves.

He glances at his phone on the oak bench. One sneaky look, and I know the truth. In the silence that falls between us everything is unspoken, and confirmed.

'You got the power on. Did you use the two-way?' he asks, dead casual. Waiting. Waiting.

He stinks of wolf, and I don't recognize him in this dangerous mood.

'Lukas,' I gasp. 'It's over. The police are coming.'

'We leave now. Don't you see what you've done? They'll be here in no time. You've put my wolves in danger.'

'You stink. The only danger around here is you

and your lies.'

Lukas flinches. He gazes at me with such pain and love that I almost take a step closer, and all the time my head is booming with terror, and I don't know what to do. I want him back, and I don't. You let Rosa drown? I need to ask, but I don't. I'm too scared to know the answer.

He reads me like a favourite book and shakes his head. 'I was trying to save her. Rosa was the closest thing I had to a mother.'

Lukas lifts his chin. On his face is the horror of that day, and I am making him relive it. His sea-glass eyes darken; they blow me away with their grief and rage.

'It was an accident,' he says, so quietly he's almost talking to himself. 'Their helicopter malfunctioned. The rotor engine died. The chopper dumped us in the fjord ... Svad planned to dump the mining waste there ...' Lukas seems in a daze. 'I got Rosa out. But the water ... ice-cold ... sucking hope out of me, and her fingers slipping from my hand and I'm grabbing and grabbing at her bracelet, my lungs bursting, lights flashing in my head, and I couldn't hold on. The quartz clasp broke. I let go of her hand. I let go of her.'

I bury my head in my hands and sob. 'Why didn't you tell me?'

'She betrayed me.' Lukas flicks open his brass lighter and stares at the flame. 'Oh, Rosa tried to protect me when I was small, but I was wild and didn't need her then. Later, she played happy families and read me bedtime stories, pretending I was you and Harper. And Rosa told herself she didn't see my burns or how unhappy I was around Svad.'

'Na na!' Pup cries from upstairs, in his *get–here–right–now* voice.

The sound triggers Lukas. He's looking at me as if hates me.

Danger. Danger, my mind screams. *He blames everyone except himself.* I make for the staircase. Lukas bolts round the kitchen bar, but I've got a head start and shove a chair in his way. The wooden legs screech across the floor. I'm at the bottom of the stairs, but he catches up, leaps over me and flies up the steps.

'Lukas, wait,' I cry. 'He's a baby. He's done nothing to hurt you.'

'He's done nothing *but* hurt me.'

Maybe I've always known Lukas hated Rosa's baby, but I didn't want to admit it. I hear Pup grumbling. A sudden scream of rage for being woken up, and then he whimpers. I don't know who is more scared of Lukas in this mood.

Lukas strolls out to the landing above me, gripping Pup by the scruff, as if he's toxic. Pup's legs pump furiously; he's bright red, gulping, choking.

'Lukas! He can't breathe.'

'Who do you love more?' he demands. 'Him, or me?'

'You.' I keep my voice very, very calm. 'You're scaring him. Give him to me. Pup's a proper pain when he wakes.' I creep up the steps. 'Please. Don't hurt my brother.'

'You don't need him,' Lukas says softly. 'Turn your back on him. Svad made your mother choose – now you can choose.'

Lukas is dangling Pup over the top banister, some metres above me. The terrified baby throws his arms round Lukas's neck for a moment. Then his tiny body jerks away, as if he'd rather die than be touched by someone who hates him.

'Did I ever show you cloudberries?' says Lukas. 'They split open like brains. You choose that death for him? It won't be pretty. No honour for him.'

'Please stop.' Pup twists towards my voice. His eyes lock on mine, and I send him a message, without saying a word. *Trust me, darling.* I tear my eyes away from his dear face and make myself look at Lukas. Pup immediately gives up on me, his limbs thrashing in mid-air. I grip the handrail to stop myself throwing up.

'You will do exactly as I say,' Lukas smiles.

'Yes, Lukas.'

Act submissive. Let him think you're no threat.

'You like to watch him so much?' He positions Pup's feet on the railing.

Oh my God.

'Walk!' Lukas roars. 'Like Svad made me.'

For a split-second, my little brother gamely tries to stand upright on the banister. But he flails, falls to one side. I can't get back down the staircase fast enough, and my body tears itself apart trying to be in two places at once.

'I said, *watch me!*' Lukas catches Pup at the last moment. His small body snaps to a standstill and then sags in Lukas's grip.

'He's only a baby,' I sob. 'Punish me instead.'

'Oh, I am.' Then Lukas's smile falters, and he looks around, confused, as if he can't remember why he is hurting me.

Pup turns on him with a snarl and sinks his only tooth into Lukas's wrist.

Lukas stares at the pinprick of blood. A single drop of his own blood. He blinks. As the colour in his face drains away, he staggers into the iron banister.

And he drops my baby brother.

Pup tries to cling on. Squawking. But as Lukas faints, he swats Svad's baby away like a bug. Then Pup is snatching at the air, a cartoon character, all whirling arms and legs.

I stand underneath him. Frozen to the spot. I see his last moments in slow motion.

He's a beanbag baby, heavy and floppy, a flash of creamy yellow onesie, falling. The air tugs at his red-gold curls and tries to save him. His dear rosebud mouth pops open in terror and still he falls. And I pray. And I pray. And I pray. I bargain my life away.

I love him into my hands. I know God heard me and He takes my Pup and He puts him gently in my arms.

Safe.

Pup thuds into me like a punch.

*

I hold on, protecting his soft head as we go over backwards, knocking into the armchair. Then we slam into the wolf skin on the oak boards. I shield him best I can, but my teeth feel like they've shattered and the back of my head turns to molten pain. I lie there, thinking how the wolf skin stinks, and I float out of my body and fly around the ceiling. *A buzzard. Flying. Slow lazy circles.* I'm watching me and Pup from above.

He doesn't move.

I command God. *Make him live. Give him back.*

Then I'm back in my body, touching my brother's face with my breath. Pup doesn't move.

I keep my eyes shut tight, so his life can't end. I collect all our moments together. Pup's sweet fresh bread smell. Pup, posh and clean, in his pram. Safe. *Until I stole him.* I see him drugged in the boot, Pup hating me in the Cessna. At the piano, his starfish hand in mine, like he'd never let me go.

Minutes pass.

I press my lips to his ear. 'Please come back to me. We're family.'

'Na na,' he whispers.

And then Pup howls. The sound is magic. We lie like that for ages, wailing, holding each other, watching dust mites trapped in a shaft of sunlight.

When he stops crying, I sit up and check him over. Nothing is broken. I draw my finger in front of him, checking for concussion. Pup follows it with his eyes, but the scared look on his face rattles me to the core. He

240

burrows into me, and it breaks my heart. *Where's my fierce little brother?*

'Shush,' I sob. His arms tighten round my neck. I nuzzle his face and replay his falling a thousand times.

Lukas staggers down down the stairs. 'He bit me,' he mutters and wraps an arm round me. 'I always faint at the sight of my own blood.'

'You monster,' I rage and push him away. 'You think your dead alpha haunts you? Hurt my baby brother again and I will haunt you to hell and back. I will sit on your shoulder and curse every minute of your living day and bleed into your sleep with nightmares. Not for one second will you be free of me.' I steady myself on the staircase. 'Call an ambulance. Pup could have a brain bleed. No more games. Ambulance. Police. Home.'

'No doctors,' Lukas says. 'Never.' He had told me wolves become psychotic when separated from their pack. Unpredictable. Aggressive. That's him all over. No wonder he hates doctors.

'Take us home,' I coax. 'No way am I staying here until you turn eighteen. I won't let you be the legal guardian over my little brother. Harper's old enough to do it right now, and if you think a dying girl hasn't got fight in her, think again. She's a force of nature. She never lets go. She will have Svad Oil so tied up in legal knots they won't be able to breathe, let alone mine Ulv Fjell. Let me go and I promise, we won't let Svad Oil develop any open pits. But we go home now, or that deal is off the table.'

Lukas flips his brass lighter. 'Tails,' he says. 'You win.'

His face looks so heartbroken, so confused, I can't bear it. Suddenly I am in his arms and kissing him. I hate myself, but it's like nothing and everything matters all together, all jumbled up at once.

38

The midnight sun is low over the mountain as we leave. When Lukas wipes his fingerprints off every surface in the cabin, somehow I know we're not coming back. We stagger down the tower. Pup's grizzling on my back. I found a baby carrier in the cabin. It's like a rucksack on a metal frame, and he sits inside it, gazing at the world like an entitled little lord.

'Ow,' I say.

Lukas turns on the step and frowns. He frees my hair from Pup's grasp and looks up, scanning the skies. He acts like there's danger everywhere; when it lurks inside him.

He gives me Rosa's wolf headdress with long mufflers.

'No. Thanks,' I say stiffly.

'But it's perfect,' he says, and places it on my head.

I sigh. Lukas Svad is like a cat that forgets it's been bad and only wants to be your friend again.

He unlocks the main gates. The goat bolts out of one of the cages and disappears into the field. We don't have time to catch it, Lukas says, and he pockets the key.

We walk across a deep meadow, yellowed by glacial

buttercups, bakkekløver, sagewort and alpine gentian. It hasn't rained in weeks and I'm glad I've got jeans, his hunting jacket and thick socks inside my biker boots to stop the ticks getting me.

I make as much noise as possible, fearful of his wolves hiding in the hip-height dry grass.

'They've gone, Nell,' Lukas says. 'Can't you feel it? The blasts from the open pit this morning scared the wolves off. They won't be coming back here. Not for a long time.'

I don't know what to say. I didn't hear anything this morning. He said Svad Oil plan to detonate that open pit, blow it up over and over, until it devours half the mountain. I don't know if that's true. But the emptiness in Lukas's eyes scares me.

It's dark in the woods. I get lost straight off – the rowans, spruces and birches all look the same to me – but Lukas greets each tree like a personal friend. He says some Norwegians still believe certain trees are sacred and hold the spirits of their ancestors.

'He's more pagan than Christian,' I mutter to Pup. Who ignores me, of course.

We come out above the airstrip, and walk alongside the ravine to the Cessna. The sharp rocks and treacherous drop give me vertigo, and my head swims.

It's a different world today. The sky sulks, the Japanese cherries lost their white blossom overnight so petals lie bruised and strewn over the airstrip. Lukas winches the Cessna round to face the runway and I lean against the crash barrier with Pup, sick with nerves about flying, and focus on the buzzards soaring above the ravine.

'Here. Take my coat.' Lukas lifts Pup and the baby carrier off my shoulders. My Dora the Explorer bag comes off with it, and all my cruddy stuff falls out. I scramble on hands and knees to pick it up, taking the opportunity to say a quick prayer to protect me and Pup when we take off. Then I realize Lukas has walked away and disappeared back into the forest.

'Lukas!' I cry. I can't let him go off alone with Pup. I stagger to my feet and snag my hair on a broken shard of metal in the barrier. I fight to get it free. But I'm well and truly caught. I panic, and wrench my hair free.

'Nell?' Lukas is standing in front of me, and hands me a sprig of wild flowers. 'Purple saxifrage. Remember?' His laugh is so infectious. He scoops me up and somehow I've got my old Lukas back. 'Storm coming. Time to leave.'

He's so compelling, and then he's pushing me into the cockpit and I'm tripping over the wolf coat, hitting my head on the ceiling, banging my elbow on the control panel. But he doesn't stop shoving and kissing me until I'm in my seat.

'Where's Pup?' I'm saying, over and over.

'Hm?' Lukas raises one black eyebrow.

'Pup!' I shriek.

'He was never here,' Lukas says quietly.

'What?'

Lukas flips the starter motor. The plane vibrates and I hardly hear my own thoughts. He's so calm; I begin to doubt Pup was ever with us. I put my head in my hands;

my sleeve reeks of sour milk and brings me to my senses.

'Stop! Where is he?'

Lukas takes my hand and he kisses the skin above the bracelet. The Cessna taxis down the grassy airstrip, the cherry trees blurring as we pick up speed.

'You can't abandon him.' My voice breaks.

'Abandonment. Abduction. It's two sides of the same coin,' Lukas says. 'You were right about Svad, by the way. The pack died because of me. If I had died, my wolves would have lived. Don't you see? I can't make the same mistake with Ulv Pup. If he lives, Asena and her cubs will die. Svad Mining will destroy them. Pup dies this time so I can rule Svad Oil and safeguard the land.' Lukas looks straight ahead, almost talking to himself. 'I played fair. I left him where Rosa found me.'

'You were *six*. Stop mucking about!' I drag at his arm, but Lukas acts like he can't hear me. And all the time we are getting further and further away from my abandoned brother. I scan the dashboard, and recognize the throttle. I shove it back in.

'Stop it.' Lukas holds me off with one arm. I struggle, but I can't move in his thick wolf coat. I lurch forwards and twist the fuel mixture knob to zero.

The engine splutters. The hatred in Lukas's eyes is worse than any blow, and I recoil into the Cessna door. It opens with a jerk. I am hanging, half in and half outside the plane, long wild grasses swishing under the wheels. Lukas stares down the runway.

'You never listen.' His voice breaks. 'I was trying to

save you.'

Did he push me? I don't know. But I am falling back-wards. The Cessna door catches me on the shin and slams in the wind. Wheels slash past my face. It's unreal, falling out of a taxiing plane, and then I land on long dry grass, my breath whacked out of me. I lie back, tangled up in his wolf coat. Gasping.

The Cessna takes off and heads off to the fjords. The whine of the engines fades. He'll be back, I tell myself. He'll be back. He'd never abandon me in the wilderness with wolves. He loves me.

I wait.

And I wait.

Soon the Cessna is no bigger than a bat, swallowed up by low cloud. I don't move. The dry earth pulsates between my fingers, and I wait. I crush purple saxifrage and wait.

He will come for me.

If I stay put, he'll come back.

For me.

He won't abandon me.

I curl into a ball and wail at the sky. Pup's miserable howl rips through the mountain night as he answers me. He sounds more animal than human. Keeping the line of cherry trees to my right, I struggle back up the slope, the wolf coat dragging through endless alpines, as I work out where Lukas came out of the forest.

I'm standing in front of trees centuries old. 'Pup!' I shout, too scared to enter.

There's no reply. I edge inside. The forest closes in on me. Spruces. Birches. Rowans. Oaks. Aspens. Pines. The ancient trees menace me in the dark. Strange shapes move between them. I see wolf-eyes everywhere, watching, stalking. Hunting me. I hurry past moss-covered rocks. Something swoops past my ear. I brush it off, screeching, 'Pup!'

Then comes an answering wail from the far side of a stream. Scrunched tight in a cradle of rocks, Pup is just another nameless shadow under a giant hollow oak. When he sees me lumber out of the gloom, my baby brother pukes in terror; a milky jet bursts out of his mouth and spray-paints my legs.

'What comes out of your body is frigging unbelievable,' I wail and hug him tight. Pup clings on to me. I clean him up as best I can, and settle him inside the hollow oak. Lukas says Norwegian oaks can survive a thousand years. This one is two metres hollow inside, full of soft leaves and mulch. Dead safe, I think, and go wash in the stream.

Darkness falls like an axe. Pale birch saplings were bang in front of me a moment ago and now they've vanished. Suddenly the forest talks to itself, and I drop Pup's bottle in the stream in blind panic. Cold stones slither between my fingers. I snag another nail before I find his bottle. I sit back on my heels and chew the broken acrylic nail off. Insects dive-bomb my face with a high-pitched buzzing. How could Lukas do this to me?

I get lost on the way back to Pup. All the paths look

the same in the dark. Then the noises start up. A twig breaks somewhere in the bushes, another one cracks like a bullet, and another one groans. I crawl in circles, gibbering, feeling my way over fungi and ferns and mulch and scurrying beetles. I'm about to give up when I stumble over the baby carrier and hold on like it can save me.

I wriggle inside the hollow tree, and half sob as my fingers touch Pup's chest. I feel it gently rise under my hand. I twist up next to him, promise to be a better sister, and throw Lukas's wolf coat over our heads.

There's a bloodcurdling scream in the night. It's nothing, I tell myself. It's nothing; it's just an Arctic fox mating. Or an owl. Not the wolves. Not a murderer. This is not the back streets of Manchester. No. Think owl. Think wildlife. The noises grow louder and louder and louder. Something or someone is walking out there. And with every sound I hope – and fear – it's Lukas.

39

I wake up next to Pup, and it hits me that I will never, ever wake up alongside Lukas again. Never.

Pup peed on me during the night. Gross. The pungent smell catches in the back of my throat. I press my toes against the hollow bark, wishing I were back home in my own walled-in bed. I throw Lukas's wolf coat off, and Pup kicks me, wailing. I blow on his cold fingers.

'I'll get you home. I promise.' He snatches his hand away and I try not to mind. He was warm and clean, happy in his pram kingdom, and now he's more miserable than me.

'Hey, don't count me out. I've watched hours of *I'm a Celebrity, Get Me Out of Here* with Dom. I'm practically a survival expert.'

Then a bug crawls over my face, and I shriek and scramble out of the trunk. I pick up Pup and sit him on my lap. He sucks on my finger in the early sunshine as I point out small birds hopping under the ferns, pulling at the worms. Lukas taught me the names. Rock ptarmigan. Meadow pipits. White-throated dippers. The morning

250

feels crisp and alive. But my skin and hair itch. And I'm starving. I drag everything out of Pup's bag; I'd make such a crap mother – I forgot to pack any goat milk or spare nappies.

Instead I have sheets of Rosa's music, the Leica camera and the temazepam. I turn the battered box over in my hands. I hid it to stop Lukas doping Pup or me again.

Then I strike the jackpot. I find a pack of Starbursts. I snaffle one in my mouth.

Pup stops gumming my finger and stares. 'Too chewy for you, darling,' I mumble. 'Shush. Shush.'

But no amount of rocking shuts up a hungry Pup.

'OK. You win.'

I pop a strawberry chew into his rosebud mouth and smile as Pup's eyes widen in delight. I'm changing out of my wet clothes, and Lukas's cashmere sweater is stuck over my head, when I hear Pup making a horrible rasping sound. I fall over in my panic, put my fingers in his mouth and pull out a stringy thread of pink goo. I sigh in relief.

Pup doubles up. Red drool dribbles down his chin. He's choking for real. My throat tightens. Dad did the Heimlich technique on me once when I choked on a Brussels sprout. How did it go? Gingerly, I place Pup over my knee and pat his back.

Nothing happens.

Pup is thrashing like a mad thing. I do another short sharp push and this time it works. A red sticky lump shoots out of Pup's mouth. He moans and curls up howling.

'I'm sorry. I'm sorry.' I kiss his exhausted tears away. I'm about to throw the chewy mess away when I think of sugar water. *Genius.* I could make him that. I drop the goo into the water bottle and shake it. I chew four more sweets and spit them into the bottle. The water turns a pale pink. 'Drink, sweetheart.' I tilt the bottle to his lips.

Pup splutters, pushes it away and howls some more.

'I don't have any goat milk,' I coax. 'You have to drink. Trust me.'

Pup's cries silence the birds. The sullen morning is darker than night and he cries all the way up the slope to the tower. Of course, the gates are locked. I cuddle Pup. He won't stop crying. I press my forehead against the chain fence and stare up at the empty tower.

How could Lukas do this to me?

I only hear the *deng-deng-deng* of the goat bell when the bloody thing takes a chunk out of Lukas's sweater. The goat smells terrible; her udder's the size of a basket-ball. I push her away. But Pup has other ideas. He roars. The goat bleats. They both butt me like I'm too stupid to understand she needs milking.

Lukas said the goat stands still if you sing to her. I didn't believe him, but she and Pup listen, dead quiet, as I sing 'Don't Believe in Love'. I tie her to the fence with a pair of my tights. She's smaller than a cow, and has only got two teats. How hard can it be?

Lukas said milking's more of a massage and not about pulling on the teat. But my fingers soon ache and I don't

252

get a drop. Pup looks unimpressed, sucking on his thumb. I watch how his mouth moves, and try again with the goat. Most of the hot milk squirts over my boots, but I fill up Pup's milk bottle.

A grey shadow streaks across the meadow.

The goat breaks free and bolts. *Deng-deng-deng*. I'm on my feet, holding a rock, heart racing. Snatching up Pup, I run to the black slatted barn next to the tower. The grey shadow disappears into the long dry grass. It's stalking me. Panic-stricken, I rock-smash the lock and push the barn door open. I hitch my little brother on my hip and step inside.

'We'll be safe in here,' I say.

The chemical smell hits me first off. I flip on the light switch. The strip lighting flickers. I get a flash of white walls. Photographs. Then the barn goes dark again.

Another flash. I see trees. Made of wire. Hanging upside down. Photos and sheet music and bells, cascading down, like leaves on willow trees. The lights flicker off again. When they finally stay on, I clamp a hand over my mouth.

I knew Lukas took a gazillion photos of me. But this is like an art gallery. I walk around the wire-trees staring at portraits of me and sheets and sheets of music. Pup pulls on the paper leaves until the bells sing, and soon the narrow blades of wire are trembling more than me.

I hold one sheet steady, and read the music for a song called *August*. My birthday. One that Rosa wrote for me?

I hum the music under my breath. It's beautiful. Full of loss and longing. It's so clearly the story of a mother trying to get back to her daughter.

I know it then. In this one piece of music. How much my mother loved me.

I choke back a sob, settle my baby brother on the straw, and take a closer look.

Each wire-tree has a different theme. The Willow Tree. Wolf Song. The Night Garden. That wire-tree has fairy lights and photos of me flying on our swing. Lukas makes me look gorgeous in every photo. Make-up or no make-up, I look happy and alive. Glorious. Mysterious. Ravishing. That's how I feel when I'm with him.

'He loves me,' I tell Pup. 'It's going to be OK.'

But I'm lying. This installation bothers me. I'm just a girl from Manchester. Ordinary. I like jelly and chips and Netflix.

And something else bothers me about the trees.

Lukas said that certain trees are sacred for Norwegians. The ones they love best. They believe the spirits of their ancestors live in their family trees. Is that why Lukas tried to capture my spirit in these? He loves me? Or deep down he wants me dead? No. No. I don't believe he'd ever hurt me. I walk down the wide aisle and study the display panels.

In these photographs, a pack of young wolves surrounds Lukas. They lick his face, nuzzle him, and he scratches their ears, hugs and plays with them. I rub the old dog bite on my arm. *How could we be so different?* I'm terrified of dogs; he was raised by a pack of wolves?

Tucked away on a high shelf, I spot his portfolio, his secret pristine photographs. I thumb through shots of Pup with his arms around a black she-wolf. Asena? Furious that Lukas risked Pup's life to get this shot, I turn the next page. The ground sways under my feet.

He's my first thought, my last thought, my every thought in between.

My journal? He took photos of my journal? He read my journal? I thumb through the photos. Yes. It's all here. *Wolfsong. Red Spider. Don't Believe in Love.* I feel sick. I blamed Harper for snooping in my journal. And it was him all the time?

The cacophony builds and builds till I think my head will burst.

Every word he has ever said to me was a lie.

A robe with pink rosebuds covers the last panel. I pull it off and my hand freezes in mid-air. The panel has photographs of Harper and me in Yellow Cottage. He's got fuzzy shots taken through the window, of her laughing as I cook supper. Photos of Harper in bed. Her meds. An unflattering shot of me asleep, open-mouthed, snoring.

He was in our home? My world spins. Anger rears up, hot and fierce. Then comes a thought so horrible that the shock of it makes my body go cold. *Was Lukas responsible for messing with my sister's meds? No. No. No. He wouldn't.*

But he took a shot of my bedroom window and a photo of me looking dead guilty, flicking a sweet wrapper.

Before we met. He always knew who I was.

Next to shots of the Dobermann in Torgallmenningen is a photograph of my smouldering British passport. He burnt it? I stare at the flames melting my passport photo, tears running down my cheeks, and tell myself that Lukas only stole it to stop me getting on that Flybussen and going back to Manchester.

With dread, I look back at the reverse timeline in the photographs. The wire-trees are drifting in the breeze from the barn door. The Night Garden installation feels like it was made with such love, but these earlier photos of me, taken furtively, without my permission or knowledge, have a darkness about them. If I didn't know better, I'd say the person who took them hated me.

Pup is snoring under the hanging trees. The wire branches spin in the breeze; the photos lift and flutter, fledglings desperate to fly.

Why was Lukas hunting me?

Think like prey, he always says, when he goes hunting. Where do they hide? What are their habits? No. No. I need to think like him. I close my eyes and feel my way into his mind. Lukas doesn't have a *room* in his head like me, to keep things sorted, manageable. Everything comes at me at once, and I feel overwhelmed with loss and chaos and menace. I feel the shadows of wolves circling, hunting me and goading Lukas to act. I see Pup sacrificed on his mountain. His blood for theirs. And the wolves coming back. I open my eyes. Shaking. Centre stage in the last panel is my missing birth certificate, pinned like a butterfly specimen by a silver rosary. I know it belongs to my mum.

My fingers take down her silver rosary, and I bite my lip as I read my mother's name on my birth certificate.

Rosary Lamb.

Lukas knew Rosa was my mum before we met.

Norway isn't like Britain, where you can leave everything to one child. Norwegian children inherit equally from their mother. I think of Harper's tampered meds and the shock of it hits me again. Does he want all of Rosa's children dead? To save Ulv Fjell?

I look back at his sacred trees and understand them now.

A Cessna is circling above the barn.

And I know it's stupid, but I really, really want my mum.

The Cessna has landed and Pup wakes up. 'Shush,' I whisper, stroking his dear face with fingers that can't stop shaking. 'Lukas will be here in minutes. You need to be quiet.'

No chance. Pup's cries startle the rabbits as we cut across the meadow, slip-sliding and skidding down the slope. But rabbits mean there are no wolves in the meadow, and I won't die as dog meat just yet.

I didn't have time to get him inside his baby carrier on my back and Pup's head drums on my chest as I lurch, gibbering in panic, grabbing handfuls of golden parched grasses to break my fall. But I go too fast and trip over Svad's wolf coat. My ankle buckles. I come down hard and pain shoots up my leg. Hiding in the long dry grass is the best I can do. Pup opens his mouth to wail.

'Shush,' I hiss. 'This isn't a game.' I feel bad when his face crumples. But Pup builds up to his best roar ever.

Lukas sprints out of the forest on the slopes above us.

A flock of speckled grouse takes to the sky, squawking in a flurry of brown tail feathers and white underbellies. I rub Pup's back to calm him down, and he stops crying, fascinated by the grouse. Lukas runs through the field to the barn and presses his hand into the flattened grass. He's calculating our departure. I slide further down the bank, biting my lip when my injured foot gets caught in alpine stalks.

Maybe I've got this wrong.

Then I think of my birth certificate and his surveillance photographs of Harper and me. No I didn't get this wrong.

Lukas wants to hate me, but he fell in love instead.

He still wants Pup sacrificed. Here on Ulv Fjell. He's going to kill every Svad as his own family was killed. And Lukas gave me a chance, to see if I could live with that. If I would choose his love over everything else.

I hug Pup to me and we watch Lukas unlock the gate, sprint up the tower and disappear in the cabin.

Go now. Run.

I hobble down to the woods, duck behind a loganberry bush, and glance back. Lukas stands on the observation deck with a rifle. He raises the telescopic sight and searches the edge of the forest. I shrink back in the bush.

And I wait.

Because that's what Lukas taught me.

Movement always betrays prey.

I hold my nerve and stay put. Pup gums my little finger. And Lukas pulls out something that looks like a firework rocket. He lights the touchpaper. The rocket flares and Lukas aims it at the barn roof. For a moment, nothing happens. Then the molten flames eat a hole in the roof and suddenly the whole barn is ablaze. Small angry flames jump from the barn and climb up the tower. Sparks fall on the meadow. In no time, fire rages through the dry grass. And the meadow ignites in flames. Then the wind catches it and the fire sweeps down the slope. Towards me and Pup.

In disbelief, I turn and run.

It's too late.

Everything around us is tinder dry, the forest ground covered in pine needles and husks. Behind me, pine branches snap and crackle as the pine needles explode. Heat and smoke billow through the forest like a gasp. I tear through the pines with Pup in my arms. But I know we can't outrun a forest fire.

40

He aims at her running figure, but even with the telescopic sights he can't get a clear shot. She weaves in and out of the trees like she knows a sniper's on her tail. As he expected, the wind changes direction and the canopy catches fire. The oil in the pine needles turns the trees into firecrackers.

Observers must not intervene to save prey.

Save her, his heart says.

Destroy her, the bad voice says.

His hands shake as he takes aim. This time he shoots.

A fist-sized hole smacks into the pine trunk ahead of her. Face height.

She stops and stares back, shocked, incredulous. He's furious she wastes time kissing and hugging Ulv Pup to her. Run, he screams. *Run.* She looks at the bullet hole again and spins, sprinting away from the pine trees and heading deeper into the forest, towards the oaks and the river.

Now she stands a chance.

Below him, flames rage through empty cages, setting

straw and bedding and the bushes alight. The land gasps in shock. Sorry, sorry, he whispers. Svad made me into this.

He looks up at the black clouds broiling above his land. His land. Not Ulv Pup's. Not Svad Oil's. And he begs the rains to come. Thick black smoke billows up from his studio, destroying the last of his photos. How could she abandon him after seeing them?

41

The skies opened and the rain powered down. A deluge. The first rain in weeks. In seconds we got soaked. Hours later, the trees are still hissing as the last of the fires snuff out.

Holy shit.

That was close.

His Cessna circles the forest. Its tail fin darts back and forth across the wet sky, waiting for us to break cover. I hide under an oak, my throat and eyes burning from the smoke. Smeared with mud ash, Pup and me are shaking so bad we're almost vibrating.

The Cessna buzzes over the treetops a few more times. The engines fade away and I have to stop myself bursting out of the trees after him. The pull of him is so strong that I feel I'm unravelling. How can I love him? Fear him, yet also want him?

The forest groans around me. And I force myself to calm down and listen to the beat of the rain slapping on the wet leaves. Drip. Drip. Drip-drip. Drip. A new song forms in my head. *Manipulation.* Yeah. I can work with that.

I get a protesting Pup in the baby carrier and I walk. And walk. A walking zombie. Except, I'm not dead. My body is flayed alive with shock. Misery. Every part of me hurts. My nerve endings scraped raw. Exposed. I trip over a moss-covered rock. My ankle screams in protest. And it hits me. I have to walk all the way down a mountain holding a baby. Days and days of walking; and already my shoulders are rubbed raw by his weight.

'I can't do it,' I wail. 'My foot hurts. We've no food. No baby milk.'

Pup pulls hard on my hair. It brings me up short. I got him into this. Focus. OK, I tell myself. Get your act together. Lukas said the key to survival is to find shelter before food.

He thought we wouldn't survive up here.

I shove my hands in the greatcoat pockets to stop them from shaking. My fingers curl round his brass lighter. I grip the smooth brass casing in my hand. This is another of his little messages. A threat. A warning not to get caught. Svad tortured him with it.

I hurl the brass lighter into the bushes, and everything in his pockets follows. Bits of string. A metal spike. His matchbox full of fag ends. Disgusting. My cut-off hair extensions? Lukas *kept* them? After a moment's thought, I stuff them back in the pocket – maybe Harper will like them. I pull out a dried-up strip of meat and roar at the sky. I'd rather chew my fingers off than eat this! I break another false nail, trying to get his cursed quartz bracelet off my wrist. But the clasp is proper stuck.

Breathe louder than your thoughts. And I push all the chaos of Lukas in my *room* and lock the door.

Pup politely ignores me, as I wipe my eyes with the corner of Lukas's wolf coat. I feel something hard in the lining. I rip the wolf skin open and pull out a phone! He has a second phone? I guess that makes sense, coming up here to such isolation. It's some cheap old-fashioned pay-as-you-go mobile, not his usual slick smartphone. But it's still a phone and when I press the 'on' switch, it lights up so there's some battery power in it.

'Yip. Yip. We're out of here,' I crow, and punch in the code to call the police. There's no signal. Of course not. Never is up here, Lukas said, as we're in the shadow of the mountain. I'm about to hurl the phone into the bushes too, when Pup's hot pee dribbles down my leg. I groan, but he looks so cold and miserable I can't be mad at him.

I pull out Mum's silver rosary to distract him. 'You know what the beads stand for?' I ask him. 'Each bead is a prayer. Early Catholics thought of the beads as a line of roses, small kisses to God. Every ten prayers to Our Lady is represented by the small beads, and then a big bead for Our Lord's prayer. My dad says prayers are powerful and I swear on our mum's rosary that I won't abandon you. Sisters outclass mothers any day. Trust me.'

But Pup doesn't trust me. He bawls with hunger. I've no idea what to do, and I just sit there, and record his crying.

*

The next morning, I wake damp and feverish, aching all over, covered in insect bites. I crawl out of loganberry bushes and drag Pup on the wolf coat after me. The sky is bruised dark. But if that was their big storm last night, I mutter to Pup, we got worse in Manchester.

He stares at me with dull glazed eyes. I can't look him in the face.

There's no sign of the Cessna. How could Lukas leave us to die out here? This horrible thought hits me. What if he is going after Harper next? He will, if he wants all of Rosa's children dead. I change Pup and throw away his soiled clothes, but we've no nappies left so I use the last of the bottled water to clean him up.

The discarded brass lighter is wedged in a lichen-covered stump. Betrayed afresh by Lukas's cruel games, I pocket it anyway. Then I secure Pup on my back, singing 'Don't Believe in Love' and an hour later we march out of the forest.

I stop dead.

Ulv Fjell drops away in steep fields of loose grey stones. No plants. No water. Just stone. Scree slopes? Lukas said they're unstable to walk on. What else did he say? But all I can remember is how happy I was flying with him when he made my night garden in the sky.

Then the pain and confusion of missing Lukas punches into me. I double over, panting, crawling on my hands and knees, sobbing, clawing at the stones and the grief inside me. The baby carrier slides over my neck and Pup squawks, grabbing hold of my hair.

'Ow, stop it, Pup,' I sob.

But he keeps on pulling and yanking me. He calls me back and back and back to my senses.

Until I can smell the ammonia pong of him, and taste the musty stones pressed to my face. I hear the beat of starlings taking off over the forest and the sky fills with undulating, swirling waves of birds. Starling murmuration, they call it. And I can feel the mountain breathing under my fingers. I piece myself together, limb by limb, and finally I get my heart going.

Gently removing Pup's grip on my hair, I kiss his fingers. 'It's OK,' I fib. 'You keep a lookout for bears, wolverines and suchlike. I've got ground transport covered.'

But as I take one step on the slate-grey scree, my foot goes from under me. Pup shouts. I land hard on loose wet stone and we slide down the sharp gravel.

I check Pup's OK, secure him on my back and try again. I hate feeling out of control on the scree, like the earth's moving under us, but soon I get a tempo going and we slip-slide down, using the odd boulder to break my descent.

My injured ankle throbs, but the pain beats thinking.

By midday, scree dust is caked in my eyes. I'm dripping sweat, the wolf coat drags me down, but we need it later for bivouacking. I was proper stupid to throw Lukas's dried reindeer meat away. Light-headed with thirst, I squint, carefully choosing my next step, and hoping Pup's tongue isn't swelling up like mine.

He's not had a pee for ages – I know that's not good – and he's too quiet. It scares me. I miss his bossy voice telling me how useless I am. Above his head, three lazy red buzzards circle the scree slopes. They scare me more than any wolf.

We stumble over the vast expanse of open pit mine before we find water.

'You'll be OK, Pup,' I say. 'Someone will help us. It's fine.'

I keep muttering that to myself. Someone will help us. It's fine. It's fine.

But the place is deserted.

No one will rescue us.

In the Cessna, this mine looked like a white flat crater. It's uglier close up. The heat is burning off the last of the rain, and steam rises off a lunar landscape of chalky white dust, littered with boulders. The hollowed-out ground is too big to skirt around. Lukas said that rutile is titanium dioxide. Is that toxic? It smells of death.

I tie my scarf round Pup's face, and strap a spare bra over my mouth. Then I risk it and we step past huge man-made grey rocks, sawn up like badly chopped eggs. The pit creeps me out. Each rock is numbered in gold paint and with the initials, U.F. That has to be for Ulv Fjell, right? So why did the guy on the radio pretend he'd never heard of the rutile mine? And why is it deserted?

I am swaying on my feet when I hear the sound of a waterfall. It's coming from behind stacks of industrial cabins.

The fast-flowing water sprays out over an outcrop of rock. But the ferns and rocks are covered with a layer of dust from the pit. When I take my boots off, my socks weep an orangey brown and a layer of skin seems to come off with them.

I get Pup off my back and scoop water into his mouth, but he just stares at me. I can't believe how fast he is deteriorating.

Don't panic. Focus. Prioritize. The weather is closing in, and we need shelter for tonight.

Something rustles in the bushes by the edge of the pit. I pick up a sharp stone and hope it's a bird or a rabbit so I can feed Pup. I touch my fingers to his lips, and we both keep still. Let prey come to you, let it do all the work, Lukas said.

The bushes move again. I hold my breath. A little dog pokes its face out of the scrub and wrinkles its nose at us. Pup gurgles. My spirits lift into the stratosphere. I never thought I'd be this happy to see a mutt. Civilization must be way nearer than I thought. I slither down the yellow lichen-covered boulders.

'Come here, little fella. I won't hurt you.'

At first the dusty black puppy keeps its distance, then prances forward on its front paws and its white-tipped tail brooms the ground with hellos. Pup's eyes follow it and he cries when the pup disappears with a *tick-tock* of its tail. I whistle and throw a stick on the ground. I see the shiny nose and then the puppy bounds out and checks to see if it is food. Pup chuckles again. He likes dogs a whole lot better than he likes me. The puppy vanishes into a tangle of bushes between smooth grey rocks.

The rain comes down, sheeting in diagonal waves. I don't hesitate; I crawl after the puppy, clumsy with one arm holding the baby carrier. Twisted branches weave into curved walls, as thick as a church vault, a sort of living basket. *Thicket?* The word pops into my head; it's a nice word, but I've no idea if it means a woven cave. There's another opening on the far side, but we're out of the wild weather. Inside the cave I can't stand upright, but it's not a bad place to hang out. My nose is bunged up from the scree and I am so covered in white dust, I feel a proper zombie.

I settle Pup on a nest of crushed leaves and he snuggles right in. I'm chuffed it's so soft, the thought of finding bedding for tonight does my head in. I wrap Pup in Lukas's cashmere sweater and tuck the mufflers of the fur headdress around his face.

Rain drums on the branches, but only the odd drop seeps through the weave. I examine my ankle. It feels hot and hurts like hell. It's twice the normal size, which is hefty at the best of times, and then I can't get my biker boot back on. I groan and lie back in the dirt. Close my eyes.

Instantly, Lukas is there, wallpapered under my eyelids. I can see every eyelash, every expression on his face. He smiles back at me. I stay like that for ages. *My Lukas.* Not like the real one. And I start to wonder if I've overreacted. Maybe I should give him a chance to explain?

The puppy yips.

I look up to see the little dog dance around my baby brother. It clambers over him, and settles down on his legs. Pup's face lights up. Lazily, I watch the dog tugging at Pup's socks. Its paws are twice the size of Pup's feet. I sit up quick. Pup grabs fistfuls of dark fur and pummels his toes into the dog's belly. My eyes adjust to the gloom; small skulls and bones lie everywhere.

Holy crap.

'We're out of here.' I push my injured foot into my boot, gather up our stuff, shove the empty baby carrier on my back and turn to get Pup.

It's too late.

The air vibrates with power; I feel it sweep over my skin. Silhouetted in the opening is a wolf. A massive black she-wolf. She's bigger than all my doggy night-mares put together. I sink to my knees whimpering. Oh my God, oh my God, oh my God.

When I dare look up, the wolf is darting back and forth across the entrance to the den, as if she's thinking the same thing.

Pup gurgles. The wolf pup wrestles out of his grasp. It wiggles on its belly over to its mum with its tail down. The wolf headbutts it behind her with her muzzle. Four other cubs squirm in the dirt, happy to see their pack safe together. The wolf's black lip curls up and all I can see is teeth: sharp, yellow, pointy teeth. I crawl backwards, dead slow.

Pup farts. Proper loud. My eyes flicker over to him. His face shines with happiness and he stares at the wolf with his arms outstretched. No fear. Not one bit. A true wolf pup.

42

The wolf growls. My stomach heaves and I puke over the small white bones. The sour smell burns the air. I cover my face, terrified to die as dog meat, and rock uncontrollably.

It's for ever before I hear the slurping sounds.

The wolf is eating my puke.

Furnace-hot breath. She stinks. A pungent foghorn of a stench. I don't move. The wolf sniffs at my bracelet. Nervous and undecided, she skitters backwards, slobbers over Lukas's wolf coat. Then she licks me, sandpapering my skin. I scrunch up my mouth and eyes, as Lukas did in his wolf photos.

And I pray. I pray like Dad; I pray for real. I pray there is a God, and He will save a sinner like me.

The wolf throws back her huge hairy head and howls.

It goes right through me. A plaintive, diminished chord.

Every hair on the back of my neck stands up and then my body is in flight, before I stop to think. I force my way through the back of the den, branches and twigs snapping at my face and hair, and I tear at them with my hands. The bushes scratch at me with a thousand claws. I think I hear the wolf lurch after me and I squeeze and slither and shriek through tiny gaps. My feet scrabble over roots and in a blind panic I keep on running and tearing at the branches to get away. At last I am outside, the fresh air burning my lungs, and I sprint over the clearing, not seeing what's ahead, just fearing what's on my heels.

I make it to the rocks and climb. My fingers scrabble at the smooth surface and I miss hold after hold. I force myself to slow down and focus on the handholds, then I am up and lying on top of the boulders, panting, my heart jackhammering in a panic attack.

Way below me, the wolf stands in the den opening and howls again.

On and on, the melancholy song bounces off the mountain, up into the sky, wave after wave, as eerie as whale music, a lament swelling into the evening. The wolf is singing her loneliness to beyond the stars. I am witnessing the performance of my life, but I cower on the rocks in shame.

I abandoned Pup.

I saved my own skin and sacrificed him. The coward in me says: you did right, you did right. No point in us both dying.

But Pup's a baby. A baby. My brother.

And I deserted him.

The wolf sits down to watch me. Panic skitters me, but

I make myself study her. Yellow eyes outlined in black, a white blaze runs down her face and narrows to a dark muzzle. Ears, big as toast and lined with soft grey fur, twitch when I move. Her coat is every shade of black and silver, electric with power.

She's beautiful.

My gut tells me this is Lukas's Asena. Bossy badass Asena. The missing wolf that now has her own pups. She was raised by Lukas, this wolf, but what did she learn? Hate or love? There's an old wound on her backside. She escaped the hunters. And she ran. Maybe she's a coward like me? I clamber to my feet.

'Come and get me,' I shout at the wolf. 'Leave Pup alone. He's family.'

Even as I entice her, my cowardly traitor hands search for ammunition, and throw as many stones as I can find. They fall short. I'm as useless at hitting a wolf as I am at tennis or any ball game. I swear if a wolf could laugh, she does. Her ears spring up, her tail high, and she pees at the side of the cave. Asena looks at me, her tongue lolling out her huge black-lipped jaws, then she turns and goes inside the den to her cubs.

And my little brother.

The stones drop from my fists. Pup will be ripped to pieces. I clamp hands to my ears and crush, crush, crush until my head is ringing. *Run*, says a voice inside me. *Run. Run. What can you do? Run. No one will ever know.* The voice sickens me. I sicken me. I peel my hands off my ears and listen.

The cave lies in shadow and is too quiet. But the mountain comes alive with shrieks. Wildlife. The night is so big, the sky luminous with every shade of red and orange cloud. But what's the point of all this beauty and a sun so bright when it should be night?

The midnight sun picks out the body of the sleeping wolf. The pups lie in a heap of paws and tails between her legs. I can't tell one body from another. I zoom in with the Leica, adjust the focus and search for my little brother.

He's not there.

Despair winds me. Stupid. Stupid me. I thought he might, just, somehow, be OK. Pup's wrapped in Lukas's sweater. Maybe Asena recognizes the smell? Maybe she really is a legend, and knows she suckles human babies? Yeah, right. Tell that to the police.

Bats swoop past my ear. I ball up. And I cry. Not for Pup. No. I'm crying for me, the shame of me, of what I've become. Lukas knows his true nature. And he is teaching me who I am. His polar opposite. A coward. Scared of life. Scared of dogs. Scared to say no to him. No wonder Mum left me. Harper's right; I was born bad.

Lukas sneaks into my head again.

Come to me. Leave him, no one will blame you. Leave him.

I scream at the night sky. 'I don't know what to do, I don't know what to do, I don't, I'm a coward, not a hero. I'm just a girl from Manchester.'

Then I hear my soul speak.

Bear witness.

I watch loads of telly. I know all about cowards who abandon a dying friend when they could've saved them. I've watched all that survival shit. I can't undo my cowardice, but I can make certain Pup is actually dead before I abandon him a second time.

And I must bury him. What's left.

The midnight sun comes out from behind the cloud and shines a silvery light on something round and white in the cave. I grab the camera and zoom in on a tiny, pale, human heel. My heart races.

The small heel moves, but I'm not sure if it's just the pups knocking it, jostling for position. Then a little foot kicks out. And a baby knee follows. Pup turns in his sleep and elbows off the smallest cub. Pup's face is wet with milk, slack and relaxed. Our cub with the white tail gives him a quick lick. Pup's arms wrap around its white ruff in his sleep.

He's alive.

Joy lifts me off my feet, and I dance on the rocks. I bet my fierce little brother had wolf howling as his bedtime lullaby. I watch him sleeping with the wolf.

And I make a vow. *Hear my soul speak,* I say to the Heavens. *I will not leave Pup behind.*

Once I make the decision, my fears melt away and I feel the universe step in behind me, like it's got my back.

Think, it says. *Out-think the wolf.*

But I don't know how.

But if you did know, what would that answer look like?

And the right answers pop in my head. Wolves can't survive without their mate. That's it. Asena can't hunt and watch her cubs. Lukas said starvation is the most common cause of death for a nursing wolf. And for now, she accepts Pup as one of hers.

Rabbits and small creatures scurry in the dusk. I drag my eyes away from the cave and watch them with the cold eyes of a predator.

Think of Pup, the universe whispers.

I can hear Harper laughing. You, catch a rabbit? You can't even run for the bus.

But I listen to the universe inside me.

Buried in the bottom of the baby carrier is the temazepam. Twelve white tablets. They would work on a wolf. But she's not exactly going to oblige me and swallow them.

Except I'm an expert at coaxing Harper into taking medicine. I will find a way.

Next problem. How do I catch a rabbit? The answer pops into my head.

Snares.

That's what Lukas does for his supper when he bivouacs. It looked piss-easy when he did it. You make a loop, a rabbit puts its head in and the snare tightens like a noose. How hard can it be? Except I don't have loops to make a noose and I threw his string away.

Think, says the universe.

I've got it. Hair extensions. And my fingers yank the red ponytail with the discarded extensions from the pocket of Lukas's coat. I lay the strands of hair in front of me and try to plait them together with wild nettle stalks. My fingers sting, and the plait looks weedy and rubbish, but soon it's as long as my arm. I make a noose and tie the other end down to a bush.

Near to the burrow hole, I prop up the loop with a stick like Lukas showed me.

And I wait.

No rabbit goes near the snares. Then the terrors come after me. What if the wolf wakes? What if Pup cries out? What if he dies?

Trust yourself, whispers the universe.

I'm bursting for a pee. I drop my jeans right there. The trickle gleams in the moonlight, a rabbit appears, hops over my snare and sniffs my pee. It's so bloody unfair that I throw the rucksack as hard as I can. For the first time in my life, with jeans round my ankles, I actually hit my sodding target. The rabbit drops, stunned by the metal frame. I jump up and throw myself over it. I feel its feet thumping into me. The rabbit screams and I feel sickened but I hold on until it stops. I lie on a rock under the stars and it dies in my arms. My first kill. I don't feel sad. I feel triumphant. I just got the wolf her dinner.

Crushing the twelve tablets between two stones, I prise the rabbit's mouth open. Its body is still warm and its tombstone teeth scratch my fingers. I try and get the drugs down. But they stick to the sides of her mouth. I put the water bottle in to wash it down. It doesn't work and next I worry that the rabbit should be skinned. If Asena can gobble it down, the drugs will work faster. Pup doesn't have much time. I think longingly of Lukas's knife.

Concentrate.

What's the sharpest thing I have?

Acrylic nails.

False nails bend and break when you use them on rabbit hide. In frustration, I bite off my broken nail. My teeth are better weapons. I don't stop to think; I pinch a roll of skin on the rabbit's neck and bite down hard. Soft fur chokes me and the taste of raw rabbit makes me heave. But I think of Pup and clamp my teeth down harder. Warm blood and pellets of fat fill my mouth. I gag and close my eyes.

But I think of Pup, and I rip the rabbit skin until I make a hole and I use my nails for the rest. I slip my fingers under the rabbit's skin and it starts to come off, like pulling out an inside-out glove. I leave the pelt dangling from her feet. The rabbit looks smooth and raw and skinny. I skewer my longest nail into her skin and push more temazepam into the puncture marks. By the time I finish, dried blood is caked under my nails. I am so hungry I suck my fingers and the blood drools down my chin.

Whoever said none of us would eat meat if we had to kill it got it totally wrong. Oh, that was me. The idiot townie.

Still panting, I stand up, holding the rabbit by its feet, and aim it at the den. I swing the rabbit a few times over my head to build momentum, say a prayer, and then I let go. The raw skinned rabbit flies in spirals. Its head yawns backwards and the legs swing round in a lazy circle. And the dead rabbit plops down between the rocks.

It's nowhere near the den or the clearing. I failed him again. How can I be so useless at everything?

I bully myself to climb down and get the rabbit. With every handhold, I pretend I am my mother, brave and strong. I pretend I'm a proper wolf girl. I pretend I'm just taking dinner to my best friend. I pretend and pretend and pretend. Until I retrieve the skinned rabbit.

Ignoring my juddering legs and the terror gripping my chest, I tighten Lukas's coat up to my neck. Rubbing his sleeves over my face, I hide my hair in the hood and pull the drawstrings tight. Mindless with fear, I stagger nearer the cave, the drugged rabbit in my hand, and call the wolf with a soft howl.

I pretend I am shape-shifting into a wolf. I feel the howl in my belly and chest, in my legs and tail, and I let it rip out through my throat. I feel her loneliness and I let her feel mine. I throw back my head and sing:

'Woo woo oo oo oo ruh.'

The sound reverberates around the night. I howl the song of a wolf who lost her mate. The black wolf pads out of the cave and stares at me like I'm a lunatic.

I say a quick prayer and throw the rabbit gently to her.

Asena catches it in her mouth. And gulps it down. A few snapping mouthfuls. And it's gone.

It took me hours to prepare that meal.

I crawl back, acting all submissive, and whimper, so that Asena knows I'm no threat to her. For the next hour or so, the wolf doesn't keel over as I expected. She paces across the cave entrance like she's got all day. The pups stir. They bounce over to nuzzle their mum. Asena bats them away a few times and then lets them feed. My heart leaps in my mouth when I see Pup, snug in Lukas's sweater and alone in the den. I want to tell him to keep quiet and wait for my plan to work.

That is so not Pup's style. He wants milk too. Now. He yips at Asena. A bossy wait-for-me yip. The wolf ignores him. I think maybe the temazepam is working after all; the wolf seems cool with this small intruder.

Pup crawls backward, rocking his body to and fro and then he manages to roll over. He does it again and again. Soon he is in the thick of the pups and pushes them out of the way to get his share. Asena lifts her huge black head, sniffs and slobbers over the baby. Then she lies down and feeds her pups.

All of them.

I crouch on my knees. The wolf hasn't moved in an age and the pups slump over her belly. I start to crawl, very low, very submissive, gibbering to myself. It's no act. I'm terrified, but I keep crawling until I can reach out and grab Pup's foot. I pull him to me.

The wolf's eyes open.

I cower and whimper. Pup thinks I am playing a game; he gurgles and rolls over to me. I wrap my body over him and I don't let him move until I hear the heavy raspy breathing. When I look up, the wolf is asleep.

43

He's alive – my lovely lovely Pup's alive and in my arms. Soggy. Stinking. Way worse than me. I stagger, drunk, scrabbling, falling, skidding down the rocks, getting distance between us and the cave. Hours later, a narrow waterfall shoots out of the rocks, drops into a pool, surrounded by green ferns, before plunging on down the mountain. My arms have cramped up. I flop down on the flat rock and pull Pup on my lap. I moan as the blood roars back into my fingers. Pup curls up tight and farts.

'Yo, stinker.' His belly's taut with wolf milk and I can see he wants to sleep off the best meal ever, without a word of thanks to me. 'You ungrateful little savage,' I whisper.

It takes all my strength not to kiss him awake. I tease twigs and bits of wolf fur out of his hair and Pup bats me away, wrinkling his nose in a snarl.

That sets me off. Even in his sleep, Pup is fiercer and braver than me. I stroke his wrists, wishing they were plump and silky like before. My own legs and arms are

283

tattooed with cuts and scratches. Inside, I'm even more of a mess, happy he's back, gutted I abandoned him. What kind of person throws a baby to the wolves?

Me.

The air feels thick and I can't quite catch my breath. I look at Pup's filthy face and, for the first time, I tell it like it is. And it's unbearable. I didn't just abandon him to a wolf. I'm way worse than that.

I stole him. I stole a baby to keep Lukas happy, and in my heart of hearts I knew he was up to no good and I didn't want to ask any questions. I was too scared to hear the truth. I risked Pup's life for a fantasy. And I didn't learn my lesson. I let Lukas back in my head in that wolf den. Let him talk to me. I was too busy imagining how my lovely Lukas, not his psycho shadow, adored me, and I never noticed the danger Pup was in. Never saw the wolf until it was too late.

I go on and on.

Blaming Lukas. Blaming me. Loving him. Hating me.

A tick lands on my arm and nips before I can flick it off. I drag myself out of my head. I'm doing it again. I'm meant to be looking after Pup. But loving Lukas is a cancer – it overpowers every other cell in my body and it hurts. A lovely cruel hurt.

The moon skulks off and the sun is up again. The mountains wake and the birds make more noise than rush-hour traffic. This is a new day. *Another day for me to burn.* A woodpecker high up in a pine headbutts the trunk.

Tuk. Tuk. Tuk.

Over and over, the bird drills the tree with its beak. Then rests for a moment and starts again. Stupid bugger. It must hurt. I shout at the woodpecker to stop. The bird looks down at me with blueberry eyes and keeps right on at it.

Tuk. Tuk. Tuk.

The far side of the pine tree is black and frazzled. It got struck by lightning and looks like it died years ago.

On my side, the tree has green needles, strong branches and fresh new growth.

Death and life, existing together, side by side.

I stare at the burnt tree for a long time.

'Pup,' I say. 'I can burn Lukas out of my heart. Every memory. Every longing. Every thought. And you'll be safe.'

I close my eyes and sing, '*Lightning. Strike him. Out of my heart.*' The woodpecker ruffles its tail feathers at me and continues beating the crap out of the pine tree. I listen to the wind bowling through the leaves, and watch a pink light come up over the mountain.

Then I open the door to the *room* and I let out Lukas.

He comes at me in a rush. I take a deep breath and push him back. I hold him in my mind and I study his face, every eyelash and every fleck in his sea-glass eyes, and every blemish that on Lukas looks insanely attractive. I see the strong iridescent thread that ties my heart to his. The pull of him. The unbreakable web he wove between us.

285

I will never love anyone like this again.

I can't do it.

Pup grips my fingers in his sleep; and I feel his strength flow into me.

I take Svad's brass lighter in my hand. I flick my thumb across the flint. The flame ignites, and I burn the shimmering threads between me and Lukas. I destroy it all. I burn Lukas Svad out of my mind as if he were just an old photograph.

I imagine the flames starting at the bottom of his face, kissing his chin, and burning it away. Then his beautiful mouth vanishes into ash. The loss of him is unbearable, but I make the flames continue up his face and torch his nose. His wolf-eyes blaze at me as the flames eat them. The whole of Lukas's face twists up, darkens and slowly, slowly, his face crumbles to dust.

And then he's gone.

It worked.

Of course, he's back in my head, in an instant. I don't give in. I torch the first time I saw him, the moment we locked eyes and our love exploded into a cosmos.

While Pup sleeps and the sun moves across the woods, I go through every memory of Lukas. I burn them all. I burn the first time I heard him speak – that's when I totally fell for him. His voice. And every word he said to me was a lie.

He's back in my head a thousand times. I knew he wouldn't leave without a fight. Finally I torch the memory of Lukas telling me to abduct my baby brother.

I feel sick now. Lukas did it with a knockout smile. No remorse. And I stole Pup while I was watching him watch me. What kind of person steals a baby to win a boy?

Me.

And the thought's unbearable.

Pup snuffles into my shirt. He smells so bad when I kiss the top of his head. But he opens his eyes and smiles at me.

Pup.

All pink gums. And yellow crusty bits round his eyes.

But he's smiling at me with his first tooth, as if I'm still a good person.

I lose it then and bawl. Pup screws up his face and bawls with me. Our sobs vibrate against my chest like we're one person.

His body goes rigid and he kicks off his last frayed sock. I can see the cubs have chewed his onesie. I hold his warm toes in my hand and can't believe he's alive. 'Oh, Pup, shush. Shush,' I hiccup. 'I'm here. I'm here. I promise, I won't ever leave you again. Next time I will lay down my life for you.'

I promise him my life and Pup hears I mean it. Soon his body relaxes and his sobs turn to gurgles. A fresh brown stain seeps through his onesie – it's not remotely creamy-yellow any more, and the smell is something else. I'll never get my head round how much shit there is in one baby, but I'm glad: it means we made it through one more day.

We wade into the green pool, furthest from the waterfall. The water's heart-attack cold, making Pup and me shriek. I soak his clothes off, wipe off bits of snot and shit, like a real mother.

Pup watches my face all the while, dozy from the wolf milk, shivering in my arms. The last of the muck comes off and he's finally clean.

And so am I.

Naked, Pup shrieks and splashes and reminds me of a thousand bath times with Harper. 'Hey, you ever been baptized?' I ask.

Pup boots me in the stomach. We both giggle. He packs quite a punch for someone so small. 'I'll take that as a no, mister. Baptism it is, then. Harper did me in the bath. She figured it'd fast-track us to heaven, despite our shoplifting habit – we couldn't stop, it gave us such a buzz. Actually, Pup, forget I said that. Stealing is wrong. Very wrong. We got caught in the end, pinching sweets, and the police said I'd be in big trouble next time.' I stop. 'They're never going to believe I didn't steal you on purpose.'

Pup looks away; I swear if he could roll his eyes he would.

I think of Lukas lying under the dirty bathwater of rose petals and wonder if he was ever baptized. 'You're a child, Pup,' I say firmly. 'You need protection from evil. I think Dad got this bit right. Here goes.' I draw Pup through the water, his red-blond curls drifting behind, and I don't feel at all silly when I say the words to the Lord's Prayer. 'In the name of the Father, the Son and the Holy Ghost . . .'

Pup burps and ruins his sacred moment. I try not to laugh, but I get the feeling he's no saint either. I start again and say, 'I name you . . .'

Shit. I can't remember his full name.

'No matter, you're my brother. I name you, Ulv Pup Svad. And I, Eleanor Mary Lamb, promise never to abandon you to the dark side. I will die before I do that again. Bless you, little child.'

Proper solemn, I dip my fingers in the water and make the sign of the cross on his forehead. Pup scrunches his face up as the water dribbles down. He does that growly thing with his nose again. Suddenly there's this huge shimmering light. Pup's face lights up as if he's been touched by something beyond; behind his eyes. Nothing in the whole world's as sweet as this smile.

Beatific.

It means touched by God. Pup grasps my finger tighter; he won't let go, and it's like he's choosing this for himself.

'Tell me what it's like, Pup,' I whisper. 'I don't remember.'

Pup smells river-clean. He lies on the bank, kicking his legs. His skin pinks up and I flick a few bugs off his face. A few days ago, they had me running for the hills.

Hidden under a stone, I find the wolf. A carved

wooden toy, its coat and ears rubbed smooth by love or neglect. I turn the toy over in my hand, sideswiped by sadness.

'Hey, you think Lukas ran away and swam here as a little boy?'

Pup grabs the wolf and clamps his mouth on it. I worry about germs, but he bats me away. I think he has another tooth coming; he locks his mouth on everything. It's like he has to taste the world to make sense of it.

I can't make sense of my world; it's enough to worry about food and shelter. I can't remember when I last ate – somehow my body's got used to hunger – but soon Pup needs to eat. And we don't have milk for him. My cuts sting like crazy when I wade into the river and wash his clothes. I scrub and scrub till the stains sort of come out of his yellow onesie. I hang it and his little vest on the bushes to dry, singing 'Baa Baa Black Sheep' to Pup.

I hum *na na* to him. My little brother makes a disgusting slurping sound and shimmies his butt; he's shameless about being naked and showing his whatsit to the world. When Pup claps his hands, giggling, I can't help but laugh.

He's got this knack of being happy with so little. Whenever I think about my heart being broken, Pup somehow slips through the cracks and keeps me alive with his laughter.

The sun shines. My foot feels better. Pup seems to plump out before my eyes. While our clothes dry, he rolls on his belly and attempts to crawl. He can only move backwards, but beams at me, like he can't believe his luck.

His determination puts me to shame. I can only curl in a ball, thinking about betrayal and our mother. I wake up, sunburnt, with a sense of dread. Something urges me to get Pup out of here. But the waterfall and pond look so magical, I don't listen to myself.

Wet ripped jeans are impossible to pull on, then I'm surprised how loose they fit and now all I can think about is food. In Pup's baby carrier, I discover an uneaten rusk. I dance around on sore feet and it takes all my willpower not to scoff it myself. I break it in half and nibble my share. It's the best meal ever. I double-check the bag. There's something hard in a pocket by the straps. A pack of tissues and a tiny tube of antiseptic cream. I'm about to slap it on my feet but Pup's got nappy rash, so I save it.

I packed no nappies. Soon Pup will pee down my back again, or worse. My ankle aches and I trip backwards over something soft. Bright green moss grows in between the flat rocks. I crouch and peel off a dome-shaped piece of moss. It comes away clean. The bottom side is brown and smells sharp, but the dense green moss is soft and spongy. I cup river water over it and wait to see if it leaks through. Result! The moss soaks it up. I wake Pup and he grizzles until I give him the half-rusk to gnaw on. And then he gives me a smile that could power the national grid.

'Nappy time.' I grin. 'This might feel a bit weird.'

I pack the moss round his bottom. Pup looks at me as if I'm crazy. Then I panic. What if he's allergic to moss? I take it off and start again. First I use a bit of the precious cream over his spotty backside and cover it with a tissue. Next, the moss nappy. I shape the moss into a figure of eight to fit round his legs. Pup wiggles as if I'm tickling him to bits. We're both laughing so much by the time I've got the poppers done up on his vest that I don't pay attention to the first splatters of rain.

Pup turns into a baby scarecrow, moss bulging around his butt and smeared rusk on his face. I feel dead chuffed by the time I get the yellow onesie on him. Now Pup's dry and comfy. I hobble over the rocks to get my clothes. It's so quiet here. The woodpecker's vanished and all the birds have stopped singing. Suddenly weird patterns appear on the surface of the pool. Shivering, I turn around.

The sun's still there, but it's mushed between black-purple clouds the size of mountains. A raindrop hits my forehead, and another. I pack and pull the wolf scarf over Pup's head to keep him dry, then limp down the track to find cover.

It's too late. Rain, big as fists, pelts us, and a neon-green light engulfs the mountainside. I feel the shock waves under my feet before the sky booms over us. My eardrums feel like I've been walloped over the head. The track turns into a torrent of mud and loose stones. I can't see where to put my feet. Pup shrieks, strangling me in his terror.

I step on a loose stone, my ankle twists under me again. 'Hold on,' I yelp.

We slither down the mudslide; stones and rocks tumble with us. Pup grips tighter and I try to protect his head, but the torrent becomes a flash flood with biting stones. I push my good foot down, we spin faster, then I manage to grab the nearest tree and hold on.

I lie back, panting, disorientated. Cold red mud oozes inside the wolf collar, creeps down my neck and cakes my hair. My head feels heavy and it's a struggle to lift it up. I flop back in the mud and feel my strength drain away.

Pup buries into me, whimpering. I wrap one arm round him and pray with everything I've got I can keep him safe.

But the next spike of lightning unzips the sky; thunder erupts on the same beat. The storm is right above us. I look up. Holy crap. We're under the woodpecker tree.

'It's OK, Pup,' I fib. 'Lightning never strikes twice, right?'

Thunder chases lightning; huge ear-splitting contractions split the sky, like the world is squeezing out a new life. I pull Pup under the wolf coat, but I can't keep my injured leg clear of the mud river plummeting down the mountain.

My fingers are sliding off the trunk; I jam my bad foot under a tree root. I bite back the scream and almost pass out, but it holds our combined weight.

Rain hoses us down like we're in a frigging car wash. Pup gets more frantic at the noise. I bellow my rage and hurt back at the sky: 'Give it all you've got. Nothing scares me now!'

It's true. After Lukas. His wolf. I can face anything. Be anyone.

Light flashes across the sky. The thunder claps on a count of four.

'Come on, Pup, give it some welly.'

For the next hour, Pup and me lift our soaking faces to the heavens and roar our heads off like we're demented.

Harper used to climb under my bedclothes during thunderstorms and tell me stories. Now I tell them to Pup. 'Thunder is made by Vulcan. The Roman god of jealous ugly blacksmiths, and he's smashing his anvil, making sparks fly, because his beautiful wife has snuck off with Apollo again. That's thunder for you. Boy trouble.'

Pup jabs a fist in his mouth, his pebble eyes blinking at me as he listens to my voice. Finally he drifts off. The thunderclaps get fainter. Lightning forks over Nøyfjord. Maybe Harper's back home worrying about whether I'm OK in the storm. I've looked after her for so long, I forget how brave my sister used to be. My stomach pinches. Harper is alone and she needs me too. And I do what I always do, when she's sick and we are apart. I imagine an orb of healing light in my hands, feel it warm up my fingers and send the light flying down the mountain over the sea rivers and fjords and press it into my sister's hands.

Hold on. Hold on. I'm coming back for you.

44

awn. Thirty black crows watch us. They sit in rows on burnt-out branches that look like black cracks in the sky, like everything is broken and rotten in this life.

I lie back, soaked in red mud, staring up at them. The crows brag and jab their beak knives at me, schoolyard bullies waiting for me to give up Pup.

They know my bad ankle is wrecked. It's wedged between the tree roots. The pain is something else, and the crows feed off it. Crows are dead smart; Lukas says they can live for twenty years, watching us, learning our weaknesses.

I rasp at the crows, 'Listen up. Learn this, birdbrains. You can't have him.'

The daylight creeps over the mountain, chasing away purple shadows in the rock. Tiny green shoots unfurl in the mud. They speed-grow before my eyes. Everywhere I look the colours of the mountains are so intense after the storm; I feel I'm hallucinating.

Pup gnaws on his toy wolf. He looks more trippy than

me, wrapped in bras and knickers with the wolf scarf on his head. He's still dry, curled up in the coat, but I'm struggling to hold him out of the mud.

My foot hurts like hell when I wiggle it. What if it's broken?

Dom says sprains are more painful than broken bones. My best friend's an expert on survival, but he's hardly been out of Greater Manchester. The only real survival skill Dom has is underage driving and his mum taught us both that.

By the time I free my injured foot from the tree root, I'm drenched in sweat. When I take a proper look, the outside of my foot is bruised screen-black and my heel has vanished in a swollen ankle. The pain is at a nine out of ten before I put weight on it. I'm so light-headed I don't know what to do. Then I see them.

Two Starburst raspberry sweets. They balance on the mud by Pup's baby carrier.

I frown. 'Didn't we eat them, Pup? You hoarding Starbursts now?'

I wouldn't put anything past him. I unwrap one. Pup squawks at me to get my attention. I chew it first and put the gooey mess in his mouth.

Then I'm dreaming there's a bottle of water jammed in the rock. I blink. It's still there. I crawl in the mud to it. The label's long gone, but the water's clean. Pup and me down it.

My neck prickles.

Someone is watching.

Adrenalin floods my body. Above the long waterfall, a light is shining out from the ferns. There's another flash of sunlight. I think I see Lukas silhouetted against the rock face. My heart goes nuts. And this voice inside me goes: *Of course, he came back for me. I knew he wouldn't stay away.* I tell myself it's just my mind playing tricks.

And I burn him out of my head. He's gone immediately. When I open my eyes, there are no more lights flashing, but Lukas sneaks inside my thoughts again. I'm too tired to keep burning him out of me and lock him in the *room* in my head.

By the time I plaster my ankle in mud and strap it with moss and a pair of tights, tears are running down my face, I'm not crying or anything, I tell Pup. It's just that the wind makes my eyes water. Not the pain, not the frigging crows waiting for me to fail, or how Pup's gone limp and quiet. He scares me how one moment he's so fierce, and the next he's so helpless. His peach-fuzz head flops against me. It takes for ever to tie him on my back in the baby carrier.

I'm knackered before we leave and I'm more scared of falling now. What if he gets injured next time?

Using a stick, I put weight on my ankle. The pain cannons up my body and I clamp my teeth together to stop the scream, then make myself relax. I blow out, panting, like I'm giving birth or something. Once my breathing is kind of human again, I try another step. The pain is something else, cruel and savage and a hundred times worse than bearable.

The crows shriek in the trees above me. Always the same three notes. *Caw . . . caw . . . caw . . .*

'I can't do this, Pup,' I moan. 'The crows are right. I'm useless.'

He feels heavy on my shoulders. One side of his face is red and wet from my sweat. But Pup beams at me and I don't know whether to laugh, or cry.

He trusts me so much.

'Fat lot of help you are,' I say.

'Woo-oo,' he whispers.

I close my eyes and breathe the sound in. Why can't I be brave, like this baby?

Stepping on to my bad foot, I throw back my head and wolf howl with him. I howl until the pain proper fades away. And with each step, the howling makes me feel bigger on the inside, the sound building in me, like the best music ever, and when the wave of pain crests, I take another step. Another howl, and I make it to the nearest tree.

Thirty-one steps. Thirty-one razor-stabbing, eye-watering, scream-howling-fuckitty-fuck-fucking-painful steps. I knuckle the birch trunk until my fists hurt as much as my feet.

Then I hear Pup, snoring in my ear, and I start laughing. I'm in agony, the crows are moving in for a kill and Pup's having a kip. He's so Lois Lane to my Clark Kent he never notices me, even when I'm the hero here. Yeah,

298

ain't that the story of my life?

'Woo ooo ou hoo roooooo.'

My ears prick up. I wrap my arms around the birch tree and listen to a real wolf howl, further up the mountain – a deep, plaintive *where are you?* howl.

Asena.

Then the tone changes and the wolf howl sounds urgent, a higher yipping sound.

A warning of *danger*.

I howl back to the wolf, louder this time, and I try to howl a sense of *we're safe, don't worry* into my wolf howls. I know, I know. It's ridiculous. I know that, but somehow, it feels like Asena has morphed into my mother and is watching over us.

A single gunshot ricochets off the mountain. Everything freezes – all the insects, the birds and the animals hold their breath to listen. We root for the wolf, but what comes next makes my blood chill. There's a second and a third shot; the sounds clap the air and ricochet off the mountain.

Is it Svad's hunters? Clearing the rutile open pit of wolves?

Tears sting my eyes. Oh dear God. Please. Not her cubs. Not Asena.

I don't risk howling again, and this feeling of dread settles on me.

No planes have flown over the mountain since the storm. If Lukas was on foot, he could find me. I left a trail a mile wide. He could track me in a heartbeat. Yet he's not here.

Why?

I know the answer. He abandoned me and Pup so we would die. Lukas assumed I'd be too useless to save a baby or myself. And I worry again he's gone after Harper.

I snap off a twig, ram it between my teeth and fix my eyes on the next tree. It's slipping down the slope, its white roots worming out of the dark earth. I concentrate on the trunk, focusing on the swirls and grooves etched in the emerald lichen.

One step.

I bite back the howl.

Two steps.

I am crying. It's so steep, stones slide under my feet. Keep going.

One step.

It takes for ever to get to the tree. Sweat is dripping down my back as I wrap my arms round the trunk and press my face into the moss. I've no tears left. *Tear deficit.* That's what Harper calls it, when I'd cry myself dry.

Dad's always telling Harper to bless pain and make friends with it. So I surrender to it. I dive into its centre; light spots dance in front of my eyes, but I pinpoint the pain in my foot and submit to its savage rawness. It takes no prisoners and I brazenly bless the pain and the message it brings. And I bless the dangerous descent pulling us to safety. It might mean days and days of walking till I get home. But I'll take it one step at a time.

One step. I can do that, I promise myself.
But the black crows follow us down the mountain too.
One tree at a time. Hop. Hop. Hop.

45

The stone farmhouse clings to this side of the fjord. Long grasses and indigo wild flowers grow on the roof. That's one of their things in Norway, turf roofs to feed the goats in winter. This family has a greenhouse and an apple orchard too.

My mouth waters. 'We've done it, Pup. We're safe.'

The evening light hovers over the water, making each tree stand out like it's on stage and the white blossom seems to float in mid-air. It looks so peaceful. Wiping the sweat out of my eyes, I study the distance again. It's about three or four miles away, as the crow flies. That makes me laugh out loud.

'Woo-hoo,' Pup whimpers.

I panic and check him over. Bundled up in so many layers of clothes, Pup looks like one of those Russian dolls that open up with another smaller doll inside. Dad always brought me dolls from his trips abroad. Who will bring Pup toys now? Silly how sad that thought makes me. He's my little brother, but Dad won't want a Svad in his home.

I can't think about that now. The crows are cawing in the trees, the creaking branches and the wild grasses singing in the wind. Now I've got him off the mountain safe, my worries crank up. What if no one believes me? What if they hand Ulv Pup back to Lukas?

It's the smell of the sea, the taste of salt on my tongue, that pulls me through the last agonizing steps. When I reach the iron gates, the stone farmhouse is silent and the ground's in shadow. 'Pup? We're here.'

He doesn't answer. My stomach twists with worry. I hobble between apple blossom trees, dripping with pain sweats. I thought I'd feel victorious to get Pup here, but he's been quiet for too long and I'm proper scared.

A figure looms out of the darkness. I scream. It's a frigging scarecrow.

I drape Lukas's wolf coat over its broomstick arms, make a sort of wigwam out of it and hide Pup inside. His head flops down on yellow marigolds. Norwegians plant them to lure greenflies away from fruit trees. I want to kip there with him, but I shove a few flowers in my mouth and keep going.

The garden feels deserted. Neglected. I check Lukas's phone for a signal, but I've turned it on so often it's dead. And I don't have a charger.

The farmhouse window buckles after the second hit with a garden spade. I crawl on to a kitchen counter, arms shaking, and moan as my bad ankle bangs into the sink. I flip on lights, wincing in the sudden brightness, my head throbbing worse than ever. I make a list in my head: 1. Phone an ambulance. 2. Call the police. 3. Call Dad. 4. Call anyone.

I keep forgetting what to do and end up muttering to myself, 'Look for a phone. Look for a sodding phone.'

There is no phone.

I crawl over to the last empty phone socket, collapse on the floor and wallow in self-pity. Why does everything have to be so tough?

Get up. Pup's alone in the garden.

I grab hold of the mahogany table, pull myself up and make it to the back door. I draw the bolts, but my eyes are too tired to adjust to the dark. Where did I leave him? My mind plays tricks and blanks out on me. I rush into the garden, like a crazy woman, calling his name. I forgot the scarecrow's wearing the wolf coat. It looks so like Lukas in the dark I grab it by the shoulders and shake it apart. I hate you, I whisper to it. The broomstick comes away in my hands; the filthy coat falls and shrouds Pup.

He wakes with a terrified wail and stares at me wide-eyed as I lug him into the house. My adrenalin is pumping so hard I don't feel my ankle. I bolt the door after me and lean against it. The garden gives me the creeps in a way that the mountain didn't.

We pass a curved staircase; boots, racks of skis – everything I touch has a layer of dust. I turn on a lamp. Pup stares into space with glazed pebble eyes.

'Come on,' I say, alarmed. 'Grub.'

We ransack the kitchen cupboards together. Cartons of formula milk, a stash of baby bottles and everything to make him one happy little pup. I rip open a jar of banana and apple sauce, spoon some into Pup's rosebud mouth and upend the rest of the jar into mine. The sweetness explodes on my tongue. I've never tasted anything so brilliant.

I go to warm formula milk in the microwave, but Pup snatches the bottle into his filthy paws and closes his eyes in sticky bliss.

'Slow down. You'll be sick.'

He doesn't listen to me.

Upstairs, I pull off his fur hood and the mud-caked bras and knickers, cashmere sweaters, shirts and socks. It was so cold last night I threw everything at the situation. Underneath the filthy layers, Pup's onesie is stained bright green by the moss nappy. I chuck the crud into the bin. I'm dead beat, but I hose Pup down in the bath with the showerhead. He hangs on round my neck like it's perfectly normal to be jet washed, drinking a bottle of milk. We find a packet of nappies in the bathroom – they're a bit small, but anything's better than Pup peeing down my back. None of the baby clothes fit him, until I find an unopened packet and pull labels off a cream onesie with an animal hood. Pup lies on the bed and obligingly puts his arms and legs in the outfit for me. 'Hey, what a team!' I kiss his snug clean foot.

'Na na,' he murmurs sleepily, and for once he doesn't boot me in the face.

I brush out his curls, alarmed how his red-blond baby hair's falling out. Then I remember, Harper used to tease me about going bald as a baby. I was born with curly blonde hair, and it all fell out and grew back dark and straight. Dad said it was normal.

The bed is heaven. Soft. Clean. Inviting. I strap my bad ankle again, then I lie down with Pup, protecting the pillow and sheets with towels. Then I pile up my last kroner notes by the bedside table. I hope there's enough there for the clothes and his milk and breaking the window.

Everything costs a bomb in Norway.

There's a prehistoric TV under the bedside table, covered with a Norwegian flag. I slide off the bed and plug it in, and the old telly glows a weird green, dangling cables over the bed like some hideous spider.

With shaking hands, I flip channels until I find the NRK news. We're the lead story. A press conference on Norway's favourite missing baby and me. I huddle under the flag and watch my life unravel on screen.

On screen, two Norwegian detectives sit bolt upright at the press table in uncool sweaters like they're on the set of *The Killing*.

Dad slumps next to them, unshaven, with the chrome crucifix round his neck. My heart lurches. Harper's in a wheelchair. I read her face like a map and frown. She looks physically OK, so what's with the wheelchair?

And she's wearing her blue scarf again. I know it means she wants nothing to do with my hennaed artwork on her head. Does she think I'm guilty too?

A spokeswoman kicks off in Norwegian. I fumble with the remote and put English subtitles on. '*Last week British schoolgirl, Nell Lamb, abducted Hagen Svad from the Oslo Shard. Miss Lamb rented a Cessna from a local Oslofjord airfield. We believe Nell Lamb concealed Hagen in her suitcase—*'

'Nell doesn't own a suitcase,' Harper interrupts. 'She only has a pink Dora the Explorer school bag. This is a set-up; Nell's too terrified of aeroplanes to fly anywhere.'

The spokeswoman sighs. 'We believe Miss Lamb obsessed over Rosa Svad after learning the identity of her birth mother.'

'Nell didn't know Rosa Svad was our mum. Dad never told us,' Harper shouts.

They ignore her. 'Miss Lamb became increasingly unstable,' the spokeswoman says. 'She played truant from Vord Skole. Miss Lamb is wanted in connection with alleged tampering of cancer medication, resulting in her sister's hospitalization.'

'Harper! Tell them it's not true,' I shout at the telly. But she keeps quiet, and I can see how much my sister resents me abandoning her in her hour of need.

The police show film of me stealing Hagen Svad, disguised as Rosa in the Oslo shopping centre. I float across the plaza in the white dress and long red curls, carefree and heartless. I am laughing with the little boy in green boots. And I walk away with the baby. I feel sick with shame. How could I do that? Reality slams me in the face, and I wake up as if from a dream. Who was that girl who stole a baby? Not me. But when I am around Lukas I become a different person: nothing matters except him – it's like a trance. How can I explain something like that when I don't understand it myself?

On TV, the detective states, 'Norwegian police believe Hagen Svad to be in extreme danger.'

I'm shocked. They can't believe that? Dad stares ahead, listening to the charges against me, bewildered, like he's seeing huge waves coming for his family, one after another, and not even his God can save him.

'In the light of these allegations,' the spokeswoman says, 'Nell Lamb should not be approached by members of the public.'

Holy crap.

I glance at Harper's face. And my heart lifts. I know that look. She's not buying into this. Harper grabs the microphone, Dad raises his eyebrow, and I can see that gets her going. 'My sister's innocent,' she says to the police.

Harper fixes her eye on the reporters and removes her blue headscarf. I grin. She's going to play her cancer card and suddenly I get why my sister is posing in the wheelchair.

'My sister nurses me,' Harper states. 'She never leaves my side. She didn't steal a baby. She felt abandoned by Mum, and separating a child from its mother is right up there as crimes go for Nell. Find Lukas Svad; I bet he manipulated her.'

The spokeswoman shakes her head. '*Nei*. Lukas Svad

is out of his mind with worry. We need to reunite what's left of his family. He is helping the police and Svad Oil to track your sister and the stolen baby.'

'My sister's no thief. She didn't do this!'

The detective in the yellow sweater says kindly, 'She has a history of stealing. We've a witness from the Svad Store who caught her shoplifting smoked salmon.'

Harper looks at him as if he's mad. 'Nell hates fish,' she hisses. 'She's a mystic, a musician, not a crazed kidnapper. And she would never, ever, *ever* mess with my meds.'

All eyes follow Harper's fingers as she taps her bald head with its hennaed angel helmet. 'My sister makes my life worth living. Nell couldn't stop crying as a baby. She missed Mum so much, and we couldn't find a way to make her forget. It's too late now. Mum's dead.' A lifetime of hope and longing snuff out on Harper's distraught face.

The NRK cameraman pushes in until my sister's distressed eyes fill the whole screen. I can't bear any more, and yank the TV plug out. The press conference shrinks to a dot on the TV screen. I crawl into bed and hold Pup. My eyelids have concrete bricks holding them down. A kip. Just for a second, I promise myself.

Don't stop, says a voice inside me. Keep moving. Danger.

And for once, I listen to myself.

An oil rig helicopter buzzes over and disappears out to sea. Now I'm scared Svad Oil will find me before the police and give Pup back to Lukas. I pack fast. The cottage must be on a small inlet that runs off Nøyfjord; it's too small for ferries and no boats have come this way, but above the cottage there are car tracks and a grey van parked in the woods. Dog-tired, I glance out the window and do a double take; the scarecrow is wearing the wolf coat. Rubbing my eyes, I look again and the scarecrow is just a lopsided boom, but I don't remember picking the coat back out of the marigolds.

It's just my mind playing tricks.

Unnerved, I go outside to the orchard, in case there's a gardener or someone who can help me. I calm myself down by taking slow deep breaths. No one is around. I grab a box of red apples from the greenhouse for our journey. I reckon it's a day's drive to Preken Rock and home. The light in the orchard and the world feels so peaceful, so full of promise that people can build happy lives together, plant fruit in one season and expect to be around, months later, to harvest it.

Suddenly ordinary family life seems extraordinary, wonderful.

For the first time in ages, I sing: *'I'll write my own life in the skies.'*

Norway is so trusting; the key was still in the ignition in the grey van. It smells of wet dog. I strap Pup into the front seat with a bottle and he beams at me. I stare at the pedals and the gearstick and feel queasy. Everything is on a different side. I try and remember Dom's instructions. ABC. Accelerator. Brake. Clutch. Yeah, a piece of piss after a Cessna. I take the handbrake off and freewheel down the first bit of the slope. We bump past a couple of trees and then the steering wheel locks and I am heading straight at a pine. I brake. Shit. I have to start the engine. The engine stalls four times in a row, it kills my ankle, and then the jabbering monkey in my brain is turning cartwheels and Pup's bottom lip is wobbling.

'It'll work this time,' I promise him, and the engine throbs into life.

The lane is very, very steep, pockmarked with muddy holes, but the treetops weave together and the leaf canopy will hide us from the sky. The grey van picks up speed and Pup nearly bounces over my knee. I pump the brakes and they make this awful squealing noise. I risk leaving the shelter of the woods and tighten my grip on the steering wheel and the van bucks on down the lane. Then I hit a groove and we go a bit smoother. I brake only for the sharpest bends. Bushes and trees fly by in a blur, my teeth rattle. Soon I am out in the open, on the fjord path, and when I let the brake off, we fly over the grass.

'Woo-hoo,' Pup shouts; even the wind seems to cheer and clap the van.

I flip on the radio and sing along to 'Don't Kill My Vibe' by Sigrid. We drive along a sheer cliff edge. For a moment, it feels like me and Pup are in an ultimate buddy movie, until I stall the engine again up the next hill and my little brother gives me this withering look, like he could do a better job.

After a day of stall-start-stop miles, my top speed is

eight miles an hour and that feels daring. Church bells ring out over the water. Every house along the fjord flies the red Norwegian flag, with its blue and white cross. Brass band music carries across the water.

Constitution Day. I forgot Norway celebrates its independence from Sweden and Denmark today. I was meant to be in the church choir.

The grey van putters up another long steep hill, and when we get down the other side, ahead of us I see the famous ledge, hundreds of metres above Nøy and the fjord.

Preken Rock.

I made it home. Now what do I do? Who will believe me?

The sun is ringed with dark cloud and the colour drains out of the fjord when I hear the motorbike. My heart twists with longing and terror. I look back up the road to see a black figure racing a bike over the fjords.

46

Visitors turn our fishing village into a carnival. I nudge the grey van through flocks of white dresses and children waving patriotic red, white and blue ribbons. Every family's decked out like they're auditioning for Heidi-the-Musical; the cheerful wholesomeness disorientates me, but Pup gobbles it all up with gleaming button eyes. His innocence makes me feel worse than ever, and I stall the engine. I'm an outsider here. A baby-stealing, medication-tampering runaway. Who'll believe me over Lukas Svad? Norwegian flags billow over the windscreen. Jumpy as shit, I look in the rear-view mirror. He's not here yet.

I kangaroo-hop the grey van up the fjord road. Police have cordoned off Yellow Cottage. There's hazard tape and red bollards, but I can't see any actual policemen. My heart freefalls, and for a moment I wonder if they've dredged up Mum's body.

TV crews are set up in our garden, stopping anyone who will talk to them. I do a double take. Even from here I recognize Gudrun's blonde plaits. What a witch. Trust her to feast off my tragedy. I want to stomp over and put the record straight, but who will believe a foreigner that Pup's in mortal danger from Lukas Svad? And I can't think how to keep Pup safe until I get watertight proof. The words pop in my head.

Sanctuary. Claim sanctuary.

It so didn't work out for Thomas Becket when he claimed protection in Canterbury Cathedral, but it's my best shot for Pup. Norwegians are more law-abiding than Brits.

Nøy Church is rammed. Music escapes through the open church windows, deafening the chatter outside. How can everyone be happy when my world has fallen apart? I park in the cemetery and turn to get my bag from the rear seat. Mum's music sheets fall out as the grey van begins to roll down through the gravestones to the fjord. Pup shrieks. I yank on the handbrake just in time. Grabbing the Leica, I settle him on my hip.

'Na na!' he says sternly, in his *don't-you-dare-forget-my-milk* voice. He bats me in the face until I hand him his bottle. How does someone so little know exactly what he wants? Wish I did.

'I need you to be quiet in church,' I whisper.

I sound just like Dad. Of course, Pup blanks my lecture and gazes at the little kids with their red and blue ribbons dancing on the spot like sandflies on a hot beach.

The church door opens and the band get ready to lead the parade. Father José has gone to town over a Madonna and Child float. Six strapping lads shoulder the heavy wooden float on poles. And in her blue headscarf Harper sits on a throne on top, decked out as Our Lady, the Virgin Mother of God, cradling my American Girl as Baby Jesus.

I almost blub with relief. Lukas hasn't harmed her. I push my way through the dancing children and hesitate in front of her. I don't know what to say. I let Lukas Svad into our life and he tampered with her drugs and nearly killed her.

My sister's sulking under her blue headscarf, but when she sees me, Harper's body jerks like I stabbed her. She sways in her chair. Then she leans down and grips me to her chest like she will never let go.

'What the fuck have you done to your hair?' she says.

We fall apart, laughing as much as crying. Pup squawks in protest at being crushed between us. The baby and Harper eye each other up.

'Hallo, Hagen, I'm your oldest sister,' Harper says. 'Pleased to meet you.'

Unimpressed, Pup extends a grubby finger and touches Doll's hair. Then he strokes it and offers Doll his bottle. He sort of sidles over to Harper. I guess she smells a whole lot nicer than me, so in no time at all Pup makes himself at home on Harper's lap, like he's known her for ever. The little traitor.

'He's just like you were,' Harper says sadly, stroking his hair.

And I think she means, before I turned out bad.

I walk alongside the Madonna float and try to bring

315

Harper up to speed about Lukas. The lads carrying the float cast sideways looks at me and study the quartz bracelet on my hand. I don't how good their English is, but I don't think they compute the child-kidnapper in the Oslo Shard with my Dennis-the-Menace haircut and filthy clothes. I'm a million miles away from that ignorant glamorous girl. And with so many small children in the church, teenage boys don't notice one extra baby glaring at them.

I tap Harper's leg. 'Lukas wants Rosa's children dead. *All* of us. I've got to prove what he's like inside. He is eighteen soon. He can become Pup's guardian. Do you understand? You and Pup will never be safe, unless I can prove what Lukas is capable of.'

'Why did you steal him?' Harper leans in and whispers, 'Was the sex so good you'd even go with a Svad?'

'I thought I was rescuing a baby.' I hitch Pup's baby carrier higher on my shoulder.

Harper grips my hand. 'You're wearing that quartz bracelet,' she says. 'It's been all over the news. It's Mum's. You know she's dead? Not that it matters – it's not like she was mother of the year, was it?'

My sister's voice wobbles, and no matter how hard she tries to be strong, the thought that she'll never see our mother again breaks her.

I pull at the bracelet. 'The clasp's stuck,' I say hopelessly.

'Na na!' says Pup, imperious as ever.

He's pointing at the roof. Roses butterfly down from the rafters, the petals swirl and dance, caught in shafts of light from the stained-glass windows.

Children are throwing bucketloads of them down from the organ balcony. The falling red and pink rose petals float down on our heads, soft as snow.

'Rosa?' I whisper, and reach out to touch one.

'No. It's not for her,' Harper snaps. 'Father José ordered ten thousand petals. He wanted a rose petal for every Norwegian lost in the Second World War.'

Pup grunts, pushes himself up on my sister's lap and tries to catch them. 'He's a handful,' she says. 'Wait till Dad meets him. You better get your story straight.'

I frown. The petals don't look like roses any more. They look like home-made confetti, fragments and pages torn from books. I catch one in my hand.

The thick cream paper is covered with musical notes written in green ink. It's Rosa's music. I get this wicked punch in my heart. I left it on the back seat. It's all I have left of my mum.

Furious, I glance around the packed church. I can't see him through the crush of children, but somewhere, in the milling crowd, celebrating their Independence Day, Lukas is here, intent on stealing mine.

Children are tearing up more pages of Rosa's music and scattering them down to us. Harper catches one of the fragments. She looks at me, bewildered.

'Music? What does it mean?'

'It's a threat,' I say. I feel Lukas's hatred in every fistful. 'He's destroying evidence that Rosa loved us. Give me your phone – Lukas's is out of battery. Then faint or something, as I need you to be the decoy.'

And I whisper my plan in Harper's ear.

'No,' she cries when I finish. 'I won't help you destroy yourself.'

'I did that all by myself,' I say, wretched.

I hug my big sister and our goodbye is unbearable. 'What if I never see you again?' She gives me a short angry hug and pushes me away like she feels the same helpless fear and rage. 'Give yourself up!' she begs.

'I will. Later. But no one will believe me right now.'

Harper helps me get Pup's baby carrier on my back, tears rolling down her face. Children jostle past and I look over their heads to the car park. 'Now pass me your phone,' I say. 'The police are here. Go straight to them. Stay safe. I'll draw Lukas away from you.'

'Come with me?' she cries.

'I can't. They won't believe me over Lukas Svad. I must get Pup out of here or they'll give him back to Lukas. I need to get proof before they arrest me.'

When I pick him up, Pup beams at me like I am the best thing in his life. His sticky, heavy, warm body melts into mine. The thought of losing him makes me giddy with terror – somehow there's not a part of him now that isn't a part of me. I take one last look at Harper and I slip out the church door with our little brother. This is my bargain.

My life for theirs.

47

There's nowhere left to run.

I climb Preken Rock. Pup's baby carrier feels heavy on my back as I scramble painfully over boulders and rocks and weave between the slender birches and spruces. Halfway up the trail, I meet a black crow walking down, patient, bored as a mother watching her toddler, but stabbing at something ahead of it on the ground. Merciless. Jab. Jab. Jab. Jab.

I hear the squealing before I realize the crow has caught a frog and its claw is gripping its back leg. Desperate to escape, the frog stretches its body until breaking point – it is all long legs and arms and looks half-human, half-alien, a naked, translucent body screaming as it's being pecked to death.

'Leave it alone,' I yell.

The crow looks at me and releases its grip, and for a moment the frog escapes and hops past me, bleating in distress. I know the frog can't escape. It can't outrun death. None of us can. I limp on but I can still hear the screaming frog and the crow. Jab. Jab. Jab. Jab.

I pass the emergency area for rescue helicopters, and the path narrows. It clings to one side of the mountain now. I step over a crevice in the rock and the trail opens up to a flat iron-shaped plateau – with a terrifying edge, as if a giant axe chopped off half the mountain and threw it into the sea. It's a sheer drop to the milky sea-glass fjord, hundreds of metres below.

No railings or anything. Lukas says Norwegians don't like to spoil the view; locals never fall, only unwary tourists taking photos. And jumpers. Last year, two German lads made a pact and leapt off together. On cue, Mum's favourite movie plays in my head. *Thelma and Louise*. The film ends on a freeze-frame of their green Thunderbird in mid-air when the two women drive over the edge of a canyon. They couldn't see another way to escape. Hounded by police. Misunderstood. Trapped. Thelma and Louise chose death over captivity. I wish I still had the grey van; I think it'd be easier to keep on going over the abyss in a car.

On the other side, green mountains plunge smoothly into the fjord. A midnight sun throws eerie, purple shadows on the water. The views over the fjords are gobsmacking. Imagine something so beautiful it calls to your soul and makes you ache with longing.

My mother lies down there.

Pain lodges like a brick in my chest. The shock of Lukas's film won't leave me alone. I see Rosa's billowing white dress, her red floating hair, and I torture myself with sick thoughts. Do the crows peck at my mother's body? Does the sea burn the flesh off her bones? A bitter grief festers inside me.

I film my last words. 'I'm Nell Lamb,' I say on camera. 'If you're watching this, I'm dead already. Don't freak out on me. It's way worse for me, and I need you to listen. I die, and this baby gets to live, but only if you listen.'

It sounds like a stupid snuff-selfie. My dyed messed-up hair and wild eyes make me look more psychotic than penitent sinner. But I don't need them to forgive me. I don't need them to get why I stole my baby brother. I need them to look after him when I'm gone. I take a deep breath. 'Harper?' I say. 'Pup likes to go to sleep in a dog basket. He loves chewing on his toy wolf; he's teething. Oh, he hates thunder and sermons and mean faces.'

My voice wobbles. 'And when he's sad . . . when he's sad . . . sing to him. He likes that. And hold him. Make him feel he's wanted. Pup should get a dog, soon as. You know, for company. He's proper brave. You look out for him. Tell him I loved him.'

I will miss his first steps. He won't understand. He'll think I abandoned him.

The howl starts in my belly.

I throw back my head, and the song lifts up into the sky.

'Arrh oou woooo oooh rooo.'

Every cell in my body is vibrating. I wiggle back from the edge, pull out Harper's phone and punch in Lukas's number from memory. 'I'm on Preken Rock,' I say to him.

'I know where you are,' he snaps. 'Everyone along the fjord can hear you and Ulv Pup. Why pick that spot? It's a dead end.'

'It's a trap,' I say truthfully.

'Prey can't fight predators!' he says.

He hangs up. I curl up by the baby carrier and wait.

I check Harper's phone to stop me bottling it. My sister has kept every bit of dirt on Pup's abduction and me. Everyone has a crack. The trolling she gets on social media is horrific. Total strangers hope Harper dies of cancer for being my sister?

Over and over, Harper replies to them: Nell is innocent, my sister is innocent.

No one believes her. No one will believe me. The papers report: 'Evil walks among us, disguised as a British schoolgirl.'

Millions have seen this trolling around the world. There's nowhere I can start over. Every room has a Gudrun, a bitch, slyly rocking her arms and mimicking a kidnapped baby. When I speak, they hear a liar. A monster. They won't let Pup grow up with me.

Who am I kidding? Lukas won't let Ulv Pup grow up at all. It's him or me. With tears dribbling down my chin, I call home to say goodbye. Harper doesn't pick up. Maybe she's safe with the police? I listen to our home phone ringing and ringing.

Pup's cries build to a crescendo; I push the mobile from me, put it away. It's time.

322

Then everything changes. A surge of power charges the air. The skylarks stop singing. The land stops to listen. Danger. Danger.

He's here.

48

Lukas Svad strides over the mountain like he owns it and the shock of seeing him, with the bedraggled wolf coat snapping around his legs, makes me forget to film it. Of course. He tracked me down to the farmhouse and stole his coat back off the scarecrow. My tears well up. And his tall figure blurs in and out of focus, so he seems real and not real. A hologram of the boy I once loved. Somehow younger and yet older; diminished by his lies.

'Nell,' he calls. 'Give me Svad's son and we can start over.'

How can someone so beautiful be so evil?

I still don't get it. No. No. I do. Lukas never stood a chance. Maybe, if Svad had let my mother take me with her, he'd have raised me like that too. Damaged. Aggressive. Unpredictable.

Even now, my body betrays me. And I can't take my eyes off his face. He was all I ever wanted. This extraordinary boy in an oversized wolf coat. I press record on the Leica, keeping it between me and his sea-glass eyes. 'Recognize him,' I say to the camera. 'Close your eyes to his beauty. Don't listen to his voice. Every word he says is a lie. He's got no heart. No soul. Stop him next time.'

'That's your big trap?' Lukas laughs and laughs. 'Photos? Home movies? The police will never believe you over me. Money talks. Svad Oil are coming. You don't have time for this.'

'I have time,' I say. 'Our first date was up here on Preken Rock, right? At dawn. When no one else would be here.'

'You never came.' Lukas sounds dead wary now.

He leaps over the crevice, sure-footed as a wolf, and lopes up to me. From habit, I step between him and Pup's baby carrier.

'Lucky for me,' I say. 'Because you planned to kill me that day, didn't you? Throw me to my death? Think you can do it today?' I know he can't. I watch the shame crush him. I'm shaking so bad; I lower the camera. For a moment, I think Lukas really sees me.

He grabs my hand and kisses the quartz bracelet. 'Give me Ulv Pup,' he whispers. 'How could you choose anyone else over us?'

'I chose to be me.' I pull my hand away from his. 'I couldn't live with myself. Pup's worth more than the world to me. He's my brother.'

Pup's cries are weaker now, and Lukas tilts his head at me, like I just don't get it. 'He's Svad's son. I must sacrifice him . . . to save the pack. Ulv Pup's an alpha, he understands. It's not personal. It's our calling.'

My hope drains away and I know Lukas won't let this fixation go. 'Pup wouldn't need to inherit Svad Oil if you hadn't let our mum die. I saw your film of her drowning. You were there.'

'I told you already,' Lukas growls. 'I tried to save Rosa.'

'Liar,' I snap. 'It suited you to let her die.'

Lukas drops his chin in the wolf fur and talks so softly I have to lean in to hear him. 'Rosa let me blame Svad all these years. But it was her who shot my wolf pack.'

'Rosa killed them?' I say, stupidly.

Of course. Her maternal instinct kicked in, and my guilt-ridden mother stopped a lost little boy being savaged by wolves.

Lukas reads my thoughts. 'She was supposed to protect my wolves! Haven't you listened to anything I said? She betrayed me.'

'My mum saved you!'

'I didn't want saving.' He closes his eyes. And I know he's with them, on the mountain, hunting with his wolves in the snow. 'Svad Oil shot Asena and her cubs,' he says. 'They're all dead now.' His voice sounds hollow with grief.

'I'm sorry,' I mumble.

'How could you leave his sock in her den? They assumed Asena killed him. Everything is your fault,' Lukas shouts. 'Svad kept Rosa from seeing you. Then he has his own son, and he finally understands; family. That's why Svad was flying Rosa to meet you.'

'What?' I lower the camera. 'My mother was coming for me?'

'Yes!' Lukas says, like he still can't believe it. 'But our helicopter went down there.' He gazes down Preken Rock to the yellow cottage. 'Rosa almost made it home to you.'

Grief turns into a monster inside me and I hurl the cruellest words at him. 'You never thought to tell me she wanted me? You bastard! I don't care about your wolves. I'm glad they died. You stay away from me and my family. I can't love a boy like you.'

'You don't mean that,' he says, aghast.

'I do,' I snarl back.

'Loving me . . . is what you do, Nell,' he laughs, uncertain, and looks up as if he hears something in the sky. I hear it too. A distant helicopter. His eyes empty. One minute he's laughing, the next he's the void. Cold. Empty. Hurting. The change breaks me.

I hold up the Leica again. 'Just confess you're a danger to Pup, and we can go home. He can live with us.'

'I can't stop Svad Oil from killing more wolves with him alive,' Lukas says. 'And I won't let them lock me up. I'll make it look like an accident.'

He darts behind me and snatches up Pup's baby carrier and he runs along the cliff edge. It happens so fast. I can't stop him.

I am screaming and lurch forward, but my weak ankle buckles, and I sprawl head first in the stones with the Leica around my neck, and I crawl to Lukas, begging him not to harm my little brother. 'Please, please, don't do this.'

He stops to sniff at Pup's wolf-fur headdress. Pulls it off. I reach out . . . and I almost make it in time . . . to save him.

But with a cry of rage, he hurls the baby carrier off

Preken Rock. It flies up, and over the fjord. Stalls in mid-air. A contrail of baby clothes, and a blue baby shoe spirals down to the sea. I point the camera, sobbing, and film it all. Pup's hysterical crying catches at me, like he's pleading for my life. Not his.

As the baby carrier falls, my American Girl doll tumbles out, padded out with Pup's dirty nappy. The sound of his crying fades, then stops, when Harper's phone hits the water.

My body is juddering as if Pup had died for real.

Lukas stands motionless on the ledge, with Pup's fur hat dangling from his hand like a small dead cat. 'Clever,' he admits at last. 'You looped Ulv Pup's crying on your sister's phone?'

'Being a musician has its uses.'

'You are so like Rosa,' he says. 'A she-wolf.'

And his voice is so sad my heart weeps.

The images of Lukas Svad rush at me. *Outside the Svad Store. 'You must really love fish.' The jolt when we first touched hands. Flying in my night garden, with a thousand candles in jars. 'What delights you, Nell?' he asked me. Delight? I never knew what that word even meant before I met him.*

'Where is Svad's heir?' he asks. 'I searched the church.'

'I hid Pup in the priest's kennel. And I recorded that little boy crying before I left him – just as he did every time he was hungry and scared. You abandoned him to starve on a mountain. I will never, ever forget what you are.'

328

Lukas flinches. He looks so lost. I almost think he'll jump and save me the bother.

The sky turns crimsom as the midnight sun drops into the horizon. The sound of the helicopter gets louder and louder.

Lukas pulls me to my feet and rips the Leica off me. He tosses it over the cliff. 'Without that film, no one will believe a word you say, Nell. The police think you're a criminal. And criminals can't benefit from their crimes in Norwegian law. You will be disinherited from Rosa's estate. You won't betray me.' He stamps his foot. 'I make the rules!'

'No,' I say. 'I do. And this time I win, if I live or die.'

The Leica memory card is wafer thin. I place it on my tongue. And part of me dies in that moment, before I swallow.

Then I remember. This film is my legacy.

It's him and me and Pup. Our story.

'Lukas, you showed me how to live,' I say. 'Pup taught me how to die.' It's a kicker line. I spent ages writing it.

Shame that I have to die, to find out how great I can be.

But Lukas simply rests his forehead on mine. 'Don't make me hurt you,' he says. 'Don't do this.'

At that exact moment, the muscles in my throat go into spasm. They tighten around the memory card. I gag. Lukas shouts. I don't listen. I imagine my throat is a boa constrictor, crushing prey, and I force the memory chip down, ignoring the pain in my throat.

Lukas pulls out his knife. 'No!' he cries.

I stare him down.

'You know me too well.' He almost smiles. And before I can stop him, his fingers are in my mouth, probing. My stomach heaves; I swallow acid back down. But he tries again, jabbing, scratching, pushing his fingers down my throat and ripping my jaws apart.

I can't breathe.

The memory card regurgitates out my mouth. And Lukas grabs it. I bite down on his fingers. Proper vicious.

He howls in pain. And I swallow the memory card down.

I wipe his blood off my mouth. 'I ate your words, Lukas Svad. Your lies live inside me. Harper begged me to give her this camera – she said not to trust you – but I had to give you one last chance. I didn't believe you could kill Pup in cold blood. Or me.'

I get to my feet and remind Lukas that his Leica memory card inside me has GPS. 'I'm not Rosa, so the divers will find my body and the pathologist will find the truth inside me.'

But Lukas is not listening to my heroic speech.

A fat, small red globule of blood spreads across his finger. The look of shock on his face sears into me.

'I never learn. How could I trust you? Rosa's daughter. You don't even like dogs.' He turns greenish-white, his eyes roll back and he's shaking as if he's gone very cold. Then his knees buckle.

I clutch at him round the waist. I try to pull him away

from the edge. I try so hard. But the dizzying height clamps my feet to the rock. The landscape dissolves around me. The fjord and the sky and Lukas are spinning together. All I can hear is a *thwup, thwup, thwupping* sound. Pine cones and leaves and grit lift off Preken Rock into the air.

A hospital helicopter lands on the flat outcrop above us. Lukas slumps in my arms; he's weighing me down and together we are tottering on an abyss. Suddenly. More than anything. I want to live. I don't want to die like this.

Voices shouting. 'We're medics. Get away from the cliff.'

Lukas groans. 'No doctors . . .'

But before the medics can get to us, armed Norwegians with dogs race along the narrow ledge to the plateau. Barking. More shouting. We can't hear them above the rotor blades. I can't hold on; Lukas is slipping and pulling me with him.

The policemen let the dogs go. The Dobermanns race ahead and jump the fissure. They form a semicircle around me and Lukas; barking, snarling, waiting for their handlers, afraid to come closer. They don't scare me. Nothing does.

They're too late.

'It's over, Lukas,' I say. 'The doctors will help you. This is Norway. They like children. The police aren't owned by corporations here. Svad Oil can't hurt you.'

'Don't bank on that, my love.' He smiles at me with such sweetness it's like I got my old Lukas back. And he pulls out a sprig of purple saxifrage from the pocket in his wolf coat.

Our fingertips touch. It sends a jolt right through us, and Lukas Svad gazes at me, as though he doesn't understand it either.

'See you in the cosmos, Nell. Write me a song . . .'

'No!' I snatch at his wolf coat, and a tuft of fur comes away in my fingers, but my quartz bracelet catches on his button. He doesn't notice it hold fast and Lukas takes one step back.

The bracelet yanks me forwards and takes me with him. And . . .

I'm falling

No

This isn't falling

I remember

This is flying

I'm proper flying. Up. And Up. Over the fjord, rising on thermals, I fly along granite skyscrapers; a warm salt wind cradles my body. I stretch my fingertips and turn, dead graceful, in long elegant loops, murmuring with the skylarks. I catch a flash of red as a robin swoops through the dark sunlight, chasing insects that shriek with excitement.

The sky runs on for ever, purple and red and lemon yellow. I float in mid-air, juggled by the thermals, rising and falling, like the sea. Time bends. I could stay like this for ever.

Safe.

From a great height, I see Lukas floating on the surface of the fjord, arms outstretched, his wolf coat drifting around him. His beautiful sea-glass eyes open, unseeing; his hair ripples into a soft black halo. I try to pull him out, but he always slips through my blood-stained fingers.

He's still falling.

Not your time, Nell.

There's a waft of rose perfume; its fragrance fills the sky with unbearable longing before I sense my mother's arms around me and I feel this wondrous, deep peace, an overwhelming happiness.

'Mum!' I cry.

I promised I'd come back for you. Remember?

And I do. I remember. My mother's grey eyes watching over me.

Her silver rosary.

Then some unstoppable force of nature pulls me back to the precipice, and police dogs are jumping up at me, barking, fastening their brutal teeth on my arms and legs, and the huge snarling black dogs drag me back, and they pin me to Preken Rock.

49

I belong somewhere else. But I wake up dazzled by clinical white lights. The hospital says I was lucky. My broken ankle, and the dog bites on my arms will heal. My voice is a different story.

The doctors think the trauma to my throat means I will never sing again. They say it like it's nothing. And when they remove the tubes from my throat, doctors seem baffled I can't speak a word.

Harper sits by the hospital bed and holds my hand.

She shouts a lot. 'Don't you dare give me the silent routine, Nell. Get over yourself. You might fool the doctors, but this is nonsense. Speak.'

I can't.

The memory chip does the talking for me, and the police drop all charges against me. Lukas filmed the abduction and he was filming on his GoPro when the helicopter crashed.

The police can't prove it, but they suspect he tampered with the rotor blades.

Norwegian divers dredge the fjord again, and this time

they find Rosa's body.

My dad had to identify her. He's not touched a drop since.

They don't find Lukas.

He never stops coming back to me, arms outstretched, falling from the cosmos, the wolf coat floating in space. He feels so alive. Maybe he's being purified by water?

Molecule by molecule.

I stare at the water jug by my hospital bed, and I won't drink. The nurses give me bottled water. It's all I drink now. Just in case it tastes of him. When I get home, I don't leave my built-in mattress. Harper is much better – she's in remission now and her future looks good. She babies me. I wake, night after night, silently screaming. Harper holds me and she never scolds.

It's summer. The dressings comes off the dog bites on my legs. And Pup visits me in Yellow Cottage. He waddles up our concrete path on jelly legs, pushing a doggie-on-wheels, batting aside the social worker's hand as he stops to admire his new blue shoes. And when he sees me leaning out of the window, his look of delight stops my heart.

I can't breathe.

Then Pup throws back his head and proper wolf howls. I crawl downstairs. He climbs on my lap and growls at anyone who tries to stop him snuggling up.

'Na na!' he says, in his bossiest voice. And he doesn't let up until he's got me back.

But he's the only one who doesn't need me to speak.

Pup talks enough for both of us. Harper sorts out the Barnevernet. Not Dad. They said an alcoholic was an unfit parent. So Harper arranges to be Pup's temporary guardian, until I come of age.

I scribble on a piece of paper. *Really?* You *a mum?*

She grins. 'An Immaculate Conception is the answer to my prayers after chemo. You OK with him being raised Catholic?'

I think of Pup's baptism on the mountain – the huge shimmering light – and nod. I'm pretty sure the universe doesn't mind what we call God.

Today's my birthday. Harper's celebrating it with an overnight ferry trip down Nøyfjord. She's paying.

'Her wolf song went viral?' Dad keeps saying, puzzled.

'It's not even her best song.' Harper smirks. 'The trolls hate her guts and they still bought it.'

Dad winces, and I feel him sending me a blessing. I try to smile but it's a sore point. Harper posted me singing 'Wolfsong' and sold it online without asking. She says I should be grateful; she's putting the money aside for my future, and now the world knows about the boy with wolf eyes.

Dad unpacks our picnic on deck. My dad's become silent like me since he's stopped drinking, but Pup makes enough noise for all of us, so no one notices.

Harper gave Dad an ultimatum. No drinking ever again. Or he can't live with us, not with a baby in the house. She's really tough on him.

Dad never got over Rosa. He told me he followed Mum to Norway and knew the exact moment her heart stopped. All these years of loving and hating Rosa? And living with me? A daughter who was the spit of her. It's enough to destroy anyone, but I made Dad swear he'll never take it out me again.

Harper kneels by her bed at night and prays for Mum's soul.

Me? I ask the universe to help Dad forgive her. I gave him Mum's silver rosary. I think it's working. On my birthday, Dad has this look of peaceful surrender on his face when he watches Pup, and he couldn't bear to look at my brother a few weeks ago.

'Na na!' Pup shrieks when he spots my birthday cake; he plops down next to Harper. The sea breeze tugs at their hair. Harper's hair is growing back. Slowly. They look more like brother and sister than me with their dandelion mops. Pup's baby hair has fallen out and is growing back blonder now too. I catch his eye and he giggles. But then Pup giggles every time he sees my new hair. Harper dyed it in the Norwegian national colours for my birthday. It's dip-dyed, so I have red on top, the next bit is blue, and the ends are bleached white. But somehow they bled together into a mermaid shimmer, so Harper plaits it. She admits it's not my best look. My sister anchors Pup's plump toddler legs to the deck. She gives him a paper plate, with the smallest piece of cake ever. And no chocolate icing. He looks super unimpressed.

Dad tries to say grace. 'Bless this food and may the Lord make us truly grateful.'

But Pup's not one to listen. 'Na na!' he roars, pointing at my portion decorated with Starbursts. Harper still doesn't believe I won't eat them any more.

'Ulv Pup! Say please,' my sister scolds.

'Na. Na?' he says politely.

I give Harper a goofy smile and hand over my cake. I soften a Starburst for him. Pup can't believe his luck and buries his face in chocolate icing. I swear his butt's wagging. In seconds, Harper's picking chocolate off her dress and opening her mouth to bitch at me. But she remembers that no one gets told off on birthdays, not even in our family.

So she tells Dad, who still listens to her every word. 'Pup has to learn his place. He thinks he's the alpha male.'

'Oh my God,' I mouth.

'I heard that,' she snaps. 'Pup must learn to speak proper.'

And she gives me a look that says: if this baby can talk, you can.

When Dad goes below deck to his cabin we curl up in a hammock with Pup. I want one night sleeping rough under the stars before we go home. Harper tucks up a sleepy Pup with the rug and opens *Jane Eyre*. We have to finish it for school, but I end up reading the same page over and over.

Tonight Harper reads the last chapter and lobs the book at me. '*Reader, I married him?*' she scoffs. 'That has to be the crappiest ending ever. Poor blind Rochester. He can't see what's coming. Marriage is worse than Insta-love for let-downs. Who do we know who's happily married?'

I shrug, and cuddle Pup, marvelling how big his feet have grown. Pup giggles and I pull the rug over us to hide from her prying eyes.

'What was the last thing you said to Lukas?' Harper says, all casual. 'Spit it out. You'll feel better. You take guilt so personally. You need to let this go.'

Lukas chose death rather than life in captivity caged up with doctors. That's what I tell myself.

'Go on, tell me,' Harper pesters, pulling the rug off me. She doesn't give up. She never does. She knows what I told Lukas. To save Pup. And it's killing me. Some stupid part of me thought Lukas Svad could fly.

Maybe we're all monsters underneath, afraid to look?

The Nøyfjord ferry glides under Preken Rock, and my sister watches me like a she-wolf. Numb with misery, I close my eyes, but nothing can stop me from seeing Lukas in his wolf coat, falling with his arms outstretched.

My Lukas.

I miss him. The Lukas in my head slays me with grief. Yeah. I know. Harper tells me all the time, my Lukas was a fantasy. An illusion. But I can't forget how it felt to be in love like that, to feel the cosmos inside, and I don't want to.

They say Lukas was proper evil. But what is evil? And

who makes us like that? How much cruelty and neglect does it take before we all crack?

Harper holds up the brass lighter. 'I found this in your stuff.'

I can't bear to touch it. Torture. Betrayal. Lukas could never let go of his past . . . I can't live there.

I toss the brass lighter high in the air. It winks in the midnight sun, before it breaks the surface of the fjord. I hold my breath, waiting for his hand to emerge from the water.

He's not here.

Of course not. I knew that.

Harper grips my knee. 'Here's your real birthday pressie,' she says brightly. 'You don't want it? I'll keep it. Hate to see it go to waste. I respect your decision never to speak again. It's big. Like your love for that wolf boy. Dom's wrong if he thinks you'll get over it. So I'll be doing you a favour.'

I know it's going to be a new journal, before I unwrap it. Harper's never subtle, but I wasn't expecting the pink Dora the Explorer pen she's waving under my nose. 'Start writing. Start living,' she says. Oh my God. She's been watching Oprah on TV. My sister grabs my new keyboard off the deck. 'Or Pup gets this.'

'Hands off, bitch,' I rasp, pinching it back. 'He can afford to buy his own.'

'*Hands off, bitch?*' she snorts. 'Your first words after weeks of silence? Classy.'

I pick out 'Wolfsong' on the keyboard, silently fuming.

The hammock quivers and I think Harper's laughing at me. But her head's in her hands. And she's sobbing. Pup wakes, wide-eyed with panic. I wrap my arms around them both. I don't have the words to make any of this OK. So I hum one of Rosa's songs from memory, until we all calm down.

'I know it's not cool, but what about Mum's money?' Harper sniffs. 'We can prove Pup shares our DNA. Let's get tested. What's the harm in that? It's only a drop of blood.'

Only a drop of blood? That's what killed Lukas in the end.

'No, I can't go there. You get power of attorney over Pup soon. As his guardian you can make Svad Oil close that open pit on Ulv Fjell. I owe that to Lukas. There will be just enough money for Pup after that.'

'You can't carry Lukas around like the Cross,' Harper nudges me. 'Let him go.'

She rocks our hammock in time with Pup's snoring; his warm body lies on my heart. It's a lovely weight. So solid. So alive.

'OK,' I say. 'You win. Give me that pen. I'll write a song.'

Harper leans back in the hammock, smirking.

But she holds on tight to my ankle in her sleep. I listen to my brother and sister breathing as the fjord ferry glides down the dark sea-river. The white night throws silver shadows over the water. Birdsong. Breathing. Wolves. Distant howls on the mountain.

The whole world is turning and shape-shifting around us. I can hear the colours in the sky, the strange pitch of the clouds, and endless rhythms in the air. The music builds and builds, drumming on my brain. Then I hear his deep voice on Ulv Fjell. Calling, calling. Nell, Nell, come back, come back to me.

I hunch over my journal and write fast. *Lukas didn't steal Pup. He stole me.* I put everything down, about him, about me, about what happened; and my part in it.

And I call my spirit back.

Acknowledgements

My gratitude begins and ends with Nick Baldock. Every day. It's tough becoming a writer, but I suspect it's a nightmare being married to one; books everywhere; the obsession, preoccupation, self-doubt; and the forgetting to cook supper. Thank you, Nick, for your never-ending support. For me, it was love at first sight three decades ago, and the idea of abduction from love was the departure point for *The Hurting*. I wanted to write a Nordic noir thriller, but I don't do violence – stealing a baby is the worst thing I could imagine. Thank you, Archie Baldock for providing non-stop delight and the inspiration for Ulv Pup.

Huge thanks to Caroline Ambrose and the Bath Children's Novel Award for their passion in supporting writers, and for my agent, their first judge, Sallyanne Sweeney.

I doubt any writer gets luckier than being published by Barry Cunningham – the legendary champion of readers and children's books – it's been an absolute delight to have you and Rachel Leyshon as my editors. I am so grateful for your courage in publishing – your kindly editorial probing unlocked so much in this book. Elinor Bagenal, for putting the biggest smile on my face with my first international sale. Sue Cook and Laura Myers for unflappable copy-editing and turning a dyslexic's manuscript into beautiful text. Rachel Hickman and artist

Helen Crawford-White for my stunning cover. Jazz Bartlett for whip-cracking publicity. My awesome fellow Chicken House authors, thanks for your beautiful books and advice.

Annie Heritage, you've no idea what your fifty years of cheering means to this debut author. Thank you. Sally Thirkettle for lifelong friendship, Amanda Fisher for showing me that broken becomes something stronger and more beautiful. Debs Exell for best chats ever over cocktails. My wonderful CBC friends – Sally Reardon and Barbara Kennedy for early reading, Gillian Dobias, Anna Gecan, Michelle Kosoy, Derek Kennedy for your Canadian creativity and integrity.

I am super blessed to have my talented MA gang – Chris Vick, Sarah Henderson, Jak Harrison, Philippa Forester, Rowena House, Eden Endfield – you are the best. My tutor, Julia Green, especial thanks for your kindness when my brother Dom died during the MA. Manuscript tutors Steve Voake and Lucy Christopher, and former students at Bath Spa. Imogen Cooper and Maurice Lyons at GEA, thanks for your swift helping hands.

SCBWI and all the writers too numerous and wondrous to mention, you know who you are, including Sara, Kathy, Candy, Mo, Tanya, Sue, Kellie, Cathie K, Pat W, Emma. Matt Killeen for song writing tips. Olivia Kiernan for making me laugh. Sophie McKenzie for inspiring me all those years ago at City Lit. Cat Muir and newer writing friends, and the screen craft passion that is Chris Jones and the London Screenwriter's Festival.

Dear Norway, nothing prepares an outsider for your breathtaking wilderness. Do forgive me for taking liberties with your geography and midnight sun to create Preken Rock and Nøy. Thank you Sigrid Anna at the Norwegian Embassy, for checking environmental information on controversial wolf culls and mining – all errors are my own.

The BRIT School and Eloise Lamb Lawrence for inspiring Nell's love of music. Sigrid for being the Norwegian soundtrack to this book. My talented goddaughter Grace Church, and Mark Ciccone for my website and inadvertently sharing your love stories.

My mum. Yikes. To be honest, I wasn't expecting you to be able to still read this at ninety-three. I hope my teenage take on religion doesn't offend you. Or Dad! Heartfelt thanks to 'Gmar' and my extraordinary family; Mel, Vashti, Jeremy, Suvi, Buck, Finn, Jez, Clem, Brian and Carole, Sirkku, Lillian, Amy, Alex, Simon, Jan, Max, Harry, Joe, Issy and my brothers Jonathan and Barney for their childhood poaching scrapes and underage driving.

Shelagh McDonough for bringing so much joy to my life and showing me how to live an extraordinary life until we die. You are a great teacher. And St Christopher's Hospice.

I'd like to single out Katy Fletcher at Dulwich Prep and wish every school had such a tireless, inspirational librarian who puts great books in children's hands. Thank goodness for publishers, teachers, booksellers and bloggers who share that passion, but we can all encourage young people to read and recommend books we love, the ones that shape us.

Please help me. Do leave *The Hurting* a review on Amazon, Goodreads, or mention it on social media. It's like clapping your hands to keep Tinker Bell alive; every word to a friend makes an enormous difference for this book to stay alive for another reader. Thank you so much for taking the time to do that. Do it for every book, if you can – enormous power lies in your hands.

To the YA reader, my blessing that Nell's story inspires you to notice your own life. And make mistakes. Loads of them. Trust and listen to yourself, not other people; I didn't know such a thing was possible when I was young.

You can contact me on Twitter and Instagram (@lucyvansmit) or via my website (lucyvansmit.com).